"A HIGHLY UNUSUAL, EXCEPTIONALLY
ERUDITE MYSTERY SERIES!"
—*Minneapolis Star Tribune*

Praise for the
Peter Brichter Mysteries by
MARY MONICA PULVER

KNIGHT FALL

"Thoroughly enjoyable . . . Highly recommended for
those who like some zany fun mixed with murder."
—*Library Journal*

THE UNFORGIVING MINUTES

"Mary Monica Pulver has exceeded herself.
The Unforgiving Minutes is a spine-tingling
thriller . . . I loved every page."
—Elizabeth Peters

ASHES TO ASHES

"The most hard-boiled book in the series; the
finely drawn characters make it one of the best."
—*The Drood Review of Mystery*

ORIGINAL SIN

"Delightful . . . Readers who enjoy good puzzles will find
a great one here . . . A sparkling, thoroughly enjoyable novel!"
—Dean James, Manager, Murder by the Book

ORIGINAL SIN

MARY MONICA PULVER

DIAMOND BOOKS, NEW YORK

All the characters and events portrayed in this work are fictitious.

ORIGINAL SIN

A Diamond Book/published by arrangement with
Walker and Company

PRINTING HISTORY
Walker Publishing Company, Inc. edition published 1991
Diamond edition / January 1993

ISBN: 1–55773–846–7

Diamond Books are published by the Berkley Publishing Group,
200 Madison Avenue, New York, New York 10016.
The name "DIAMOND" and its logo are trademarks
belonging to Charter Communications, Inc.

PRINTED IN THE UNITED STATES OF AMERICA

10 9 8 7 6 5 4 3 2 1

For Aunt Mamie, Aunt Velva, Aunt Pete,
and all aunts everywhere who
keep the family albums
and tell the family stories

Only the Lord can understand,
When first these pangs begin,
How much is reflex action and
How much is really sin.

—Rudyard Kipling

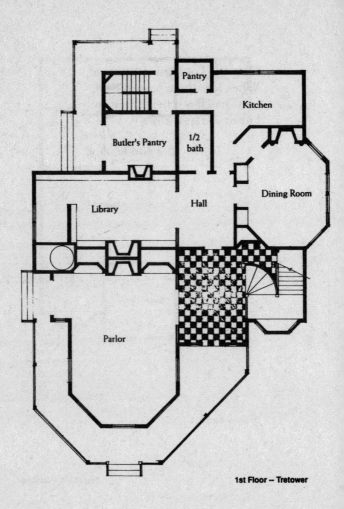

Pantry

Kitchen

Butler's Pantry

1/2
bath

Dining Room

Library

Hall

Parlor

1st Floor -- Tretower

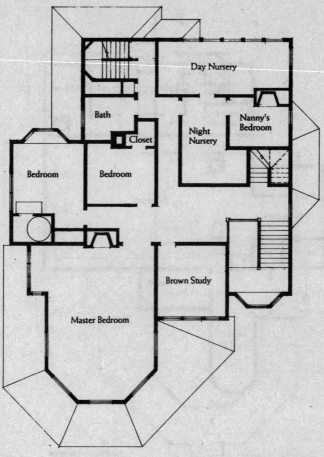

Day Nursery

Bath

Closet

Night
Nursery

Nanny's
Bedroom

Bedroom

Bedroom

Brown Study

Master Bedroom

2nd Floor – Tretower

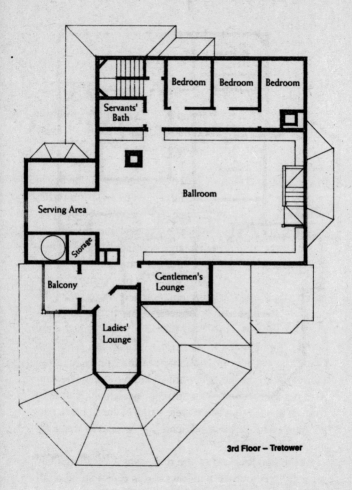

Bedroom

Bedroom

Bedroom

Servants'
Bath

Ballroom

Serving Area

Storage

Balcony

Gentlemen's
Lounge

Ladies'
Lounge

3rd Floor — Tretower

Chapter
1 †

Because I have to know if it's still there, thought Evelyn Biggins, as the plane began to settle heavily downward. *And stop her if necessary.*

The sound of trumpets faded away, and a guitar began quietly summoning all the faithful, joyful and triumphant. The music had a crystal edge that meant it had been recorded digitally; and despite the low volume, it filled the living room, an unusually large one in a fine old house. The room was decorated in a contemporary style, the walls a rich peacock blue, the deep plush carpet forest green. To offset the dark colors, there were two long couches identically upholstered in champagne silk, facing each other in front of a fireplace made of pale gray stone with a small carved frieze of galloping horses. Flames sent cheerful flickers over the faintly textured fabric of the couches and warmed the fur of a black standard poodle sleeping on a strip of cheap black carpet in front of the hearth. (There were strips of cheap black carpet all around the house; Michael D'Arcangelo was a famous sleeper.)

At the opposite end of the room was a very large bay set with three outsize windows. In its center stood a tall balsam, whose Christmas fragrance filled the room like the music. Kneeling by the tree, and bent laughing over a baby in a plastic carrier, was Kori Price Brichter, a lovely

1

young woman whose pale complexion was set glowing by the cranberry-red cocktail dress she wore.

In the narrow space between the tree and the middle window stood Frank Ryder, a short, stocky man with white hair. He had lifted one of the heavy champagne drapes and was peering out.

"Turning into a real old-fashioned Illinois blizzard out there," he remarked with the complacence of one who does not have to go out in it.

"Too bad you and Mary didn't get married two days ago," teased Kori. Her words were for Frank, but she spoke as if to the baby, grimacing and shaking her head to make him laugh and wave his chubby arms. "Then you could be walking the white sands of Cancun instead of watching the white snows of winter sift across the porch of my house."

"Oh, well," said Frank, his complacency unbroken, "it isn't as if this were a real honeymoon." He came out from behind the tree. He was not two hours from St. Therese's and was still wearing the vest and trousers of his wedding suit, a navy pinstripe. His dark necktie had been pulled loose, and his boutonniere of white roses and baby's breath had been removed from the coat and pinned to his vest by a loving hand. He caught his bride's eye, smiled, and said in a broad brogue, "Tiss is mahr like taking up where we left off, am I not right, *mo chroide*?"

Mary Ryder was short and frankly plump, a Mrs. Claus in a gray suit and ruffled blouse, her silver hair done up in a bun. She smiled back, lifted her camera and flashed a picture of him. "As if we were never apart," she said. She cranked to the next frame, turned and took a picture of the young woman kneeling over her baby. "Kori, it was very kind of you to offer us refuge from the storm while we re-arrange our reservations. Christmas among friends is so much better than a last-minute motel."

The blizzard, which was at that moment building, had earlier closed Denver's airport, where they were supposed to make their connection to Mexico.

"Where's Peter?" asked Frank. "He isn't going to skip out on the tree-trimming chores, is he?"

Kori, reminded, turned from her baby to the cardboard box marked "lights" and began picking at the masking tape holding its top closed. "He's at the airport, picking up our last guest."

Mary said, surprised, "Is our airport still open?"

"When I called to check, they said yes." Kori checked her watch. "That was half an hour ago. Her plane should just be touching down now."

"Who's the guest?" asked Frank. "I thought this little party would be just Dr. Ramsey and Mary and me."

Kori pulled the tape loose, then turned with the smile of a person about to reveal a happy surprise. "No, there's another guest, a very special one. It seems I have a cousin."

"You mean one of Peter's relatives?"

"No, my very own. Remember how I always said I didn't have any living relatives? I was wrong; I have one. Her name is Evelyn Biggins. She's a cousin once removed, actually. She was my mother's cousin; her maiden name was Evelyn McKay."

Frank said, "As in Evelyn and Inez, the sisters?"

Kori nodded. "You've heard of them? Yes, isn't it wonderful?"

"You're related to *them*?" asked Mary, in a peculiar voice.

"Yes; my grandmother and Evelyn's father were brother and sister."

"Well, I'll be damned!" Frank shook his head. "But you know, I would have guessed they'd both be dead by now. Evelyn and Inez. Christ, I haven't thought of them in years! How the hell did you find Evelyn?"

"Peter found her for me. About all I had was her name. I've been thinking about redecorating the house, this time with me in charge instead of a professional, and doing something to make it reflect its history. So I started researching, and I found out that we've always lived out here at Tretower—my mother's side, anyway. Right from the time this house was built in the 1870s. But I can't find out anything about them as people; all I'm getting is begats—you know, Charles begat William, who begat Ferris, who begat Evelyn, like that. Charles and his wife Eugenia were my great-great-grandparents. Now I have Evelyn, who actually remembers Eugenia—she must have lived to an enormous old age."

"It would be nice if you had told us she was coming," said Mary, and this time the edge on her voice sliced into Kori's happy excitement.

"Mary, what's wrong?"

"My God, I can't believe you actually expect me to sit down and be pleasant to Evelyn McKay!"

"Biggins," corrected Kori, too startled to think. "Evelyn McKay Biggins."

"Whatever, I won't do it!"

"Now, hon—" began Frank, as surprised as Kori.

"No, Frank! I couldn't be responsible for my actions if I had to spend a weekend with a McKay! I'm going upstairs for our bags; you go start the car!"

"Um," said Kori, "that won't be possible." She got to her feet in a single unhappy motion. "Peter's car is in town having something expensive done to it; so he took the Bronco to the airport. Danny borrowed the pickup for the Christmas weekend, and my little MG is up on blocks for the winter. There isn't any other transportation available, at least until Peter gets back."

Mary's face was pale and cold, a frozen sculpture. She said through stiff lips, "Frank, as soon as Peter arrives, tell him we can't stay after all. I'll be upstairs; I don't want to see her, even accidentally; and I won't stay in this house one minute longer than I have to after she arrives." And Mary turned and walked out of the room.

Charter's airport was small and backward; Evelyn found she had to disembark onto the tarmac. The wind grabbed at her as she stepped away from the stairs, pushing her rudely; snow stung her cheek as she hurried with the others toward the glowing rectangle that marked the gate to the terminal.

Inside, she slowed and looked around. Hot air wrapped itself around her legs in a marble-cake mix with the icy air from outside. They were in a hallway built of plywood; a string of full-size Christmas tree lights surrounded a steamy window. A voice was announcing in a tone that would indicate this was the fourth repeat that bad weather had forced the closure of all runways, and no more flights would be arriving or taking off. Outbound passengers were instructed to report to the ticket desks of their respective airlines. A white board sign pointed with a single arrow to the main terminal and baggage retrieval.

Evelyn started in the direction indicated. She was tall for a woman of seventy-nine, erect and looking even taller wrapped in her gray wool coat. Her gloves were lined, and her black felt hat sat well down on her head, but she had forgotten overshoes. Her oxfords were sensible, but hardly warm; she hoped she wouldn't have to stand outside to wait for a taxi.

Now that she thought about it, it might be hard to find a taxi at all. Her destination was a farm, and, with the airport closing, there would be a rush of others wanting a ride into town, where still more customers waited. Better get started. She looked for another sign pointing to baggage retrieval.

"Mrs. Biggins?"

She turned around. A slender man with sharp-drawn features under fine, straight, colorless hair was studying her with the palest eyes she had ever seen. He was five ten or eleven in his good Burberry, hatless, and carrying thick leather gloves in one hand. She hadn't a notion who he might be.

Her face must have shown her puzzlement, for a wry smile tweaked his thin mouth. "I'm Peter Brichter, and I've been sent to pick you up." Her host, she realized.

She put out a gloved hand and said in her cultured falsetto, "How very nice of you to come out in such unpleasant weather."

He took the hand politely and went with her to retrieve her two suitcases, then led the way as they threaded a path back to the main entrance. His manner was courteous, but not forthcoming. Evelyn, sensitized to any hint of trouble, began to wonder if something was wrong.

Don't be silly, she admonished herself. After all, it's Christmas, a time for family, and I'm a stranger coming into his house. Men, she knew, could be funny about events that spoiled their treasured routine.

But maybe he knows. That thought made her hesitate when he turned at the door to the outside, holding it open for her, looking back with those strange cold eyes. But she gathered her courage and sailed through. There was nothing wrong, nothing.

Kori was kneeling by the fireplace, preparing to put another log on the flames. Michael was sitting beside her, a twig in his mouth. Peter had taught him to "help" at the fireplace, and he took his job seriously. Kori said to

Frank, "I don't understand. I didn't know she had ever met Evelyn."

Frank nodded agreement. "I don't think she has. After all, neither my folks nor hers were of a class that got invited to the same parties the McKays went to."

"No, I didn't mean—" Kori began.

"Hush, I know what you meant. And it's all right; we weren't destitute, or trash. But Mary's family, especially, was at that social level that hopes someday to rise into the middle class. I can't understand how she managed to get close enough to any McKay that it would still hurt fifty years later."

Kori push-dropped the log into the fire, then stood and reached for a poker. "Did you ever?"

"Get hurt by a McKay? No."

She glanced at him with flawless gray eyes. "Did you ever speak with one."

"No." He hesitated, looking around the beautiful room. "I've been out here quite a few times, first as your husband's boss, then as his friend and yours. This is an interesting old house, and I can understand why you want to know about the folks who used to live here, especially since it turns out they're kin." He looked at Kori. "But I thought Peter might have warned you about poking into the history of this place, because he can tell you from his own experience that there's sour apples on many a branch of the family tree."

Poking at the log, she said, "You do know something about the McKays, don't you?"

"All right. I don't know why Mary's taking it so personal, but Evelyn's old man was Ferris McKay; and he was, pardon my French, the ripest bastard in the country. He was a banker by profession, and a meaner, harder man never foreclosed on a mortgage."

Kori looked startled, then she laughed. "Okay, so my

great-uncle was like Ebenezer Scrooge before the Ghost of Christmas Past worked him over. That's . . . interesting, and something I didn't know about him." She put the poker back into the rack of fireplace tools, dusted her hands. "Maybe I should have come to you looking for stories about my ancestors."

"You want more? His wife was a snob, his daughter Evelyn was a cold-hearted bitch and his other daughter, Inez, was a tramp." He saw real shock and dismay flood Kori's face, sniffed and rubbed the underside of his nose with the edge of one hand in an embarrassed way. "Now I've gone too far. I'm sorry, I shouldn't have said that."

"It's all right," said Kori, but her face and voice said it wasn't.

"Please, forget it, okay? I was speaking from gossip I overheard as a boy, so it's kind of dim and was probably exaggerated to start with."

"Strange to think so many members of your own family could be held in such low esteem."

Frank, trying to heal the breach, said, "Especially when others, like your parents, and you, are very highly thought of."

"I wonder. Frank, can you talk to Mary? I mean, I wrote to Evelyn about an old-fashioned Christmas house party, and if you leave, there will only be Gordon, Peter and me. And Gordon's in one of his marathon cooking moods, which means the meals will be delicious, but we won't see much of him. I don't know how I'd explain. Jill will be so disappointed, too."

Frank blinked. "Why will your nanny be disappointed if Mary and I aren't here?"

"Because she's going to be a maid. She made a costume and she's all excited about it. It won't be nearly as much fun if she can only be a maid for Evelyn."

"She's excited about being a maid?"

Kori's eyes kindled with amusement. "Well, she watches a lot of old movies, so her idea of what a maid does is from what she's seen in them. She's been expecting an audience, and was all cast down when I told her Cris and Laura's plane was stuck in Denver. She was the one who suggested I check about your flight, since you were booked through Denver; and she was really happy to hear you and Mary were taking Cris and Laura's place. She can hardly wait to make her entrance." Kori sobered. "Frank, you know Mary much better than I do. Is this some kind of delayed bridal vapors, or is she serious about refusing to share a roof with a McKay?"

Frank shrugged. "I never heard anything about a feud between the O'Briens and the McKays during the thirty years we were married: maybe it's something that started during the twelve years we were divorced. I'll go and talk to her."

Peter Brichter was an excellent driver; still, between the blinding whirl of wind-driven snow and the ice that lurked beneath it, the drive to the ranch had been a serious adventure.

But now, nearly at the end, the struggle up the narrow lane to the ranch was proving even more slow and difficult; here the Bronco had to bully its way through real drifts. The lane ran between the same fence rails she remembered from her youth. Seeing them, Evelyn suddenly was impatient to be at their destination. She leaned forward, looking for a glimpse of the house, but snow drew teasing curtains across her view.

The lane widened abruptly, and there was a big drift right in front of them. Evelyn saw it only soon enough to brace her hand on the dash before the front tires buried themselves in it.

"Damn," muttered Peter. He tried backing up and

crunching forward again, but he couldn't get up enough speed to force a passage. He sighed, shut off the engine and got out.

The wind paused as if to take a breath, and in the break Evelyn was surprised to see they had come nearly across a racetrack. She had been sure it would be gone, but there was the curve of the rails, white shadows against the snow. She and her sister Inez had loved racing their ponies on the track, which had been built by her grandfather to encircle the house and other buildings back around 1915—and still did, apparently. How reassuring to find it still existed! She leaned forward and in another brief glimpse saw the multi-roofed outline of the house on top of its rise, white against the dark sky, windows glowing, and her heart thumped painfully against her ribs.

The door opened and Peter was there, looking up at her with those cold gray eyes. He appeared interested in her reaction to her glimpse of the house, but she could not otherwise read his expression. *What an awful man you are,* she thought angrily.

She allowed him to help her out, and they began to wade through the snow, which was wet, heavy and more than knee-deep in places. The wind was blowing hard enough to blind them, and she staggered under its onslaught until he got her steadied and aimed in the direction of the half-seen house. He kept hold of her arm, but she insisted on making a team effort of the struggle, and by the time they arrived on the big old porch, she was feeling vindicated, as well as breathless. *Not so old as he thinks,* she told herself.

He opened the elaborate front door—she remembered the original as rather plainer—and she walked into the big entrance hall. The black and white tile floor was the same as she remembered from her childhood. The wallpaper had been replaced with mauve and cream paint, but the beautiful wooden staircase, with its curve-away lower segment, that was the same too. A real holly garland had been woven through the railings of the banister where they met the steps, and the air was fragrant with the safe and familiar Christmas smells of roast fowl and evergreen. She felt a sudden sting of tears, and was glad Peter was behind her. He began to help her off with her coat.

"Here we are, Katherine," he said, lifting the coat free, and Evelyn, turning to correct him about her name, had her eye caught by a figure standing in front of the parlor door: a young woman with a sleepy infant in a green jumpsuit tucked into one arm. The woman was dressed in cranberry velvet, and her long dark hair was pinned up in braids, tendrils of which had escaped to curl in front of her ears and down the nape of her slender neck. She was exquisitely lovely, and Evelyn, who had never been even pretty, felt a familiar stab of envy.

"Mrs. Biggins?" said the woman. "I'm so glad you're here; I was starting to worry. Welcome back to your old home." The infant made a fussing sound, and the woman put it up on her shoulder, patting its back. Though her poise was that of mistress of the house, the mistress was Kori, not this Katherine person.

Evelyn looked around at Peter, who explained, "Katherine is her real name; Kori is the nickname everyone else calls her."

So this *was* Kori Price Brichter, the woman she had been writing to for the past four months.

Evelyn turned back to extend her hand. "I've been so looking forward to meeting you, Mrs. Brichter," she fluted.

The woman came forward, devouring Evelyn's face with eager gray eyes, free hand extended. "Please, call me Kori." She, like Peter, pronounced it Koh-REE, and Evelyn corrected the mental pronunciation she had been giving it during their correspondence. Kori continued, "This is our son, Gordon Peter," turning around to show the baby's disinterested face. "He's ready for bed; I kept him up to show him off, just for minute." She said to Peter, "Is it as bad out there as it looks?"

"Getting worse by the minute," nodded Peter, putting Evelyn's coat away in a tall antique armoire. "I hope Danny got off all right."

"He left about a half an hour ago. I wonder if I shouldn't have told him to call when he arrived at his parents' house."

"Who is Danny?" asked Evelyn.

"Daniel Bannister, my groom."

Evelyn's eyebrows lifted. "Bannister?"

Kori laughed. "Lots of people say that. Yes, his father is the famous lawyer, and his grandfather was the famous judge. Danny says he prefers the barn to the bar. But first things first: let's get you upstairs; your feet must be soaked. We can catch up on local names later. Peter, why didn't you bring up Evelyn's luggage?"

"Because I was hoping Danny'd had the sense to change his mind about driving home in this weather and I could send him out for it." He had taken his gloves off; now he pulled them back on. "If I'm not back in twenty minutes, organize a search party."

"All right. This way, Evelyn." Kori started up the stairs, the baby resting his head on her shoulder, sucking his thumb. When Evelyn followed, he lifted his head and regarded her judgmentally. She looked away, and around.

How gracious and beautiful everything looked, and better maintained than she remembered it from her youth. The railing of the stairs had been stripped, smoothed and refinished in a lighter color, and the carpet on the stairs was deeper, more luxurious. But the large and beautiful

stained glass window on the landing was the same, and
Evelyn paused to admire it. A red and green dragon with
a lance down its throat writhed in the center. A knight in
silver armor pressed the lance home from his half-rearing
horse, and a fair maiden with long, spiraled curls clasped
her hands anxiously in the background. It was a superb
and original example of Victorian work. The central picture was surrounded by framed squares of spurious coats
of arms. Evelyn gestured, frowning. "I seem to
remember—aren't two of those panes different?" The
two she meant were, in fact, different in expression from
their fellows, as well as from what she remembered.
"Broken, I suppose."

"On, no," said Kori. "We just decided to put our personal arms up there. We're members of an organization
that studies the Middle Ages, and one of the things they
encourage is the design and registration of personal de-
vices. The horse on a blazing sun is mine, and the lit candle is Peter's. I saved the two panes we took out, in case
of restoration, but I couldn't resist the opportunity."

A portent of other, more major, changes? Evelyn wondered. They continued up the stairs, then turned down the
hall.

"I hope you like your room," said Kori. "I wanted to
give you the study, because it's a big room with lots of
windows, but the bed in there folds down out of a chair. I
gave it to Gordon, who can sleep on anything. The oriel
bedroom I gave to Captain and Mrs. Ryder, because it has
the big bed."

Evelyn slowed. "You have guests other than myself?"

Kori kept going. "Yes, of course; the other members of
the house party. Except they aren't exactly the ones I told
you about. Cris and Laura McHugh got trapped in Denver, where this storm hit yesterday, and we've added
Frank and Mary Ryder." Kori opened a door and flipped

on a light switch, then looked back and waited for Evelyn to catch up. "Frank and Mary were supposed to be on their honeymoon in Mexico, but they have to spend Christmas here instead, poor things."

Her face showing her confusion, Evelyn stepped into the room, which was small and windowless. It had been a storeroom in her time, but now it was beautifully decorated in a soft lavender and silver gray. The bed, not quite full size, had high, scroll-topped head and footboards that curved into the sideboards, giving the effect of an old-fashioned sleigh.

"This is charming," she said, because it was, but she turned and asked again, "You have other guests in the house?"

"Yes, you remember, I wrote and told you about my idea for an old-fashioned Christmas house party. It was in the same letter that said Peter would pick you up at the airport."

Evelyn said, "I was wondering about a taxi when your husband came up and surprised me."

Kori's face registered dismay and distress in equal parts. "You didn't get the letter? I wish I'd called—no, that wouldn't have helped, because—you'll like the others, they're good friends, except—oh, well, never mind. I mean, sit down and get those wet shoes off. I'll bring you a towel, then put Jeepers down for his nap and we can talk about it."

"Jeepers?"

Kori smiled and turned again to show the baby's sleepy face to Evelyn. "Gordon Peter. But the original Peter lives here and Gordon's a frequent visitor, so it was GP for a while, and that sort of turned into Jeep. I decided to let him take a late nap so he could meet you right away. Say hello to Cousin Evelyn, Jeep."

The baby, hearing his name, smiled briefly around his thumb, then resumed sucking.

Kori left, and Evelyn sat down in a comfortable little chintz chair to remove her shoes. Kori had written earlier that she wanted to invite some people to meet her, day and number unspecified. Evelyn had agreed, asking that it be a small gathering. She'd assumed Kori would arrange for it to happen on an evening close to her departure day, since they'd agreed they would need several days to share the stories of the house and its family. Instead, she'd walked into a house party already under way.

A Tucson neighbor's grandson referred often to the Post Awful, and Evelyn felt a sudden, angry kinship with his generation. Mind? Yes, she minded. She minded very much indeed.

Chapter

2 †

Evelyn changed her stockings and selected the purple suede laceups with cuban heels, then exchanged her brown dress for a purple knit skirt, a plain gray blouse and a purple sweater jacket. There was a pretty antique oval mirror on one wall which she used to powder her nose and apply the pale lipstick she wore only on important occasions. She smoothed her yellow-gray hair with a large hand, tucking a few stray strands into the bun at the nape of her neck.

She was nervous about meeting strangers, but, even more, didn't want to meet someone who might remember her. Frank and Mary—what was the last name? Runner, or Rider, neither one a name she recalled from her youth. Honeymooners, Kori had said, so they were probably very young. And there was a Gordon, who could sleep on anything, another trait of youth. Very likely none of them had ever heard of her; this generation was less interested in the gossip of its elders than any before it.

She looked around the little guest room, seeing nothing shabby or cheap. *Well,* she thought to herself with a little moue of envy, *it appears some of us are doing very well indeed.*

"So what are we going to do?" asked Kori, exasperated. They were in the oriel bedroom, she, Frank, Mary and Peter. Mary was standing by the bed as if guarding the open suitcase in its center. Frank and Peter were near the massive and ornate antique wardrobe; Kori, on the other side of the room, by the beautiful oriel window that gave the room its name.

Frank said to his wife, "Hon, we're going to have to trust Peter on this. He's a racing-class driver, and when he says the roads are impassable, they're impassable."

Peter said, "Mary, I don't understand why you won't face Mrs. Biggins."

"I don't think I owe anyone an explanation. Obviously you don't know the McKay family like I do, and that's all there is to it."

Kori said, "But with the blizzard out there, we may be stuck here for days! You can't stay in this room the whole time! What will Evelyn think?'

"I don't care what she thinks! If you don't want a scene you'll never forget, you'll arrange a schedule so we never meet."

"Mary, you're upset, and I'm sorry. On the other hand, Evelyn isn't very happy, either. She didn't expect to find guests other than herself already here. It seems she didn't get my last letter about the house party, and was hoping there'd be just her and me for the first couple of days. So fine; to give everyone a chance to adjust, I'll spend some time with Evelyn alone, at least until supper. We'll use the library, out of everyone's way. Then if you're still unhappy over her being here, I'll have Jill bring you up a tray and we'll tell Evelyn you're indisposed. That's all I can think of for right now; we'll take the rest as it comes. Okay?"

There were unhappy nods all around, and Kori left the room.

Kori seemed to be taking her time putting the baby to bed, so Evelyn did some unpacking while she waited. In lifting out her small jewelry box, she was reminded of the beautiful silver and amethyst earrings, all that remained of the good pieces her mother had left her. She opened the box and took them out.

She was putting the second one on when someone knocked on the door. "Yes?" she hooted.

The door opened, and it was Kori looking just the littlest bit strained. "I want to apologize," she said, "for surprising you with this house party—yes, I know it wasn't on purpose, but still . . ."

"Oh, my dear, it's all right. I'm just shy, and in a strange place . . ." She stopped, and suddenly smiled. "Isn't that an odd thing to say? I grew up here, this is—was—my home. But that was long ago." She gestured and confessed, "Oh, and I did hope I could have some time to renew my acquaintance with this house, and get to know you better, before I met all your friends."

"Not all of them," objected Kori, grimacing as if at a private, uncomfortable joke. "I'm a little shy myself, so I can understand how you feel. I have an idea though: how about we just ignore my other guests and spend the rest of the afternoon together, just we two? Then if you feel up to it, we can meet the others at supper."

"But it's Christmas Eve, and if you're the hostess . . ." said Evelyn, and paused, because she yearned to agree.

"No, truly, they won't mind. They'll have Peter to talk to, and Gordon's famous shrimp puffs to eat, and the tree to decorate. They'll hardly miss us. And I'm just dying to start hearing all the stories about this house."

"Well," said Evelyn and paused again. When Kori said nothing, only looked hopeful, she surrendered. "It's very kind of you to give up spending Christmas Eve with your other guests to listen to an old woman rattle on."

As they came down the front stairs, the sound of voices and recorded Christmas music was heard, faintly, from behind the closed parlor door. Kori paused, obviously listening to be sure the sounds were happy, and Evelyn, stopping beside her, had her eye caught by the newel post at the bottom of the stair railing. The top third of it had been deeply carved into a twist of leafy tree branches set with birds and their nests. Adult birds sang or brooded their eggs, a fledgling teetered on the edge of one nest, and hatchlings lifted bulbous heads from inside another, mouths agape for food.

Evelyn stroked a swift holding a mayfly in its beak. "I remember liking this even better than the window," she said.

"My decorator says it's unique," said Kori. "Is it original, do you know?"

"Oh, yes. My great-grandmother said her generation felt the home was a temple in which the family was worshipped, which explains this—and also their use of stained glass. I didn't care about the explanation, of course; I just thought it was beautiful."

Kori said, "Yes, but what a wonderful thought."

Without looking at Kori, Evelyn said, "You are very young, my dear."

"Come on," Kori said. "The library's this way. But you know that, don't you?"

The library was a pleasant, square room with a rectangular bay on the far wall so deep it was nearly another room. The bay was partly cut off from the rest of the library by a half wall of bookshelves. It was a traditional library, somber with old books in matched leather bindings. What wasn't bookshelf was painted in an old-fashioned, quiet green. A fine old circular table stood on lion-claw feet in the middle of the room, and steel engravings of famous authors and poets leaned down from the narrow stretch of wall above the bookshelves.

Blue tiles surrounded a small fireplace that shared its

chimney with the fireplace in the parlor. Two worn
leather club chairs were pulled up to it. Branches of pine
in the coal scuttle were the only comment on the season
in a room that remarked on the seasons as gently as it had
been marked by their passing.

"Why," said Evelyn, surprised, "this room is exactly as
I remember it!"

The round table stood on a very faded oriental rug,
double bordered, the medallion and the space around the
inner border made up of every imaginable kind of flower.

"Even this old rug," said Evelyn, coming to stand on it.
"I never thought this would still be here."

Kori said, "Still? I found it rolled up in the barn and
had it brought in. I didn't know it belonged in the library.
It—just felt as if it did. Maybe my parents had it taken
up."

"It's too bad you have no memories of them," said
Evelyn, touching the shining surface of the table with the
palm of her hand in a tentative way. "It would be interesting to know if your mother and grandmother were anything like the earlier women in our family. I, of course,
didn't know either of them."

"But my grandmother was your aunt," protested Kori.
"Surely you knew her!"

"No, she was away at boarding school when I was
young, and went from there to college, where she met the
man she married. I suppose I must have seen her on occasion, but my only real memory of her was at her wedding."

Kori, who had never even seen a photograph of her
grandmother, asked shyly, "Did she look anything like
me?"

"Well . . ." Evelyn studied Kori. "Not much. She was
taller, for one thing, and her hair was a lovely light brown
with reddish highlights. Rather like mine when I was a

girl." Evelyn reached up to touch the dingy gray knot at the nape of her neck, caught the little sardonic glitter in Kori's eyes, and looked away, saying, "My mother said she was mad about horses."

"Which must be a family trait. My mother bred ponies, I breed Arabians. And there's that racetrack out there that predates any of us. Who built it, do you know?"

"Yes, it was built by William McKay. He was the son of Charles McKay, who was my great-grandfather and your great-great-grandfather. Charles married Eugenia Klee and they had—" Evelyn touched her fingers as if counting, "—five children, including my grandfather, William. William married Annie Stuart, and their children were Ferris—my father—and Margaret. Margaret died having her one child, Katherine—that was your mother. Katherine married—," Evelyn paused and looked at Kori.

"—David Price, who had one child, me. But tell me how the house switched from your side of the family to mine."

"It was her husband—Margaret's husband—who bought this property when my father put it up for sale."

"Do you know why?"

"Because it was too much work for my mother, I suppose. This was well after the time when servants were cheap and easy to come by. And they had done a lot of entertaining when Father was vice president of Commercial and Property Owner's Bank, but in later years, when my father had accepted a different, less strenuous position, there were less demands made on them. Then father retired, and soon after they sold the house and moved away, first to Chicago, then to Florida."

"No, I mean, why did my grandfather buy this house? If it was my grandmother's people who had lived in it, and she was dead?"

Evelyn looked surprised. "I'm sure I couldn't say."

"Did you ever meet my grandfather? What was he like?"

"I saw him only once, when he married your grandmother, my Aunt Margaret. He was shorter than she, with dark hair that was thick and unruly. I distinctly remember it was a mass of curls, so unusual. I think someone said he was a deacon in his church."

Kori, touching the braids that were all that kept her own dark and curly hair from total anarchy, said, "But until he bought it, he was never in this house."

"Oh but he was! I was sent to Arizona for my health when I was twenty-two, but my parents lived on here for a long time after that. I remember my mother mentioning in her letters now and then that Aunt Meg and Uncle James had come for a weekend. Aunt Meg was very fond of this house." Evelyn gently patted the rug under her feet with one foot. "My father said grandfather—William— used this room as his den, and would allow no changes to it. He would not allow a woman in here except in the spring, when the housekeeper could come in to dust.

Kori brightened and came closer; here was something more than begats. "Is this room still something like it was in William's day?"

"Oh, yes. I fact, I'm quite sure what you see now is very much what you would have seen when the house was first built. Except the lamps, of course; we didn't get electricity out here until after my great-grandmother— 'Great-Jean' we called her—died. How interesting and how wonderful that it has survived unchanged." She turned to Kori and took her arm in a surprisingly firm grip. "I do hope you are not planning any changes to this room after all these years."

"No, of course not." Kori pulled free as gently as she could—she did not like being held fast. "This room is perfect just as it is. Anyway, Peter loves it as much as William did. He won't let me do more than replace the occasional light bulb."

Evelyn smiled, relieved. "I am very pleased to hear that." She walked around the table and past the half wall into the bay and said, "Yes, these are the same books that were here when I was a child."

Kori followed and glanced around at the old children's books, early mysteries and Edwardian romances that filled the shelves. "I learned to read using these books. People who wonder where I got my outdated values need look no farther than here."

"The cozy corner." Evelyn, relaxed now and smiling, turned to Kori. "That's what Great-Jean called this. She said that every proper house should have its cozy corner."

"You remember her well?"

"Oh yes. She didn't die until I was nearly sixteen. She outlived her husband and all her children."

"How sad," said Kori.

Evelyn gave a little shrug. "Yes, because it wasn't so much that she was very old as that the children all died before their time." She sat on the tufted leather seat under the window and stroked the tufted leather. "Whenever I was ill, I would be propped up with a comforter and lots of pillows right here."

"Me, too," said Kori, pleased to find another link with this family she owned, but didn't know. She pulled out a small black enamel chair that was pushed up to a tiny matching desk against the half-wall of bookshelves. "And on rainy days, when I couldn't go riding, or when I was just blue, I'd crawl in here with blankets and pillows, and Gordon would stack the window sill with books for me." She sat and opened a shallow drawer of the desk, rummaged briefly and found a sheet of paper. "I took what little I knew of the McKay family and added what you told me in your letters to draw up this genealogy chart. Can you tell me more about the people? They're mostly just names to me."

Evelyn took the sheet of paper.

CHARLES McKay(1828-1906)
married EUGENIA KLEE (1851-1928)

Lloyd	Phyllis	William	Margaret	Andrew	Alice
1867-74	1869-?	1871-1919	1875-	?	?
	married	married	1875		married
	George	Annie			Terence
	St. Clair				O'Brien

Ferris	Margaret
1890-1961	1891-1930
married	married
Lydia Campbell	James McLeod

EVELYN	Inez	Katherine
1911-	1912-?	1930-1973
married		married
Henry Biggins		David Price
		1928-1973
No Children		

Katherine (KORI)
1967-
married
O. Peter Brichter
1955-

Gordon Peter (Jeep)

KORI'S CHART

"Well, let's see. This is correct, Charles McKay, born in 1828 and died in 1906."

"Was he from around here?"

"Oh, no. He was born in Aberdeen, Scotland. He came to America sometime in the early 1840s, determined to turn a small inheritance into a great fortune—and indeed he did. He bought some land, and some stock, but the cleverest thing he did was to back forty-niners on their way to the gold fields of California. He'd pay their expenses for half of anything they found. Most found nothing, and two even died, but one discovered a perfectly enormous vein of gold. Charles was still one of the richest men in the state when he died."

"When did he marry Great-great-grandmother Eugenia?"

"In 1867—but no one ever called her Eugenia. She was always Jean or Jeannie. She was a Klee, a proud family rumored to marry one another's cousins to keep the money in the family. True or not, they all looked alike. Handsome people with blond hair and the most peculiar light brown eyes, though in Jeannie's generation there was very little money left to go around." Evelyn inclined ever so slightly toward Kori, eyes twinkling with amusement. "When she married Charles McKay—who by the way was *not* a cousin—she was sixteen and he was approaching forty, a scandalous difference. Worse, he had bright red hair and a *frightful* Scottish accent. On the other hand, there was all that lovely money . . ." Evelyn made a sound dangerously near a titter, and Kori laughed. Evelyn continued, "Great-Jean once confided to me that her parents' objections became mere formalities when they realized just how well off he was. And the marriage worked out very well—she kept a daguerreotype of Charles by her bedside to the day she died."

"And they had—you said five, but wasn't it six children?" said Kori, moving to sit beside Evelyn so she could point to the row of names under Charles' and Jeannie's. "James was the oldest and Alice was the baby . . ."

"No, no, there were only five," corrected Evelyn.

"Lloyd, Phyllis, William, Margaret, and Andrew." She rubbed the last name with a forefinger as if to erase it. "There was no Alice, no Alice. But here, let's see." Evelyn traced the dates under the first name with her finger. "Yes, Lloyd died in 1874, age seven, so that date is right."

"What did he die of, do you know? Diphtheria? Whooping cough?"

"No, it was an accident, a fall down some stairs. Probably the back stairs, they're so very steep. Before electric lights were installed, it was very dark back there. And little boys are so often in a rush, aren't they? Never taking time to be careful."

Kori said, "Are you sure there was no Alice? I found a page from a Charter marriage register that showed an Alice McKay, spinster, married one Terrence O'Brien in 1920. If she's not a daughter, could she be a niece or something?"

Evelyn grew thoughtful. "Do you know, I remember hearing about a woman named Mrs. O'Brien—" She paused. "Yes, I think that was her name. She came to see my father in 1930 or 1931, claiming to be a cousin, he said, or maybe it was an aunt. She was destitute, so Father gave her ten dollars, but he warned her not to come back. I wonder if she was this Alice."

"Could she have been a relation?"

"I doubt it. For one thing, an O'Brien would be Catholic, and in those days we didn't marry Catholics. I remember my dear mother being doubtful over my Henry because was he a . . ." Evelyn leaned sideways and whispered, "Lutheran."

Kori bit her lip. Keeping her head down, she tucked a forefinger into the folds of the tufted leather seat and said, "This is cracking in the creases; I'll have to replace it soon. I hope this shade of oxblood is a standard color."

She looked up and found Evelyn twinkling again at her, and the two broke into laughter.

Liking her now, Kori asked, "What was the house like when Jeannie lived here?"

Evelyn lifted her hands in another well-bred shrug. "I don't know. When I was born she had already moved into the cottage William built for her. It was on the property; I visited her every day. I don't suppose—"

"Oh, the cottage is still here; Danny lives in it. What did she look like? Great-Jean?"

"I remember her as old, of course. And tiny. But bustling, always busy." Evelyn's odd hoot became deliberate as she fell into narrative. "She had masses of snow white hair it took her an hour to comb out and put up in the morning. She wore button shoes, and her skirts came to her ankles. She wore purple in the winter, brown in the summer. She had a black straw summer hat trimmed with brown silk flowers. In winter she wore a bonnet." Evelyn sat back, smiling and instructive, remembering. "She had an electric car that had to be charged up at a service station in town, and if some Sunday we didn't go to church, she'd drive that car in alone and be angry with Father the whole next week for making her do it. I haven't thought of that car for years; it looked like a phone booth somehow, being so tall and not having much of a hood or trunk. She enjoyed taking it on little jaunts, but Sundays were different; she wanted to enter church on the arm of her grandson. We were far less likely to miss church when the weather was bad than otherwise, because Father would start thinking about Great-Jean setting out on the road by herself in that old car, and hurry us all into getting dressed for ten o'clock service."

Kori said, "How real you make it; I can almost see her! Would she scold Ferris if he didn't drive her to church?"

Evelyn gestured deprecatingly and said, "Great-Jean

wasn't the sort to raise her voice; she was strict, but not stern. She would just remark that she was *very* disappointed in my father, and pretty soon he'd come by the cottage and be especially nice to her for an hour or so. Then she'd offer him tea and cookies, and they'd be friends again. I remember Great-Jean and I shared a love of wordplay. I specialized in riddles, she'd make puns. Hers were very clever; she'd lead me right into a pun and laugh. I would groan and say what my mother always said, 'Puns are the *lowest* form of humour!' "

"Why is it we're supposed to groan at puns? Do you remember any of them?"

"Oh, let's see. There was one, something about a young lady returning her fiancee's gift of the rarest necklace on earth. Ah, yes; it was made of matched pearls of a unique color, and she sent it back, saying she wouldn't have any yellow peril." Evelyn's eyebrows went up expectantly.

Kori frowned. "I don't get it."

"In the early part of the century, before we learned to be afraid of Germany, our biggest worry was the Japanese, who were called the yellow peril."

"Oh," said Kori, "that's right, I remember reading about that in an old novel called *Her Father's Daughter*. The heroine was bright and talented and terribly bigoted, especially against the Japanese; all with the author's warm-hearted approval."

"Oh, that's how everyone was back then," said Evelyn, waving dismissively. She continued, "Most of Great-Jean's puns were homemade. We had a cook who came with the house when we inherited it. Great-Jean used to say that Sarah Friar—and she led us all in jokes about *that* name—she said Sarah had an electric personality, by which she meant her stormy moods. And she continued the joke even after she died in 1928, because she left

Sarah her electric car in her will. Sarah's husband died of drink in 1929 and her son Jimmy joined the Navy the Christmas after that, but Mrs. Friar drove that car around town until she died sometime in the thirties."

"I think I like Jeannie."

"I loved her. And I was her favorite."

"You mean between you and your sister?"

"There were three children out here then, me, my sister and little Jimmy. He was Sarah Friar's son, but Great-Jean treated him like one of the family. I asked her once why she liked Jimmy more than Inez, and she said he was trustworthy, with that sly smile that meant she was making a joke. Only I never got the point, and she never explained it to me, though she repeated it more than once."

"Trustworthy. No, I don't see a pun in that. Unless—did she leave Jimmy something in her will?"

"No, she didn't even mention him."

"Odd. I'm glad you got to know her, and that you came here to share her with me. And that William built her that cottage so she would be nearby. He must have liked having her nearby."

"Oh, no. And she didn't like him. I remember her saying that—" again Evelyn leaned over to share a confidence "—he had been a difficult person, from a child."

Kori smiled. "What made him so difficult?"

"Oh, the usual I suppose, being stubborn and disobedient. And later there were the horses. Race horses, you know. They were flashy, and they drew flashy people—and they were terribly expensive. William spent a great deal of his inheritance trying to make a go of his thoroughbreds. Great-Jean felt William's wife was to blame for not taking charge of him, settling him down."

"I suppose Jeannie had settled her own husband down?"

"Well—" said Evelyn, and they both laughed.

"How did Charles and Great-Jean come to build this house?" asked Kori.

"Oh, that's a famous family tale! Charles announced that Charter was too small for his cultivated tastes and that they would move to Chicago. Typically, Great-Jean decided at the same moment that her children would be happier in the country. Without consulting Charles, she began to discuss plans for a house with a local architect, and found it necessary to call on him frequently. Someone told great-grandfather, who went to speak to the architect, horsewhip in hand. But, as proof of the innocence of their meetings, their architect displayed the floor plans—and Charles liked them. He bought forty acres of land and ordered the house begun without telling her about it. The basement was dug and the frame of it up before he took her for a drive in the country and showed it to her, as a birthday surprise." Evelyn stopped and her head twisted a little to one side.

"Now that I think about it, I wonder if a move to the country wasn't what Great-Grandfather wanted all along, and this was his way of getting it." She chuckled. "Nevertheless, it cost him a great deal of money to do it this way, because Great-Jean hadn't finished thinking about what she wanted in the design of her house. She changed her mind constantly while the house was going up, and Great-Grandfather insisted the architect adjust his plans accordingly. It took nearly two years to get the place finished enough so they could move in. And that's why there are so many clumsy features about it; the front parlor so large there's no room for a back parlor, and no closets in the bedrooms, and the back stairs so steep and narrow.

"Dear Charles—she always called him Dear Charles; when I was very small I thought his first name was Dear—he died in 1905, and left the place to Wild William, who married that namby-pamby Annie Stuart."

Evelyn cleared her throat. "That's how Great-Jean described them. She was strong in her estimations of character."

Kori, delighted at the images Evelyn was creating, asked, "Was Wild William still wild when you knew him?"

"I don't think so. Actually, all I remember about him is that he was rather stout and always in a hurry, and that he had a big red mustache and a loud laugh."

"What was the house like when Wild William and Annie the Namby-pamby lived in it?"

"I remember pink and yellow roses on the wallpaper and an itchy red horsehair couch in the parlor. And the most beautiful blue polka-dot curtains in the kitchen! I was quite pleased in 1919 to discover we had inherited the house—and those polka-dot curtains—and rather sad when mother took them down first thing and made rags of them. My mother redecorated often until Father put his foot down in 1931. Except the library, of course." Evelyn looked around. "Father loved this room, and it's so exactly what it should be, that it would have been foolish and expensive to change it. When father wasn't using it as a study, it served as a back parlor; Mother served tea here, sometimes, and Inez entertained her chums."

"There's a mystery about Inez, isn't there? She—disappeared?"

Evelyn bowed her head. "It was a terrible thing, a mystery that was never solved."

"What happened? Tell me about her."

"Well, Inez was a pretty child, very tiny and blond, with beautiful light brown eyes, just like Great-Jean's. But as she grew up—well, 'fast' was the word for girls like her in my day." Evelyn sighed. "Father called her his whirling dervish, because she was full of energy, never still. He would laugh at her antics, but as she got older

Mother got after him to slow her down, because her behavior was making people talk. Dancing and parties had become roadhouses and liquor. But, she had talked Father into buying her a secondhand car for her sixteenth birthday, and there was no keeping her home. She'd be out till all hours, would sneak in tipsy and stinking of cigarettes. She and Mother used to have terrible quarrels. Inez often threatened to run away, but that was a common sort of threat in her set; and since she had no place to go, it wasn't taken seriously. Great-Jean said over and over that she'd come to a bad end, but what her end was, we don't know. She packed a suitcase one night and left, and we never saw her again."

Kori suggested, "Perhaps she eloped. Did she have a boyfriend?"

"Oh, dozens. And that's what we decided, finally. Someone she'd met in another town, because none of the local boys were missing. And someone recent, because the boy's parents never came inquiring. We never heard from her after she left, not so much as a postcard. My parents were frantic, of course; they called the police and put advertisements in the papers offering a large reward, even hired a private detective. But to no avail. It broke my father's heart."

Kori, taken up by the romantic images of a moonlight elopement, said, "Suppose there was an accident? After driving all night, laughing and sleepy, they lean toward one another to kiss, and miss a curve. And the bodies, burned beyond recognition, are buried in a pauper's grave somewhere."

Evelyn said, more pragmatically, "Or, once the honeymoon was over, he proved to be a bad sort of person, and she was ashamed to bring him home."

"Did she hint to you about a secret boyfriend or that she was planning to elope?"

"No. But we weren't as close as sisters should be, because we were so different. I don't remember the actual disappearance; I didn't know she'd gone until it was long over."

"Why not? Were you away when it happened?"

"No, I was very ill. It happened the night I was to go to an important dance with Henry Biggins. But I'd come down with a bad summer cold a few days before, and that night it turned into pneumonia. Mother and Father were out at a party, and came home to find Inez gone and me out of my mind with fever. Mother said later she was sure she'd lost both daughters, but after a week of it the doctor said I might live, and so I did."

"Pneumonia was much more dangerous in those days than it is today, wasn't it?"

"Yes, this was before penicillin. When I was well enough to travel, they sent me to Tucson—so good for the lungs, you know—and I fell in love with Arizona. Henry wrote me there, such nice letters, and he was so handsome and charming that—well, I invited him to visit and he did, and after we married he moved his law practice to Tucson, where we bought the house I still live in." She looked around the alcove. "It's a nice house, but not the equal of this one. I'm glad this stayed in the family." She shifted in her seat, shifting verbal gears as well. "Do you know, if I'd had my wits about me I would have thought to bring that photo album down with me. Remember I told you in one of my letters that I would make one up for you, with selections from all the family albums? Well, so I did. There are several of Great-Jean, and a wedding photo of William and Anne, and some of my parents. Oh, and there's a big photograph, taken in 1918, of everyone standing on the lawn in their Sunday best, including Mr. and Mrs. Friar and their little Jimmy.

I drew up a family tree a little more detailed than yours, with comments here and there; and put it in the back."

"And you wonder if I'd like to see it now?"

Evelyn smiled. "I unpacked it; it's on the bed in my room."

Kori jumped to her feet, and hurried to the library door. "Wait right here; I won't be a minute."

Chapter

3 †

Kori went back to the front entrance hall. The door to the parlor opened and Jill came out, a heavy silver tray balanced precariously on one hand. She was wearing a startlingly unflattering maid's costume.

Jill was scarcely twenty, short, a natural blond, and very pretty. The dress was a shapeless black sateen that came nearly to her ankles, with long sleeves ending in white cuffs. Clunky, low-heeled black shoes, and a ruffled white apron and cap, the latter with broad ribbon streamers, completed the outfit. Kori could not help smiling; if she had dared to suggest Jill wear such a uniform, Jill would not only have refused, but been highly insulted.

Jill, seeing Kori, assumed an erect stance, put both hands under the tray, and bobbed a respectable curtsey. "Ow, there you are, madom," she said in a bad imitation of Cockney. "Oi was wonderin' where you 'ad got to. Is you and the guest h'ov h'onor going to come into the parlor? Hi was just goin' for more *horse durvies*."

Kori giggled, but Jill properly repressed a responsive chortle. Kori said, "Oh, Jill, you are wonderful! I'm sorry Evelyn and I won't get to see you in action until later. We're going to be in the library until supper, and we don't want to be disturbed, okay?"

"Ow, that is too bad, for Oi can't wait to see 'er!" said Jill, then amended her enthusiasm with, "Oi mean, I've 'eard so much about 'er. I—Oi don't have no personal in-

terest in 'er at all, I don't." Jill started to walk past Kori,
but stopped and said, the accent gone, "Do you think you
could talk Dr. Ramsey into being the butler for a while?
I've tried, but he says he's too busy. His English accent is
real, and he'd be just perfect."

"Jill, when Gordon is cooking, it's best just to stay out
of his way. Besides, if he comes to join the party, it will be
as a guest."

"Oh. I thought—Oh well, too bad; he'd be really
great." And Jill went clumping off down the hall in her
ugly shoes.

Kori smiled after her. She was right, Dr. Gordon Douglas Ramsey, PhD, was genuinely English, and could feign
an attitude supercilious enough to deflate a duke. Which
was, he claimed, why he was a fully tenured professor of
medieval history at a local private college.

Gordon had known both Peter and Kori well before either knew the other existed. He served in the role of wise
and kindly uncle to both of them, had been responsible
for bringing them together, and was godfather to their
son. Kori could not imagine any major celebration in her
house without his presence.

Jill, who had come to Tretower just ten days ago, had
apparently mistaken Gordon's activities in the kitchen for
those of an employee, rather than a member of the family.
Jeep's first nanny had been a dull but competent care-
taker, and Kori was prepared to put up with a certain
amount of theatrical posing if Jill could prove herself the
same.

Kori ran up the stairs, down the hall, and into Evelyn's
room. She didn't see the album at first; she rechecked the
dresser and chair, frowning. Then she saw a corner of it,
sticking out from under a bathrobe on the bed. She pulled
it free.

As she was coming out the door, she could hear a rapping coming from down the back hall, then Frank's voice, "Mary? You in there?" Mary must be in the bathroom, she thought.

She turned and closed the bedroom door, took two steps toward the front stairs, then changed her mind and turned instead down the back hall, toward the nursery. Frank was nowhere in sight.

The nursery was a complex of three rooms. Jeep's crib was in the nanny's bedroom, with Jill's brass bed. A night light shaped like a clown holding a bunch of balloons, each balloon containing a tiny bulb, glowed softly on the dresser. By its light she could see Jeep on his back, arms upflung, safe asleep. She kissed her hand to him and hurried back down the hall to the front stairs.

Coming down, she saw Jill making some kind of tucking adjustment to the holly garland wrapped around the banister. She looked up and said in that silly accent, "Ow, am Oi glad you're here! I'll plug the lights in and you can tell me if they're ool raht." There were white fairy lights twisted into the garland, but they were not plugged in.

"I'm sure they'll be fine," said Kori, but she obediently paused to watch.

Jill stooped out of sight. There was a pause, then every light in the house went out.

"Hey!" said Jill in a perfectly American voice, then, *"Aaaaaaaaaaaaaaaaaa!"*

A door opened, and Peter's voice said, "What the hell?"

Kori had to raise her voice to be heard. "We've blown a fuse, I think! Jill, stop that noise!" She could hardly see; it was getting dark outside, and the fading light was further sieved through the stained glass. Kori groped her way down to the landing and put the photo album on the deep windowsill. "Peter, where are you?" She could make out dim shapes in the hall, but could not tell furniture from people.

"Parlor door—Mrs. Brichter said that's enough, Jill!"

The noise stopped, and Kori said, "Thank you. Now, Jill, if you'll feel along the baseboard behind you, you'll find a rechargeable flashlight. It's a big one, with a handle. . . ."

Jill sniffed and said, "Yus, madom, Oi've already got it." A square of light came on, and went sweeping upwards to catch Kori in the face, blinding her.

"Turn it onto the stairs, not in my eyes!"

"Sure. I mean, yus, madom." The light moved.

A woman's voice came from upstairs, distantly. "The lights have gone out up here!" Mary.

"Oh hell, upstairs, too?" said Peter.

Jill said hastily, "It wasn't me! I didn't even have the stupid plug stuck in when everything went dark!"

"Is there anyone else up here?" came Mary's plaintive voice.

Kori called, "We're down in the front hall, Mary; come here!"

"I can't see!"

"Okay, just a minute!" Kori came the rest of the way down the stairs. "Jill, hand me the light." There was some fumbling confusion before she got hold of it. "Mary?" she called, turning and splashing the beam against the wall near the top of the stairs.

But Mary didn't answer. Gone, feeling her way back to her room, probably, thought Kori.

"Ooh, I'm frightened, I am," said Jill, searching for her accent.

Another voice was heard, this time from the downstairs hall. "Jesus sufferin' Christ, where is everyone?"

"We're in the front hall, Frank!" called Peter.

"Who turned out the lights? And what's all the uproar?" By his voice and footsteps, Frank was approaching. Kori turned and threw the beam of the lantern on the floor of the downstairs hall to guide his way.

"Line down, must be," said Peter, "if the lights are off all over the house. Wasn't Gordon in the kitchen?"

"I was," said Gordon, from a little behind Frank. "Who was that screaming?"

"It was me, Dr. Ramsey," said Jill. "I was being the maid, and they always scream at things. Was I too loud?"

"Only for anything made of glass," remarked Frank, coming into the hall and pretending to unplug one ear with his little finger. "I thought someone was being killed."

Gordon came up beside him, a stocky figure with graying fair hair and baggy brown trousers, wrapped in a professional white apron. "Are the lights fused?" His accent was not Cockney, but that of an educated Londoner who has not been home for a long time.

"The lines have gone down in the storm, I think," said Peter.

"Ah, that was to be expected, I suppose. The stove, however, is fueled by bottle gas. I'd better get back to it, I left food cooking." He turned and went away.

Peter said, "Let's go into the parlor; the fireplace will give us some more light."

But Kori said, "No, I want to go get Mary right away; she sounded frightened—"

"Where is she?" asked Frank, his voice sharp with concern.

"Upstairs. It's only because it's dark, Frank. And the baby; I'd better bring him down too."

"I'll come with you," offered Jill.

"Let her go alone," said Peter. "Because one of us should go down and start the generator while the other keeps company in the parlor."

"All right." Kori started to hand over the lantern, but said, "No, wait, how's your night vision, Jill?"

"My mom says I inherited her cat eyes."

"Good, because I want you to go up without the light. There's another one at the top of the back stairs. Get it, then get Jeep and Mary. I'll go make sure Gordon's found the kerosene lamp in the kitchen, then go down to the basement and start the generator. Go on now."

"Yes'm." Jill lifted the rustling skirts of her maid's dress and clumped up into darkness.

Peter said, amused, "Come on, Frank; let's stir up the fire in the parlor. The ladies, as usual, having things well in hand out here."

Kori started down the downstairs back hall. She splashed the lantern's beam on the library door—and remembered Evelyn. "Oh, gosh," she said and opened it. "Evelyn, it's me, Kori. Sorry about the lights." There was no reply. "Evelyn?" Kori pointed the light toward the "cozy corner" and saw the soles of a pair of purple suede oxfords.

"Hey, what happened? Did you fall?" Kori hurried to look, and stopped, rooted with shock, the beam of light trembling along the too-still figure lying on the strip of carpet that marked the bay.

Evelyn lay partly on her left side, between the bench seat and the little desk and chair. Both desk and chair were shoved out of place, and the carpet was rucked up, as if by them and by Evelyn's fall. There was a minor trickle of blood coming out of the old woman's left ear, running down her cheek and under her chin. An open book lay facedown under an outstretched hand. She did not appear to be breathing.

Kori stooped by Evelyn's legs to squeeze hard just above one ankle, but got no response. She stood and pushed past the desk and chair to stoop again. The hair on the top of Evelyn's head was dark and wet, as was the carpet under her cheek. Kori pressed two fingers into Evelyn's neck, searching for the carotid, a test Peter had taught her. She felt no answering bump-bump. "Dear God," she muttered, "please let it be stupid me, can't find the right place." She stood and thrust her way quickly to the door.

"Peter?" she called, and repeated, louder, "Peter!"

"Fy'n galon?" came his voice from the parlor door, using his reassuring pet name for her.

She aimed the light so he could see his way, and when he arrived she held it out to him. "Evelyn's hurt. Back in the bay."

Peter took the lantern and went into the library.

"What is it, what's wrong now?" called Jill, coming up the hall from the other direction, sweeping her light before her. She had Mary and Gordon with her. Jeep was awake and crowing on her shoulder.

"It's Evelyn," said Kori. "She fell, I think."

"Is she hurt bad?" asked Jill.

"She's unconscious. Peter will see to her. Gordon, take Jill's light and go back to my office and call an ambulance. Jill, you go on to the parlor with Mary. Frank's waiting there."

"But the snow," said Gordon; "I'm not sure an ambulance can get out here."

"Go call anyway," said Kori. "We may need a doctor to give us advice."

Kori groped her way back into the library, to one of the leather club chairs in front of the little tiled fireplace, and sat down on the very front edge of it, pressing thighs and ankles tight together, clasping her hands in her lap.

"Damn," she heard Peter mutter.

"Is she . . . ?"

"Oh, yes. The top of her skull's like a smashed egg."

The light bounced around the bay. "I don't see what she hit it on," he said. "Did you move anything when you found her?"

"The desk and chair, getting to her. But they were already out of place. Oh, Peter, are you really sure . . . ?"

"Yes." This was followed presently by, "No, there's no blood on the desk or chair."

"Then what happened?"

"I can't say." Peter came out of the bay and flashed the light around the room, then heard the sounds of crying and came to her. She was trembling as he lifted her to her feet and embraced her.

"Th-this is terrible!" she sobbed. "My last relation, my last link with my family! Oh, Peter, why? What happened? It was that strip of carpet, wasn't it? It's not tacked down; she must have slipped, or tripped and fallen."

"*No, fy'n galon*; if she had, the injury would be on the side of her head, or the back, not the top." Still supporting her with one arm, he moved the light more slowly across the fireplace irons, the chairs and the angled, parchment-shaded lamps that stood like kibitzers behind them; then across the shining surface of the round table and up the bookshelves. He was looking for a stain, or fragments of something fallen from a height. But everything was as it should be; Wordsworth, Longfellow and Kipling stared down from their intact frames.

"What do you see?" asked Kori, rubbing her nose with the back of her hand like a child.

"Nothing unusual," said Peter, fishing for a handkerchief. "That's what worries me."

She took the handkerchief and blew her nose, and sat back down. She followed the lantern's beam as Peter walked with it around the room. "You can't be thinking—," she began, and stopped.

"Well," he said. "There's a body over there with no obvious explanation for how it got that way."

"No! Not murder, not Evelyn!"

"Did I say murder? But whatever, or whoever, hit her does not seem to be present any longer."

Kori pulled her knees up so she could wrap her arms around her shins. "This is impossible," she said, no longer teary. "Should I cancel the call for the ambulance? I mean, since she's. . . ."

"We need to report her death. Are you all right?" He knew she had a place beyond crying when she was badly shaken.

"I'm fine," she said, having reached that place and feeling falsely calm.

"All right. Go tell Gordie to report we've got a body on our hands."

Kori went to the door and opened it to find Gordon just arriving in front of it. "Phone's out," he said, and raised his voice to ask, "Peter, is there anything I can do to help?"

"No," said Peter.

"Is she dead?" asked Gordon.

"Gordie, please take Katherine to the parlor with you."

Kori began, "But Peter, I think. . . ."

"Not right now, *fy'n galon*. Go and see if you can persuade Frank to come in here without telling him why. And don't either of you tell anyone else what's happened, for now. And one of you go get that generator started; I want more light than this damn lantern can give me."

The bay was about six feet deep by eight feet long, and between the padded bench under the windows and the little desk and chair, there was not a whole lot of floor space. Evelyn Biggins took up most of it, lying with her head toward the closed end of the bay. Frank was getting past her body by moving along the bench on his knees. Snow blowing across the porch outside the twin windows made a sandy sound. He lifted the heavy drapes and looked out, but it was completely dark now and he could see nothing at all.

Peter stood at the open end of the bay and shone the light for him. Its beam caused the lettering on the spines of some of the old novels to gleam.

Their movements were coordinated and professional, which was not surprising, as Peter was a detective sergeant with the local police department and Frank had been, until six months ago when he retired, a police captain and Peter's supervisor.

"I wish we could get a real crew out here," said Frank.

"We probably will, but not for a day or two. Meanwhile, things may change or be changed. The body, for one. We have to do what we can right now."

"I'm sure she tripped and fell against something," said Frank.

"If it was an accident, you'd think we would see what caused it."

"Maybe that book under her hand hit her on the head," suggested Frank. He got off the bench and stooped near Evelyn's head, bending at queer angles trying to see its title. The book lay open, facedown, under her hand. It wasn't a very thick book. "I don't see any blood on the spine," reported Frank. "But, if it fell from one of those top shelves. . . ." He looked up at the half wall, lined solidly with books.

"No, look behind you," said Peter, "at the shelves on the far end of the bay; there's a gap on the right end of the third shelf down. But that's not nearly high enough, unless she was stooping or squatting when it fell."

Frank rose and looked where the light's beam played

over the end of the alcove. The shelves there were framed in the same dark, fluted wood that framed the door of the library. He lifted and released a volume that leaned across a narrow gap to touch the vertical end of the shelf. "Yes, this isn't even over my head, and you can see she was taller than me." He ran his finger along the other shelves at the end of the alcove, and Peter tried to follow his movement with the light. Frank said, "It looks as if she pulled out and replaced books from all the shelves at this end; see how they're out of line? I wonder what she was looking for."

"I wonder if she found it."

Frank turned, squatted, and carefully lifted the two fingers that covered the spine. "*Blind Corner*, by Dornford Yates," he said. "What kind of a book is that?"

"A thriller from the twenties. A good yarn even today, once you get used to the dashes for the swear words."

"Maybe she wasn't looking for a book, but something hidden in one. An old will, maybe, or a compromising love letter. But who actually ever hid something valuable in a book? Not that it wouldn't be a good idea in this place; it'd take a burglar a week to open every book in here."

Peter said, "On the other hand, the current owner has opened every book back in here not once, but several times. And never found anything more significant than a dried flower."

"Huh," grunted Frank. He returned the way he had come, by way of the bench, and stood looking back at the body. "No blood on anything but Evelyn and the rug. I don't like this."

"Me either." Peter tugged an earlobe. "But, dark as it is, we could be missing something obvious. What's taking them so long to get the generator started?"

† † †

The generator was a surprisingly small motor in a green metal shell. It was in the basement, on the floor next to the furnace.

"Where's the fuel tank? Better check that first," said Gordon. He had taken off the apron and replaced it with a shabby cardigan with leather patches on the elbows.

"It runs on bottle gas," said Kori. "See that pipe?" She ran the lantern's beam up and along the ceiling. "It comes in through there, and here." The beam traced another pipe, this one wrapped in insulation, to where it ran out the corner of a window. "That's the exhaust. And the tank is full; the man came and checked it day before yesterday."

"Very well. Now, how does one start it?"

"First, we make sure the master switch is thrown to off." The beam shifted to a small gray fuse box on a pillar, and Gordon stepped over to look.

"Off," he said. "Correct."

"Then we take hold of this handle and pull." Kori took the handle of the rope, kicked off a high-heeled shoe, and braced her foot against the motor in a lightly scuffed place that indicated this was normal procedure. She pulled one-handed, grunting, and the light danced across the walls and ceiling. The rope came halfway out, and that too slowly to do any good. "Uff!" she said. "Stiffer than I thought. Here, hold the light for me."

"No, if you please," said Gordon. "You hold it for me." They changed places. Using two hands, Gordon pulled, the rope came all the way out, and the motor went bub, bub, in an unenthusiastic way.

"Hell," said Gordon, and braced himself for another, harder pull. Bub, bub, bub, went the motor. "If this were a gasoline engine, I'd say it needed choking," he said, releasing the handle.

"Yes, but it's not," said Kori.

"Well, then," said Gordon, and he heaved again. And again. But all he got was a sullen bub, bub, bub.

"This isn't any good."

"Let me try again," said Kori.

Gordon started to say no, but instead took the light and held it while Kori again braced her foot on the place indicated, took hold of the handle and pulled hard. She was attractively slender, but had spent a lifetime working with horses, and the rope came out as fast and smoothly as it had under Gordon's efforts. And to as much effect.

Gordon squatted and said, "When in doubt, read the instructions, hm?"

"The instructions *say*," said Kori, getting out of his way, "take the handle in a firm grip and pull smoothly to the end of the rope! That's what we're doing; why won't it start?"

Gordon had come to Tretower Ranch when Kori was nine, staying until she was twenty, serving as her companion and private tutor, coming in that time to understand her in a way no one else could, not even Peter. He heard the real question she was asking, rose, turned to invite her into an embrace. "I am so very sorry this had to happen," he said. "I know how much you were expecting of this visit."

She put her arms around his well-padded shoulders and said to his sweater, "It isn't right, you know. I'd only just found her. It was so important to me, having a relative. What am I going to do?" Her voice, on the last question, rose to a ridiculous squeak, and she made a sound half laugh, half cough. "What if . . . Peter seems to think it might be . . . but it just couldn't! I mean, why?"

"Peter's wrong; there's no one who had any reason to kill her. As soon as we get him some light, he will see what really happened at once."

"You're right," said Kori, stepping back, wiping her

eyes with the palms of her hands. "So how about we get back to work and get them some?"

"Right." Gordon turned, stooped and began unscrewing a wing nut. He put it carefully into his cardigan pocket and lifted off the air filter, then put his palm over half of the carburetor intake. "Pull," he said.

"What are you doing?"

"Choking the engine. Pull."

Kori put the lantern on the floor, came and grasped the handle. She pulled, and the engine went *bub, chuff, whak, whak, bam!* and took off in an uneven, noisy run. He looked up at Kori with a triumphant grin and she grinned back—it was too noisy to say anything and be heard.

Gordon took his hand off the intake, and the engine stuttered, backfired again, then smoothed itself into a baritone snarl. He picked up the filter, fitted it back into place and screwed it down, while Kori went to the fuse box and threw the switch. The furnace cleared its broad throat and began an airy hum. A dim light halfway between them and the door leading back to the stairs came on. She turned the lantern off.

Halfway back up the stairs, daring the "told you so" she was glad he hadn't so far offered, she said, "You've started one of these generators before, haven't you?"

"No, I haven't." He put an arm around her. "But I was starting motors when your horses were still the rocking kind, so I know what an engine that needs choking should like. And now so do you."

The generator powered the furnace, the water pump, the kitchen and its appliances, and the parlor, the upstairs bathroom and the halls. All other rooms, including the library, remained in darkness.

"So now what?" asked Frank.

"First we turn off every unessential light and appliance," said Peter, "so we don't burn the generator out when we run extension cords to the lamps already in the library and to one or two more we'll bring in."

As Kori brought the last extension cord in the house to them, she asked, "How long is this going to take? And what do I tell the others? I don't think they believe this is only an accident any more."

"I'll talk to them," said Frank, "while Peter sets up the lights."

"Ask Mary for her camera," said Peter. "Send Katherine back with it. I want to talk to her about Evelyn."

Frank waited while Kori went upstairs with Mary to get her camera, and until Mary came to sit on one of the couches. Then Mary, Jill, and Gordon waited expectantly for Frank to explain things. Baby Jeep, bundled warmly in Jill's arms, made gurgling noises in the silence, and the black standard poodle, Michael D'Arcangelo, sat up on his strip of carpet, watching with interest as Frank assumed a policeman's stance at the other end of the couches.

"All right," Frank said, "I think it's time we told you what's going on."

"Hear, hear," said Gordon.

"Mrs. Biggins is dead," he began, and they nodded, having by now deduced that much. "She appears to have died of a skull fracture. Kori found her lying on the floor in the library bay. Did any of you hear a crash or thump that seemed to come from that direction?"

The three looked at one another, each waiting for someone else to say something, but no one else did, so they all shook their heads.

"All right," said Frank, pulling out a pen and a sheet of paper folded into quarters, in lieu of a notebook. "Where was everyone when the lights went out?"

"In the dark," said Gordon promptly, and Frank

frowned at the rebellious grins until they faded. "Sorry," said Gordon. "I was in the kitchen slicing carrots and building a Béarnaise sauce." Gordon's culinary skills were such that if he ever lost tenure, he could immediately double his salary by working as a cordon bleu chef.

"I was just about to plug in the lights for the stair garland," offered Jill. "Mrs. Brichter was right there, watching me." She gently pulled one of the ribbon streamers from her maid's hat out of the baby's hand and tucked it out of reach behind her back.

When his eyes lit on her, Mary said aggressively, "I was upstairs in our bedroom, for heaven's sake! You know that, Frank!" He quickly gestured agreement and went back to Jill.

"Kori was on the stairs watching you plug in the lights, right?" he asked, and Jill nodded. "Where was Peter?"

"In the parlor. I was still being the parlormaid, so I screamed at the dark, and he came to the door and told me to stop it."

Frank wrote that down.

"Why are you acting like this is a murder investigation?" asked Gordon. "Certainly I understand how when someone's died the facts need to be learned, but who needs an alibi for an accident?"

Jill said, "I agree with Gordon; you're acting like we're under arrest. Is something wrong?"

Frank said evasively, "Peter and I are conducting an investigation into some puzzling aspects of Mrs. Biggins's death, that's all."

Jill, alarmed, said, "There's something funny about the way Evelyn died, isn't there? Maybe it wasn't an accident!" Jeep made an abrupt, unhappy sound.

"Oh, for heaven's sake, Jill!" exclaimed Mary. "Who'd want to kill Evelyn Biggins after all these years!"

Jill bent over Jeep. "I only thought—" she muttered, "—I mean, we're being asked like this is murder."

"She's right, you know," said Mary to Frank. "I suppose you enjoy pretending you're back in harness, but that's no reason for you to get all bossy and nosy. I think we're all upset enough without you interrogating us." She got to her feet. "I'm going upstairs to lie down until supper," she said, "and I'd appreciate it if you'd join me."

"Now, Mary," began Frank.

"And there's a perfectly good sauce that's going to go bad if I don't get into the kitchen and tend to it," threatened Gordon, also standing.

Jill, smiling now, chimed in with, "It's getting on time for Jeep's supper. If you keep us here until he decides to really start complaining about it, you won't be able to hear our answers to your questions."

"Okay, okay, okay," said Frank, stuffing his square of paper into his pocket. "I guess the kind of weather that would keep a murderer at home will keep all of us here. All right, everyone can go about his or her business. Except stay out of the library."

Jill gathered the baby onto her shoulder and stood. Mary, starting for the door, said, "Frank, aren't you coming? I want to talk with you."

"Sorry, hon, I've been drafted to help Peter."

She turned and took two steps in his direction, index finger aimed at his face, an angry Mrs. Claus. "Oh, no, you haven't!" she said, "I won't allow it! There was an accident, and I'm sorry, and it's unfortunate, but there's no need for you to get involved! You're retired, remember? You aren't a policeman anymore. That's why I remarried you, and that's why I want you to come with me!"

"Now Mary-me-love, this won't take long," began

Frank, turning pink. "I promise I'll be up in just three shakes of a lamb's tail."

But Mary came closer, finger waving. Gordon, anxious to avoid a scene, inserted deftly, "If it's all right with you, Frank, I'd like to borrow Mary for a while. The sauce will need constant stirring once it gets under way again, and there are bread sticks to prepare. All this fuss has thrown me behind schedule, so I really do need an extra hand. Jill's about to become busy with Jeep, or I'd ask her."

Mary looked at him, then at her husband. In the silence, an angry, probing wind made one of the windows tremble. She knew this was a ruse to calm her and allow Frank to have his way. She wanted to ignore Gordon's peacemaking, but old memories told her this could end with her in tears and her husband in the library nonetheless. Frustrated, she turned angrily on Gordon, but caught herself and only said, "Oh, very well!" She took a deep breath and even forced a smile. "I'll stir while you bake, all right?"

"*Fy'n galon*, did Mrs. Biggins seem angry or frightened any of the time you talked to her?" Peter had finished taking photos, and was slumped in one of the club chairs, rewinding the film. His bright red sweater with six black and white penguins marching across his chest was a cheerful contrast to his sober expression.

"No," said Kori slowly, looking into the dead fireplace from her matching chair. "Well, she didn't like the idea of houseguests already waiting for her. She didn't get my last letter, in which I told her about my plans for a weekend Christmas party, so she was surprised. Dismayed might be a better word. She was shy, poor thing. Did you notice that when you were driving her out here?"

"Hmmh," said Peter, remembering the stiff, dark figure who rode beside him in the Bronco. "I was thinking she was scared, being out on a country road in a blizzard. I know I was."

Kori made a gesture meant to be at one of the windows beyond the half hall, and indicating the howling storm beyond. "This was shaping up to be a totally grim weekend anyway, wasn't it? Trapped out here by the storm, with Evelyn not wanting to meet my other guests and Mary threatening . . ." She stopped. "I didn't mean that."

"I know you didn't. But I'll have to ask her what she had against Evelyn McKay."

"How could it matter? She couldn't have done it; she was in the parlor with you and Frank and Jill when it happened."

"As a matter of fact, I was alone in the parlor. After you left the oriel bedroom, Mary said she had a headache and was going to take some aspirin and lie down. Frank gave her half an hour, then went up for her and still hadn't come back when the lights went out. Then Jill went away, discouraged at her lack of audience. Unless they got together somewhere else, none of them has an alibi. Who knew you were going to be in the library?"

Kori's face was frightened. "Everyone. I told you, Frank and Mary in the bedroom, and Jill when I saw her come out of the parlor on my way upstairs."

Peter asked, "Did anyone knock or come into the library while you were in there with Evelyn?"

"No."

"What did you two talk about?"

"Family stuff. The generations of McKays that lived here. She was one of those women who make a hobby of genealogy. Every time she mentioned a name, she gave the pedigree. 'Wild William, he would be your great-grandfather, built the racetrack,' that sort of thing. Only, of course, it's important to me right now too. And she mixed in some gossip about the family, not enough. . . ."

Kori stopped, gulped. "Oh, Peter, I can't bear this! There's no one left, no one, only me and the baby. . . ."

"And me," he said.

"You're not blood. There's a greatness to family. That's why they use the image of the tree, with its spreading limbs and many branches. Distant cousins and great-aunts and grandparents, all branches on the same tree, sharing the same roots. My tree is all chopped down. I can't make you understand how awful that is, can I?"

"Probably not," he said, but gently. Peter had a number of relatives, but none had bothered to rescue him from a terrifying childhood with an abusive father, so he had never felt any need to reach out to them as an adult. She herself had never been interested in family until their son had been born. Of course, now that the second-to-last bough of her family tree had been lopped off with violence, he had become interested, too, in a professional way. "Tell me more of what she said," he asked.

"Well, Great-Jean—that's what Evelyn called Eugenia McKay—was a tiny, bossy lady who left her electric car to the cook as a joke and called her daughter-in-law a namby-pamby because she couldn't keep her husband from wasting the family fortune on race horses."

"What kind of joke does an electric car make?"

"It was a final pun. The cook's name was Sarah Friar. . . ." Peter snorted and Kori said, "Yes, I know, isn't that dreadful? Anyway, Sarah was moody, excitable, and Great-Jean often said, in addition to the predictable jokes, that she had an electric personality, and underlined it with the bequest. She also said Sarah's boy Jimmy was trustworthy, but she didn't leave him anything."

"Hmmh. What else?"

"We covered a fair amount of ground considering we didn't have very long to talk. Great-Jean's second son, William, begat Ferris and Margaret; and from Ferris we

got Evelyn and from Margaret we got Katherine, who begat me."

"If there was a first son, how did William end up with
this place?"

"Because his first son fell down some stairs—the back
stairs, Evelyn thinks—and died when he was just a boy.
There was an older sister, too; and a younger sister and a
younger brother. But, out of five children, only William
had children who survived him, and now I'm the sole surviving descendent of the children."

"Hey, wait a minute. Didn't you try to interest me in a
genealogy chart a few weeks ago that said there were six
children? Or is that another branch?"

"No, I found a marriage license application that indicated an Alice McKay married one Terrence O'Brien.
She was the right age to be a tail-end baby, so I thought
she was a sixth child. But when I showed Evelyn my
chart, she said there was no Alice, and anyway she
couldn't be one of our McKays because none of us would
marry a Catholic back in those days. Oh, speaking of
charts . . . !"

"What is it?"

"There's a better one; Evelyn brought it. It's in the
back of a photo album she put together. That's why I went
upstairs, to get it. I left it on the landing, on the window
sill. The lights went out, and I wanted both hands to guide
myself. I'd better go get it."

"Hurry back," he said.

She was gone about three minutes, but came back
empty-handed. "It's gone," she reported. "I looked and
looked. Someone's taken it."

Chapter

4 †

Kori came into the kitchen not long after her talk with Peter, wearing thick socks, old pants, heavy working jacket, wool cap and a scarf. Fat mittens hung out of one pocket, dirty cotton work gloves from another. There was about these garments the pong of horses, and Jill, who was nearest, wrinkled her nose.

Mary looked up from the stove, where she was stirring a pot with a wooden spoon, as did Gordon who, flour to the elbows, was punching down a large pottery bowl of dough. A radio on the counter featured the unmistakable fruity accents of a BBC broadcaster explaining something in a low voice.

"Oh, I'm going to miss the *Nine Lessons and Carols*!" mourned Kori.

Gordon turned around. "Sorry, pet," he said. "But must you? I don't like your going out in this."

Mary asked, "You're going out? In this storm?"

"I have to feed the horses. Hunger isn't called on account of weather. Speaking of which, it smells wonderful in here."

"How can you tell?" asked Jill, her upturned nose still wrinkled. She was seated on a tall stool, stirring a small glass jar of green mush. She had exchanged the ugly dress for a tight red sweater printed with green bows and her favorite faded blue jeans. She was short, not really plump, but full figured, a somewhat pejorative phrase considering the reaction her figure stirred in a good number of males in the neighborhood. Like the dress had disguised her figure, the ribboned cap had disguised the shape of her face, which was square-cut, set with large, beautiful eyes of a peculiar light brown color. Her upper lip was thin and sharply recurved, and a decided contrast to her lower lip, which was sensuously rounded.

Jeep, in his plastic carrier on the counter, waved his arms and made his motor sound in an attempt to get the green mush moving in his direction. Jill dipped up a spoonful and laughed at Jeep's sudden silence and anxious clenching and unclenching of his small fists as she brought the spoon to his waiting mouth. She was a volatile person herself, leaping from merry to woebegone in the space between breathing in and out. But Kori had yet to find a trace of cruelty or meanness in her.

"I heard them moving something a while ago," said Jill, sober again. "Was it—her?"

"Yes."

"What did, I mean, where did they put . . . ?"

"They wrapped her in a sheet and took her out to the side porch," said Kori.

"But, she'll freeze out there, won't she?"

"Well, it's not as if she's able to notice such things any more," cut in Mary.

Kori added, more kindly, "And they can't leave her in the house, Jill. It may be a day or so before the snowplows get out this far, and—well, it's warm in here."

"Oh, ish! Never mind, I'm sorry I asked!" said Jill. She turned back to feeding Jeep.

Kori went to the refrigerator and opened the door. "Gordon, you didn't use both bunches of carrots, did you? You know I—no, here they are." And she pulled out a bunch by its leafy top.

"If you're looking for a snack," said Mary, "I can make you a sandwich. But supper will be ready soon."

Kori shook her head. "No, these are for the horses. There's not one of them who wouldn't exchange a pound of sugar lumps for one fresh carrot." She said to Gordon, "Remember when you told me the legend about the animals gaining the power of speech for one hour at midnight every Christmas eve?"

"And you've been bribing them every Christmas Eve since to say nice things about you. You be careful going out there."

"I'll take one of the rechargeables with me."

"And Michael."

"Don't worry," she said with a grin, "going without him takes the skill of a sneak thief." Kori went back up to the front hall and, opening the bench seat that formed the base of an old coat rack, took out a pair of Wellington rubber boots with traces of mud and worse on them. As she closed the seat and sat on it to pull the boots on, she became aware of a soft whimper coming from behind the parlor door. Michael knew what the sound of the bench seat being lifted meant. "I hear you, Michael," she said, and he whined louder.

She picked up the rechargeable light from beside the bench and opened the parlor door. Frank and Peter, seated facing one another on the two couches, fell abruptly silent. "Just me," she said. "Heading down to the barn." Michael, standing close, tail wagging, gave another soft whine. She smiled down at him. "All right, Mikey, let's go."

"We're going to have to talk to every one of them individually," said Peter. "I'll take Jill and Mary; you take Katherine and Gordon." Peter never called his wife Kori; it was a nickname that had been given to her by her uncle and therefore not a name he liked to find in his mouth. To him, she was Katherine.

"How about I take Mary," said Frank. "She's really upset by all of this, and she'll take some special handling. You can take Kori."

"Come on, Frank; who was the one who taught me about letting personal feelings affect the job? If I wanted this to be easy, I'd have taken my wife and my oldest friend, Gordon."

"Personal feelings have nothing to do with it," argued Frank. "It's simply that she won't say a word to you. She's scared because she let everyone know she didn't want to spend Christmas with a McKay."

"Why was that?" asked Peter. "Did she tell you what the quarrel was between her and Evelyn?"

"It wasn't a quarrel with Evelyn. She said it was the McKay family she didn't like."

"Did she say why?"

Frank shrugged uncomfortably. "No."

"So let me talk to her."

"If she wouldn't tell me, what makes you think she'll tell you? She keeps reminding me I'm not a cop any more, so being questioned by a real cop is going to make her clam up even tighter."

"I take it that means you're talking to her like a husband, not a cop. Asking me to allow that means you want special privileges for her. I can't do it, Frank. Mary's right, you're not a cop any more. So I'll talk to each of them myself, including Mary. You stay out of the interrogation part of it altogether."

It was far worse out than Kori had imagined. It was completely dark, and the driving snow made the lantern nearly useless. The wind blew her off balance, and the slope of the hill encouraged frequent falls. "Whew!" she laughed after picking herself up for the fourth time. "They were right; I shouldn't be out in this!"

Michael bounded over to see why she was dawdling. Twenty-eight inches high at the shoulder, he was nearly that deep into the drift she was struggling out of. Michael loved snow, and she had let his kennel cut grow out for the winter, so he had no problem with the cold. His top-knot of curls, so weighted with snow it hung sideways, looked sillier than usual. He stuck his pointed muzzle into her mitten to extract a caress, then bounded away again.

She had only gone a few yards more down the gentle slope toward the barn when Michael began his come-and-see bark. She ignored it; she felt no need to waste any effort in going to look at the dead bird or fallen branch or whatever other anomaly he had discovered in his territory. She wanted to be in the warm safety of the barn.

"Michael! Come!" she ordered, and Michael, who was obedience trained, came at once. But when she reached to take him by his broad leather collar, he bounced away, tempting her to chase him, and a few seconds later she heard him barking come-and-see, come-and-see.

She looked around, pointing the light, but the snow was so thick she couldn't find him, so she turned again toward the barn—or where she guessed the barn to be; she couldn't see that far, either.

Then, suddenly, Michael was back beside her. He grabbed the edge of her jacket with his teeth and pulled. She fell, and he leaped out of reach and stopped. "Whuff," he said, looking off at something he felt needed her immediate attention. She struggled to her feet and again swept the lantern's beam in the direction he was looking. Nothing.

"Whuff!" he insisted, and moved off without looking back to see if she would follow.

"This better be good, Mikey, old pal," she muttered, starting after him. But in two or three steps she could no longer see him. She stopped and waited for him to begin barking again, and when he did, she followed the sound.

When he saw her coming he dipped into the snow and came up with a piece of cloth, which he commenced yanking at, shaking his head to pull it free. But it was fastened to the snow somehow, and wouldn't come loose. He dropped it when she arrived beside him. His tail was wagging madly. "What is it?" she asked, and bent to pick it up.

It was a sleeve, the sleeve of an army-green coat. But heavy, with an arm inside it and pale bare fingers just visible at the end of it. Not a stranger's arm; Michael would be standing on a stranger, not trying to help him up. She bent further to brush the snow away from the person's face, and fell to her knees.

"Danny, oh, Danny!" she cried, shaking him by the shoulder. "What happened? Are you hurt?"

Her groom pulled his other arm out of the snow and moved it in some sort of gesture, and his eyes opened. "Round," he muttered, and the eyes closed again.

His hat was gone as well as his gloves. His skin was so cold the snow falling on his face was not melting. She took her own hat off and put it on him, pulling it over his ears.

"Danny, listen to me! Can you get up?" She shook him again, and he mumbled something. "Come on, the house is just a little way from here! Danny?"

But Danny was not paying attention. She began to lift him, trying to get him to sit up, but he was a stupid, top-heavy bundle that fell over as soon as she let go.

She turned to her dog and said, "Michael, go home! Get Peter!" The dog immediately ran off.

She pulled her mittens off and forced them over his hands, a task made difficult by his limp lack of cooperation. That done, she began again to pull at the young man's shoulders. "Come on, we can't just sit here." She pulled him into an upright position and squatted to shout into his face, "What's the matter? Can you hear me?"

"Central mercy," he muttered, sagging awkwardly away from her.

Frightened at his helplessness, his gibberish, she let him collapse, then pulled him the rest of the way over, onto his face. "Crawl then!" she ordered, pulling at his coat. "It's not far, come on!" She pulled harder, fruitlessly, then leaned to shout in his ear. "Crawl, Danny, *crawl*! I can't carry you!"

"Flintsy," he said into the snow.

"The house is this way," she said, starting to pull again. "See? Look!" She groped for the big flashlight, wiped his face with an elbow and straightened, pointing with its beam. But the light bounced off the flying curtain of snow in front of her; she couldn't see past it. She shut off the light and then there was nothing but darkness and the wind ruffling her hair, taking cold nips at her ears and through the thin work gloves she had worn under the mittens. She turned the light on again and looked around for a tree or other landmark, trying to orient herself. She had been floundering an unknown while toward the barn, then followed Michael's barking—to the left? Back uphill? To here, with Danny. She didn't know where in the big yard they were. "Oh, help," she said.

Michael had a flapper entrance around back that was barely big enough for him to crawl through, a necessary stratagem to slow him down enough for the electronic device on his collar to trigger its lock. It also scraped some of the snow off as he went through, and he paused in the back hallway to shake more of it off before trotting into the kitchen.

"Hey, Michael's back!" said Jill.

Mary hurried him through by flapping at him with her apron. "Out, out, out with you!" she ordered.

But Gordon, frowning, followed him as he trotted up the hall.

Scent and voices led him to the parlor, where he barked until Peter opened the door. As soon as he did, Michael turned and ran to the front door, barking, ordering that it be opened at once. When no one complied, he came back to look up at Peter. "Waw-waw-waw!" he barked again, then looked at the door.

"What's wrong?" asked Peter.

Frustrated, Michael ran to the door again. "Waw-waw-waw!" he barked, anxiety now adding a falsetto edge to the sound.

"What's the matter with that dog?" asked Frank in an annoyed tone, coming to the parlor door.

"What's he doing back without Kori?" asked Gordon. "I told her to take the dog with her to the barn."

Michael reared onto his hind legs to emphasize his demand that they let him back outside. "Waw-waw-waw!"

Mary came up the hallway from the kitchen wiping her hands on her apron, Jill following with Jeep in her arms. "Can't you make him stop it?" said Mary. "He'll set the baby crying."

"I think something's happened to Kori," said Gordon.

Peter went to the armoire and found his coat, actions that made Michael fall silent, though following every move with desperate anxiety. "Is it Katherine?" Peter asked. "Is she hurt?" The dog turned and pressed his wet nose against the edge of the door and whined.

Peter reached over him and opened it. Michael shot through, across the porch and down the steps. Peter stepped onto the porch and stopped. The snow was flying horizontally across the edge of the porch, blocking any view of the background into which Michael had already vanished. "Michael!" he called.

"Waw!" barked Michael. "Waw, waw!" Very faintly, he heard another voice: "Help! Help!"

His heart, prepared, nevertheless lurched. *"Fy'n galon?"* he called.

"Here, oh here, hurry!"

He tumbled down the steps and fell to his knees in deep snow. Rising, holding the front of his coat shut against the wind, he called, "Where are you?"

"Where is she? What's happened?" asked Gordon, from the porch.

"Shut up!" said Peter, gesturing savagely over his shoulder. *"Fy'n galon?"*

"Over here! Speak, Michael!"

Guided by the barking, Peter waded through howling darkness until he saw her lantern and found her—and someone else.

"It's Danny," she said. "God knows how long he's been out here. He's almost unconscious, and I can't lift him."

He stooped to touch her head, whitened with snow. "Are you all right? Where's your hat?"

"I'm fine. I put it on him, and my mittens. But I couldn't leave him; I didn't know if I could find him again. That's why I sent Michael."

Peter turned to the boy, who was sagging against Kori. "Danny, what's happened to you?"

Danny did not reply, and when he shook him only groaned.

"Come on, on your feet!" ordered Peter, shaking him harder.

"Stupid," mumbled Danny.

"Here, wake up!" Peter said, half lifting him by his coat and striking him hard on his face. "Snap out of it!"

"Go 'way," insisted Danny, trying to brush away the blow with a hand. "Tha's hard to tell."

Kori said, "He's not drunk, he's—what's it called when you go crazy with cold and take off your hat and gloves?"

"Hypothermia. Let's get him inside." Peter moved around to Danny's back. "You take his legs," he said.

"Which way?" she asked, tucking Danny's knees under her arms and straightening.

Peter lifted and called, "Gordon!"

"Here I am! Where are you?"

"Stay where you are! Can you see the house?"

"Yes, of course!"

"Well, we can't! Talk us back!"

In a few minutes, the warm shape of the front door began to show through the falling snow, Gordon's silhouette looming up in front. When he saw them, he came and took Danny's legs from Kori. With Michael following close behind, Danny was taken into the house.

Jill, Mary and Frank were waiting in the hall for them. "Blankets!" ordered Peter. Jill handed Jeep to Frank and ran up the stairs. Jeep, startled, began to cry.

Gordon and Peter carried Danny into the parlor, where he was dumped on the floor in front of the fire and unceremoniously stripped of every article of clothing. Kori watched through the open door as she took off her own jacket and boots. Michael shook himself hard, sending snow in all directions.

Jill came tumbling back down the stairs with a huge bundle of blankets, including, Kori noted, the down comforter from the master bedroom. She followed Jill into the parlor, took Jeep from Frank. "There, there, Jeepers," she soothed him. "Hush a baby." Jeep, taken from the scary stranger and made secure in his mother's arms, changed note, but continued voicing his concern at the frantic activity swirling around him.

Danny was lifted onto the farther couch, naked, still unaware. The light from the fire gave a spurious warm glow to his white flesh. Jill dropped the blankets, flipped open the comforter and hurried to tuck it around him, seeming as anxious to cover his nakedness as to start his warming.

Peter, putting wood on the fire, said, "What's the matter with that baby?" and Kori left the room.

In the welcome silence Peter ordered, "Here, Mary, take this blanket and hold it up to the fire, get it warm. Gordon, go heat some water and make some nice strong tea."

Jill, still tucking, asked, her voice husky, "Is he going to be all right?"

"If we can get him warm, yes," said Peter. "We need to get him aware enough to drink something warm. It's his internal temperature being low that's got him like this."

Jill said in a low, furious voice, "This is Kori's fault! She shouldn't have let him try to drive home!"

"Jill, are you and Danny—," began Peter.

"So what?" interrupted Jill. "You don't mind, do you?" She sounded as if she'd bite Peter if he minded.

"I guess not," said Peter, surprised. "Mary, bring your blanket here. Jill, take that comforter off and start heating it. Frank, keep that fire going. We'll work this in shifts. Don't let the comforter get too hot; we don't want to burn him." He went to help Mary tuck the warm blanket around Danny.

"She wouldn't have let one of her horses go out in this," said Jill from the fireplace, holding the blanket wide. "They're at the top of her lists, and Danny's at the bottom."

"That's enough, Jill," warned Peter.

Mary said, "Jill, be glad Kori loves her horses. It was for love of them that she started out to the barn, and doing that got Danny rescued." She picked up another blanket and came to stand beside Jill, arms spread. The two enclosed Frank, who, on his knees, was feeding splints of wood to the fire. Michael suddenly thrust his way in, carrying a bit of kindling. "Go away, get out of here!" ordered Frank, and the dog, surprised, obeyed.

Jill tested the front of her blanket with an elbow. "Danny better be all right," she said. "You won't like it if he's not all right."

Chapter
5 †

Peter sat on a couch in the living room across from Danny, who was asleep on the other couch. Sleep was a natural part of recovery from hypothermia, but in a little while Peter would wake him to see how he was doing.

Not long ago Danny had been sitting up, ruffled and confused, trying to understand why everyone was so pleased with him, and why Peter insisted he drink a mug of hot, strong tea laced with milk and sugar. He had managed to down nearly all of it before getting sick into a plastic bucket Peter had not been surprised he'd need, but the second had stayed put. The room was silent now; the others had found tasks to occupy them. The refilled mug was keeping warm on the hearth until Danny was awake again.

While waiting, Peter recorded all he could remember of the events of the past few hours in a fat little notebook, printing because his writing was all but illegible, even to him. That finished, he stuffed the notebook into a back pocket and slipped off the couch onto his knees beside Danny.

Danny was a skinny young man of twenty-four, with mud-colored hair, high cheekbones and narrow eyes. He had come to Tretower still shaky from heroin withdrawal, desperate for a job because with one he might get probation instead of a jail sentence. Kori had hired him because she had awakened that morning to find herself with a still-useless broken arm, all her regular help gone, and her five hungry horses standing ankle-deep in muck. Now, five years later, he had gone from stable hand to groom to trainer and only this past summer he had taken her stallion Copper Wind all the way to the Nationals, showing him brilliantly in the finals. But, his law-oriented family still considered him a failure, and Danny himself was surprisingly offhand about his talent with horses.

"Danny?" Peter touched the young man's shoulder. "Danny, wake up."

"Wassa mare?" Danny's eyes opened. He stared at the ceiling a while, as if trying to think where he'd seen it before.

"Danny?"

He looked over, blinking, then recognized the speaker. "Oh, hi, Sergeant." Danny had had several run-ins with Peter before his reform, and had never felt comfortable enough around the detective to call him by his first name. Nor had Peter asked him to after the one time.

Danny stretched and yawned, then froze. "I'm naked," he said, and reached out with a bare arm to touch the top of the pale wool blanket that covered him, as if to confirm its presence.

"Yes."

Danny moved his head back and forth experimentally and swallowed, making a face. "Did I get sick? I feel like hell."

"You came real close to knowing how accurate that comparison is."

"I did?"

"You nearly froze to death earlier this evening."

Danny stared at Peter, then his eyes unfocused as he explored the past few hours. He twisted his head up and back, in the direction of the bay. "It's snowing, isn't it?"

"Yes."

"I thought it was a dream." He rubbed his face, glanced

at his thin bare arm and shoved it under the blanket. "Where are my clothes?"

"We took them off; they got wet from you burrowing around in the snow out there. Want to tell me what happened?"

"I was walking in from the road and got lost in the snow." His voice was slower and softer than usual. "How did I get back in the house?"

"We carried you in. You were found unconscious in the front yard. Why did you come back? I thought you were going home for Christmas."

"Not home, to my sister's. But yeah, so did I."

"Where's the pickup?"

"In the ditch, maybe a mile west of here. My bag and a pile of presents are still in the front seat."

"Tell me how that happened."

Danny frowned and thought. He shivered suddenly. "I guess I am cold," he said, surprised.

"The shivering is a good sign," said Peter. "You were too cold to shiver a little while ago."

"Kori said maybe I shouldn't go, and I should've listened to her." Danny pulled up his knees to shiver some more. "It's terrible out there. Just going down the lane, the snow was blowing so you couldn't see three yards in front of you. I turned on the fog lamps, but they didn't help. I thought once I got onto the road, I'd be all right, but it was worse. I couldn't even tell where the damn road was, and I was fishtailing all over the place. I knew I'd never make it, so I decided to turn around and come back." He shook his head, remembering. "I swung over and came around, then stopped and tried to back up. I felt a tire drop off the pavement and I hit the brakes, but the wind had caught her and she just drifted back and sideways, kinda slow, into the ditch. I punched her hard to stop it, but there wasn't any traction. I was thinking, don't tip over, please, don't tip over. And we didn't; she settled in solid at about forty-five degrees. I had to stand on the steering wheel to get out."

"Did you see anyone else out there?"

"Uh-uh. Maybe, if I'd've been heading toward town, I would've seen you coming in from the airport and not had to try that walk. . . ." Danny fell silent; Peter began to think he was falling asleep, but he was only remembering. "It's real dark out there," he said. "Snowing like it's the last chance it'll ever get. And the wind takes your breath away, and knocks you down and blows snow up your sleeves. No, no one with any sense is out in that. That's why I didn't stay very long with the truck; I was pretty sure no one was going to come along and offer me a ride."

"How did you find your way back to the house?"

"How close was I? I knew I was in the yard."

"I mean from the road."

"Oh, that was the easy part. I kept falling in the ditch, so I finally just stayed there until I came to where the lane crosses it, then came up."

"Could there have been someone in the lane with you?"

Danny yawned, shivered and sniffed hard. "No, that lane's too narrow to sneak a car up it, even in a blizzard." He frowned. "Is there someone here I don't know about?"

"No. But could someone have slipped past you on foot?"

"Well—I was keeping one hand on the top rail to find my way, so I suppose there could have been someone doing the same thing on the other side." He smiled suddenly, amused at the notion of two lost souls feeling their way up parallel fences, neither aware of the other. "But I doubt there was someone doing that, unless he dumped himself in the ditch like I did." He squirmed under the

blanket, making some invisible adjustment, then struggled to an upright position, putting his wrapped feet on
the floor. His dark hair was ruffled into angry peaks, but
his face was slow and dull, the narrow eyes puffy.
"What's this all about?"

"Evelyn Biggins is dead."

"*She* went out in this?"

"No, she was found dead in the library."

Danny hazarded, "Heart?"

"Skull fracture."

"She fell?"

"Apparently not."

Danny looked away, baffled. Then his eyes came back,
questioning, and saw no denial in Peter's face. "Holy
sufferin' Christ!" he murmured.

"Funny words from an atheist."

"Hey, holy cow doesn't make it when you want to say
something that means oh my God."

Peter got up from his couch and went to bring the
warm mug of tea to Danny. "Drink this."

Danny reached out over the top of the blanket, careful
not to open it more than necessary. The blanket was a
thick wool, stiff as leather, not inclined to cling or drape.
He took the mug, looked into it, sniffed and made a face.
"Do I have to?"

"Yes."

"Has it got medicine in it?"

"No, it's just tea with milk and sugar. It's warm, and
we're trying to get your core temperature up."

"What's that mean?"

"Instead of ninety-eight point six, your internal temperature was probably down around eighty-seven degrees. It's close to normal now, and this will help bring it
the rest of the way up."

"I don't feel cold inside." Danny brought both arms out

of the blanket, holding it in place with his elbows. He wrapped his hands around the mug but didn't drink. "You know, if some guy sneaked up on the house, he must have built-in radar. Because once I crossed the racetrack, I was out of fence, and lost. I couldn't find the house or the barn or a shed or even a goddamn bush to crawl under. I mean, I've lived here for five years, and I was really lost. I kept thinking, did the whole place get up and walk off? That's when it started getting like a nightmare. I was mad and cold and scared, but I just kept walking, thinking I'd run into somewhere I could hole up sooner or later. There were snowdrifts up to my elbows, and I kept falling, and every time it got harder to get up. I got so cold it stopped being important to try to keep warm. And then—then—I kind of forget what was next, and then I was wearing something hot and my hands wouldn't work—I had a cup of something, and Jill wrapped her hands around mine so I could hang on to it—did that happen, or was it a dream?"

"That happened."

"Is Jill gonna be able to stay out here?"

"Why shouldn't she?"

"I dunno. Kori is funny about who gets to take care of Jeep. Not that she shouldn't be, but Jill hasn't got a degree in child management or anything. She just likes kids."

"If she leaves it will be her choice; meanwhile, Kori likes her, and so does Jeep. I understand you and Jill are . . . close."

Danny's eyes dropped and he consulted the contents of the mug with his nose, but still didn't drink. "Jill tell you that?"

"Yes."

"Well, okay then, yeah. I met her late this summer, and we sort of hit it off. I told her after Kori hired her we should let you guys know, that you'd find out and maybe be pissed we didn't say something, but Jill wasn't sure Kori would approve, and to be truthful neither was I, so I agreed not to mention it."

"Drink your tea."

Danny lifted the mug to his lips but winced when he opened his mouth to accept the beverage. "Hey!" he said, lowering the mug. "Someone slugged me! I remember now! He hit me right here!" Danny probed his jaw and winced again.

Peter leaned forward, "Did you get a look at him?"

"Huh-uh. I had my eyes closed or something. There was a dog barking, he wouldn't shut up. Was Michael out? How come he didn't take hold of that guy who hit me? Or was it the guy's dog barking? Maybe that's how he found the house; he had a dog with him."

"It was after the dog barked that you were hit?"

"I think so. The dog was barking right in my face. He wanted me to snap."

"The dog?"

"The guy who hit me. Or rap. He hit me and said, 'Rap on it.'" Danny frowned. "Or something like that. Then I think he dragged me off to someplace."

Peter sighed and sat back. "That was me. I hit you and said, 'Snap out of it.' When you didn't, we carried you into the house."

"Oh, I guess I was pretty gone, huh." Danny took a tentative sip of his tea and made a face. "Could I have something else to drink? Coffee? Cocoa? This tastes like stewed string."

"Sure." Peter took the mug and put it back on the hearth. "So you don't remember running into anyone else out there."

"Not if it was you who hit me." Danny sat back with a

sigh. His nose twitched. "Can I eat something? What time is it? I think I'm hungry."

"Not quite eight. Supper's nearly ready. One of Gordon's specials."

Danny inhaled to double-check an aroma. "I thought I smelled bread baking. Can I have my clothes back?"

"They're not dry yet. And we can't use the dryer while we're running on the generator."

Danny's eyebrows lifted, then he grinned. "*That's* why I couldn't see any lights! The lines went down in the storm, right? I wasn't going blind or crazy, after all." He hitched the blanket closer around him and shivered again. "Can I borrow something to wear? This blanket's drafty."

"I'm sure we can find something. Danny, did you know who Evelyn Biggins was before Kori told you about her?"

"Nope. Never heard of her."

"Who did you tell that she was coming for a visit?"

Danny shrugged and sat back. The surge of energy his nap had given him was about to run out. "My folks. Jill."

"Anybody else?"

"Nobody else I can think of."

"When did you tell Jill?"

He yawned and his eyes stayed closed. "Right after Kori told me. Jill was so interested, I figured maybe it was news or something, so I told my mom and dad." His eyebrows lifted, though his eyes remained closed. "And my old man did perk up when I told him. He said he thought both girls were dead—Evelyn had a sister, do you know that?"

"Yes. Don't go to sleep until you drink something." Peter stood. "What else did he say?"

Danny shrugged. "He asked me if I was going to stay out here for Christmas, and I said no, I'd come to my sister's—it's her turn to host the family Christmas. I guess he wanted me to say hi to Mrs. Biggins or something." Danny wriggled himself deeper into the couch. "Not that she'd know me—or even him; my dad was probably about three weeks old when she left town." He started to smile, but yanked another yawn instead.

"I'm sure the Bannisters were friends of the McKays."

"Oh, they were. My grandfather was their family lawyer. Dad thinks I've smudged the family reputation, becoming a farmhand. But I'm not a farmhand, I'm a horse trainer. I said that if it would make him happy, I'd let Evelyn know my sister was a hot-shot lawyer, just like her dad and granddad." He did smile, then.

"He didn't hint he'd like to meet Evelyn and tell her himself?"

"Oh, no. He wasn't making a serious point of it, he was more like teasing. Like it didn't really matter."

"What about Jill? Why was she interested?"

Danny sighed. "Beats me. I only know that when she found out a McKay was coming home, she decided she wanted to be a nanny. Better go get that coffee. And make it strong; I'm falling asleep right before your eyes."

The table in the dining room of the big house was a massive affair. With all its leaves in place, it could seat twenty; without them, it seated Gordon, Jill, Danny, Mary, Frank, Peter and Kori, with room to spare.

The power was still out, so they were eating by candlelight, which Kori and Gordon had made into a virtue by bringing out two elaborate silver candelabras. The candles' warm light softened the strained expressions on everyone's face.

There was a big white tureen with geese marching around it at Kori's end of the table, and she was ladling soup into shallow bowls and handing them left and right to be passed along. The supper was a tomato broccoli soup, cold chicken with hot Béarnaise sauce a la Ramsey, carrots cooked with ginger and honey, and bread sticks.

"So long as I have you all in one place," said Peter from his place at the head of the table, in a tone that sent ripples down already rigid spines, "I'd like to ask if anyone saw or moved a photo album that was left on the windowsill of the front stairs landing."

There were blank looks all around. Kori said, hands moving to indicate size, "It's just a cheap one, black pages and a light-blue imitation-leather cover." She had changed back into her cranberry cocktail dress, but had added a soft patterned shawl against the room's chill.

More blank looks, this time accompanied by a solemn shaking of heads. Gordon started the bread sticks around. "Is it important?" he asked.

"I wouldn't have thought so," said Peter; "but the fact that it's missing, and none of you admits taking it, makes me wonder." He looked around at the wary faces. No one looked back; they didn't even look at one another. "This won't do, you know," he said. "One or more of you must have seen it, and someone moved it. I want to know who." He waited.

After what seemed an eternity, he made a faint sound of exasperation, and said, "It was you, wasn't it, Jill?"

To everyone's surprise, she jumped up, her chair scooting back and nearly tipping over. "What is this, arrest-the-nanny time?" she cried. "You think because I'm just the servant out here you can pick on me? Well, I didn't touch that old album, and I won't stay here and let anyone accuse me of stealing! Good-bye!" She stormed out of the room.

Danny said, "I can't believe you'd just accuse her like that, especially in front of everyone."

"I wasn't accusing her of stealing it," said Peter, still looking at the door she'd slammed behind her. "I don't think it was stolen." His eyes came back to the table. "I think someone took it, perhaps casually, and then hid it to keep someone else from seeing it. I was going to go around the table and see what each of you had to say on being accused." In the silence that followed that remark, the wind could be heard whistling under the eaves and making the ill-fitting storm windows shift in their frames.

Then Kori said, "But how can it be of interest to anyone but me? No, Peter; it'll turn up tomorrow and someone will say, 'Oh, that thing! I was afraid someone would trip over it, so I put it up there, out of the way.' "

"Maybe you're right," said Peter. "So how about we try to fix where everyone was from about ten minutes before the lights went out to right after?"

Danny said, "I was somewhere between the road and the house, falling down in the snow."

Peter nodded and looked at his wife, who said, "I was in the library with Evelyn. From there I went to the front hall where I saw Jill and spoke to her. Then I went up the front stairs and when I came down, I saw Jill again. She asked me to wait while she plugged in the fairy lights on the holly garland, and I did. Then the hall went dark, and I thought it was because there was a short in the lights."

"Did you see anyone besides Jill and Evelyn?" asked Peter, who had put down his soup apron to pull out his notebook and a ballpoint pen.

She thought. "Frank. Except I didn't see him. I heard him. He was knocking on the bathroom door calling Mary's name."

That brought Peter's head up. "I thought you told me you saw Mary in the bedroom, Frank."

"I did. She said she was going to try to take a nap."

Peter looked at Mary, who was nodding emphatic agreement. "I had a terrible headache."

"Why did you knock on the bathroom door, then?" Peter asked Frank.

"I looked in there first."

Kori frowned and said, "No, you didn't; you couldn't have. I was standing outside Evelyn's bedroom, which is next to the oriel bedroom, when I heard you knocking. Then I went down to the nursery, which is across from the bathroom. If you'd gone from the bathroom to the oriel bedroom, we would have passed each other. But we didn't. In fact I didn't see you at all. I thought you must have gone down the back stairs."

Frank smiled aggressively. "I *said* I looked in there first. And since she wasn't in there, I did like the Queen of England does and took advantage of the opportunity. Okay?"

Kori repressed an embarrassed smile. "Oh," she said. "Sorry."

Frank said to Peter, "And Mary *was* in the 'oriel bedroom', as Kori calls it. She said she had taken some aspirin and wanted to try to sleep. So I came back down the hall and took the back stairs—thank God the lights didn't go until after I made it down, they're the steepest stairs I've ever seen in a house. I was in the kitchen and was wondering where Dr. Ramsey was, when it went dark. Someone let out a yell like the devil had her by the hair and I came up the hall to find out what the hell was going on. Kori was there with a big flashlight, and I saw Jill and you too. And you saw me."

Peter frowned and asked Gordon, "Where had you gone to, Gordie?"

"Nowhere," said Gordon, surprised. He had finished his soup and was putting slices of chicken onto his plate. "Frank must be mistaken; I was never out of the kitchen. I was alternating between scraping and slicing carrots and building a Béarnaise sauce." He reached for a gravy boat, poured a little of its contents over the slices of chicken. "This very Béarnaise sauce, my own adaptation of a complex and difficult family recipe." He set the boat down in front of Kori's plate hard enough to spill a little onto the damask tablecloth. "Sorry," he said.

"Now wait just a minute," said Frank. "I came into the kitchen just before the lights went out, and you weren't there."

"I *was* there," insisted Gordon. "I was working in there well before the lights went out, and I didn't come away until I heard Jill scream."

Frank said heavily, "When I came into the kitchen, the lights were still on. And you weren't there. I remember wondering where you were, because you'd left the radio playing."

"If I left before you came through," said Gordon, "then why did I come up the hall to find out what was going on behind you? Remember, Peter? He arrived ahead of me."

"You damn betcha I remember," said Frank, suddenly looking like the cop he used to be. "So if you weren't in the kitchen, and you weren't in the hall, where the hell were you?"

"The dining room," suggested Kori. "Setting the table."

"We set the table together, by candlelight," said Gordon to her, surprised. "I hadn't gone in there before that."

"The only other room off that hallway is the library," said Frank. "Maybe you were in there."

"What would I be doing in the library?" asked Gordon; and the answer hung heavy, unspoken, in the air.

"Oh, for heaven's sake!" said Kori, angry and frightened. "Gordon never heard of Evelyn McKay Biggins until I told him about her five or six weeks ago! This is stupid; there must be a simple explanation!"

"If there is," said Frank, "I think we should ask Dr. Ramsey to give it to us."

"You don't mean to suggest I might have sneaked into the library and coshed that old woman on the head?" Gordon seemed only now to be understanding that Frank might be serious about accusing him of murder.

"Now, Gordie," said Peter. "I've known you since I drew you for freshman history in college, and I'm sure that if you murdered someone it wouldn't be like this."

"Thank you very much, I don't think!"

"Dr. Ramsey," said Frank, "Peter can tell you anyone will murder, if motive and opportunity connect just right. I think you'll agree we need to look into this further."

But, instead of replying, Gordon stood, draped his napkin over his forearm, put his silverware on his plate and lifted it with one hand, took his wineglass with the other, turned and walked through the swinging door to the kitchen.

As Danny came down the hallway, he could hear a baby crying. He opened the door to the night nursery, wondering where Jill was, but as he crossed the floor toward the nanny's bedroom he heard the deeper, softer sounds of a woman weeping.

He put a hand on the doorknob, hesitating, then opened it. The light in the room was soft, almost too dim. It came from a small lamp whose base contained a six-volt battery.

Jill, sitting on the narrow brass bed with her back to the door, twisted around, startled, when he came in. Jeep was on her lap. She blinked, surprised a second time, and said, "Oh, it's you."

"Who were you expecting?" he asked.

"I—I thought. . . ."

"They were coming to arrest you?" She nodded word-

lessly. Danny forced a light chuckle and took the baby
from her. "Poor kid," he said, not meaning the baby. He
held Jeep awhile, patting his back, then put him into his
crib, offering him a pacifier and a fabric ball that tinkled
when shaken. Comforted and sleepy, Jeep let his heavy
eyelids close even as tears still leaked from their corners.

When Danny came to sit at the foot of the narrow bed,
Jill had stopped crying. He was wearing a set of dark
green sweats borrowed from Peter, which were only a little too big, two pairs of heavy socks, and no shoes because his feet were two sizes smaller than Peter's. The
dim light made interesting shadows around his high
cheekbones and small narrow eyes.

"Your hair's a wreck," she said, gulping one last time,
wiping cheeks that were already dry.

"My hair can be fixed," said Danny, brushing at it im-
patiently. "What's with you? That was quite a scene you
put on downstairs."

"Oh Danny, I'm so scared," she whispered and put her
hands over her eyes. "Peter thinks I took that album."

"He doesn't suspect you any more than the rest of us."
Danny explained the tactic Peter had been about to use.
"It's an old, old trick, but it still works."

She went from sad to indignant in a single sharply
drawn breath. "Is that legal, tricking people like that?"

"Probably. Cops have a job to do, and most of the people they work with have good reasons for lying. You
should've just said you didn't know anything about it. Or
at least not blown up like that. That was a mistake." He
made an effort to keep the question light. "Did you take
the album?"

"Oh, Danny!" she whispered, "how can you think
something like that?" She bit her lower lip and her chin
began to tremble.

"Why did you really come out here?"

"You know why! To be near you!"

He sighed and looked away. "I don't know what I know anymore."

She gave a tiny sob and two very real tears overflowed. He looked around and his expression changed. She began to lean slowly toward him, and he took her in his arms. "Aw," he said, patting her on the back. "Aw, now."

Chapter

6 †

Kori sat on one of the couches in the living room, untangling a string of lights. Peter and Gordon were near the tree. Gordon had several strings circling his neck like a wreath; they were plugged in and his hands moved in and out of the nimbus of light as he unwrapped and fed one string to Peter, who was putting it on the branches.

"No, no, Peter," said Gordon, "you're putting them all on one side. You should try to distribute them evenly."

Peter was the sort of person who as a bachelor ignored all the holidays, especially Christmas. Had this world been arranged for his comfort, rather than his education, he would have met and married a woman who marked Christmas with a rendition of Tom Lehrer's "The Christmas Song" (". . . Brother, here we go again!").

But he had married Katherine McLeod Price, and so found himself standing in front of a nine-foot balsam, taking criticism on the way he was putting a string of miniature lights on the smelly thing. Though he did not make caustic retorts to that effect, by the muscle working of his jaw it was obvious he was thinking plenty.

Kori put down her tangle of lights to regard the pair who had just entered the room. Jill had resumed her maid's costume. "We've come to 'elp," she said in her dreadful cockney.

"Danny, shouldn't you be in bed?" replied Kori.

He shrugged. "I feel fine."

"Still," remarked Peter from over by the tree, "I think he should at least be resting."

"Sit down," said Kori.

"Yes'm," said Danny, and he backed until his knees were buckled by the cushions of the other couch.

"Now, what inspired that outburst at the supper table?" Kori asked Jill.

Jill hesitated, then abandoned her accent to say, "I was scared, I guess. I mean, your husband's a real policeman, right? And the way he was talking I was sure he was gonna arrest me, so I just kind of overreacted. I'm sorry, I apologize."

"Did you take the album?"

"No, ma'am!" This was said emphatically, with eyes sincerely wide.

"All right. Here, you sit down and take over from me. I don't know how it is that every year I wind these up very neatly and put them away, and the next year I take them out, they're in knots."

Jill plumped herself down. "I know. Ours do it too. It wouldn't be Christmas if you didn't have to spend at least an hour untangling the lights." She was being determinedly normal.

With Jill's energetic help, the tree was soon twinkling all over with multicolored lights. She wore a path in the carpet, bringing untangled strings one by one to Gordon—Kori liked a lot of lights on her trees.

"What was she like?" asked Jill after a while, handing a string to Gordon, and plugging it into the bamboo stem of plugs hanging near his left elbow. "Mrs. Biggins, I mean."

Kori paused and thought. "A little shy," she said. "She had a funny voice, like Eleanor Roosevelt's."

"Who's Eleanor Roosevelt?" asked Jill.

"President Franklin Roosevelt's wife."

"Oh, back in the olden days. What do you mean, her voice was funny?"

"As if she were talking artificially high."

"You mean like Aunt Bea?" frowned Jill.

"Who?" asked Gordon.

"On 'The Andy Griffith Show.' Old reruns. Aunt Bea, who took care of Opie and Andy's house." Jill paused, lifted her chin, raised her eyebrows, and called, her voice cracking upwards, "O-oh-pee! Suppah's ready!"

"Well, almost something like that," said Kori, laughing. Then she sobered, closed her eyes, took a steadying breath, and asked briskly, "How many more strings of lights to go?" She looked over toward the couches. "Is Danny asleep?"

"Yes, he went to sleep before I even finished the first string. There're two more strings left."

"Is the futon set up in the nursery for him?" Kori asked, turning to Peter.

"Yes." Peter started for the couches. "I'll help him up to bed."

But Jill was there ahead of him. "Danny? Wake up, time for bed."

"Huh? Oh, hi, baby." He pulled her down by an arm for a kiss.

"No, listen a second," said Jill, glancing toward the others. "I'm going to take you upstairs. The futon's waiting for you in the nursery."

"Huh?" Danny followed her look. "Oh. Okay. Sure." He got to his feet, a little unsteadily, and allowed her to lead him out of the room. "G'night," he murmured, yawning, as she opened the door and maneuvered him through it.

Their going out was complicated by the coming in of Frank and Mary, who looked after them briefly, nonplussed.

"What was that all about?" asked Frank, coming in.

Peter explained that Danny was still suffering from the effects of hypothermia, and Jill was taking him to bed.

"Could he be faking that?" asked Frank.

"The behavior, yes," said Peter. "But I took his temperature after we got him conscious, remember? There's no way to fake a thermometer down to ninety when it should indicate ninety-eight point six."

"Thank God that dog found him," said Mary.

Peter said, "I wish we could persuade him to find the weapon. What was it? And where did it get to? How about you and I do a search, Frank?"

Mary took Frank's hand in a pointed way, and Frank snorted, "Now? During a power outage? In this big old house? With all of that howling darkness to toss it into? I think you should offer us a round of drinks, let us hang a bauble on the tree, and send us off to bed." Frank smiled at his wife. "I have done enough police work today, considering I am a retired cop on my honeymoon. What say you, *ma chroide*?"

Mary noticed that Frank kept closer to her after his speech, and lightly interrupted every time the talk drifted toward the case. They helped decorate the tree, but before it was finished Frank was pleading weariness. God knew Mary had had enough, so she joined him in the excuses and they went upstairs.

Now, some while later, they lay side by side under crisp sheets in the oriel bedroom. Frank was asleep, his slow exhalations marked by a thin whistle, but Mary was wide awake.

How nice to have him back with her, hear the dear, familiar whistle—was it a bit more emphatic than it used to be? Well, he was a bit older than when she had last heard

it. The warmth of his presence hadn't changed
though—he was always so toasty in bed.

She'd never loved anyone else. She'd divorced him because she loved him, because she couldn't bear the waiting, every day, for the doorbell to ring and some kind,
shamefaced young cop to be standing there, waiting to
tell her Frank was dead at the hands of a piece of trash not
worth one of Frank's fingernails.

But then he had retired. And two days after retiring,
he'd come ringing her doorbell himself.

She wished with all her heart they had been able to fly
to Denver and make that connection to Mexico. Bright,
cheerful Mexico. Was it like the travelogues and posters?
White beaches under a hot sun, clothes that glowed with
color? And the sightseeing, churches and Mayan
ruins—or was it Aztec? No matter, they would have been
climbing the ruins, staring at the cryptic stone carvings,
tipping the guide to take a photograph of them holding
hands in front of some alien god. They'd have been that
harmless cliche, the American couple on vacation,
avoiding the water, peeling the fruit, sending postcards to
their friends back home.

Instead here they were, trapped in this old house, be-
sieged by snow and wind, with a dead body wrapped in a
sheet on the porch. And everyone knew the blizzard made
it impossible that some stranger had come and got away
again.

How could Frank sleep?

Because he was used to murder, she supposed. But also
because he didn't know who the lady beside him really
was, not even after all these years. Poor dead Evelyn Mc-
Kay Biggins, wouldn't your jaw have dropped if I had introduced myself? I mean *really* introduced myself? You
stupid, silly, oblivious old woman!

Mary rolled over and felt hot tears of—what? Anger?

Shame? Pity?—spill from her eyes and soak into the lavender-scented pillowcase. Poor old Evelyn, it wasn't her fault. Maybe she hadn't even known.

Jill settled under the blankets in the narrow brass bed in the nanny's bedroom. She was far too frightened and angry to think about sleep. Kori might have been friendly in the parlor, but she had come along later to check on Danny— she said—and had taken Jeep away. Oh, not grabbed him rudely, but so cool it was even more insulting. "I think it would be better if Jeep slept with me tonight. I'm sure you understand."

You bet she understood. Jill was a suspect in this murder business.

Jill wondered if she shouldn't slip out of bed and go get some advice from Danny. He was curled under a comforter on that Japanese mattress Peter and Gordon had dragged down from the third floor, sleeping in that restless way sick people do.

When Jill had brought him up and got him undressed and settled, he had stolen a kiss, asked for—and gotten— another, and then—but she'd said no, not now and for sure not in this house. Even sick, Danny was something else. Honestly, why it always had to be the girl saying no. . . . So it would probably be a bad idea to go wake him up. Anyway, Danny never showed much sympathy for people complaining about messes they got their own selves into. Serves you right, he'd say, coming out here asking for that job.

Maybe it did. Though it was kind of surprising how much she liked a job she'd come looking for under false pretenses. Big old houses were nice, and the work wasn't all that hard. But there were undercurrents even in this ritzy place.

For example, why didn't Peter like Jeep? Most men

she knew liked babies, or only pretended not to. But Kori had given her strict instructions to keep Jeep out of his way. And Peter hadn't come to visit the nursery once so far. Wasn't Jeep his? No, he must be, because if he wasn't, Peter'd be mad at Kori too. And she'd seen the two of them together enough to know they were still in love. It was weird to think of someone as beautiful as Kori falling in love with someone like Peter Brichter. He wasn't exactly homely, but his hair was falling out, and he had those mean eyes. What did Kori see in him? It wasn't like the money was his. And he was a lot older than her too. Danny said he was a really good cop, a hero who had saved Kori from her uncle who was a crook. Maybe it was opposites attracting: she was rich and gentle, he was cold and dangerous.

But now he was really dangerous to Jill. Was there any way she could fix that?

Gordon lay in the bed that unfolded out of a brown leather easy chair. He was in the Brown Study, a room that served Peter as a den and was decorated in his favorite color. Though there were big windows on two walls, it was utterly dark in the room. Perhaps he should have accepted Kori's offer of a kerosene lamp; he had gotten used again to living in a city, where utter darkness is unknown.

He rolled over, closing his eyes against the dark, willing sleep to come. No use. It wasn't just the darkness; it was this house. He had suffered much at the hands of Kori's villainous uncle, who had ruled this house in which he, Dr. Gordon Douglas Ramsey, had spent many an unquiet hour. It was too bad that he, who loved quiet and order, had found himself so often in the midst of noise and fury. He still sometimes had dreams about the screaming sirens, the sudden bomb that smashed his Lon-

don home when he was eleven and sent him with his
mother on a flight to Canada and safety, praying every
night that his father would survive his enlistment in the
Air Corps to join them. He had, but only just, and the frail
old man who came to live with them after the war had not
survived his second winter in Winnipeg.

They had moved again, he and his mother, to Chicago,
where he had bent his keen mind to the road of orderly
scholarship, earning degrees up through his doctorate,
and further honors as a professor of history at the Univer-
sity of Chicago. All was serene until Nick Tellios sought
him out wanting a tutor for his mad niece.

All right, that was his own fault, he had provided the
indiscretion Tellios used to lever him out of his safe little
niche. And in one respect it had turned out not so badly,
because the niece was Kori, who was not mad after all
and had become the daughter he would never otherwise
have had. But even so, those years in the hands of Nick
Tellios had been a desperate time, full of dread.

And now this. Held again in this unhappy house, with
murder afoot.

Fortunately, there was nothing to connect Gordon with
Evelyn Biggins. Gordon knew it was that total lack of
connection more than his friendship with Peter and Kori
that made Peter look slantwise at Frank's outrageous suspicion. Still, the wretched memories, the thick darkness,
and the knowledge that the stilled heart of a silly old
woman was stealthily turning to ice out on the porch,
stopped his downward drift into sleep.

He rolled again, seeking something less ugly to chew
on. He wondered if the power failure and consequent
heavy darkness bothered Peter, who was also a product of
the city. Probably not; Peter was never much on environ-
ment, especially now that he had Kori.

Interesting that their marriage was working so well.

They shared that potentially bad kind of love, where each focuses on the other instead of finding a common, outward, viewpoint. She was a country girl born and bred, a member of the horsey set, a good works and country-club type, an Episcopalian of good standing. Peter, on the other hand, was a cop, with all the cynicism and souring of the soul that can bring, an agnostic—how could he be otherwise?—with the mind of a philosopher. Not exactly a matched set. Yet couples more poorly matched fell in love, while couples even closer never found the spark.

He sighed, beginning at last to relax. Love was a thing of chance. "The life so short, the craft so long to learn; The assay so sharp, so hard the conquering; The dreadful joy . . ." wrote Geoffrey Chaucer on the subject, in his marvelous *Parliament of Fowls*. Yet love was not the key to bliss, concluded the birds; hearts desired something even more elemental: mutual respect. Strange, that something so base . . .

It was after midnight. Kori and Peter were still in the parlor, decorating that blessed tree. Or rather, Kori was. Peter was taking hooks out of his sweater, fitting them into the ornaments and handing them to her. Jeep was in his plastic carrier seat, rubbing his eyes and whining without quite breaking into real tears.

"What's wrong with him?" asked Peter.

"He wants to be up in his crib," she replied, taking a clear glass ball with a bit of silver tinsel in it from him.

"Then why not put him there?"

"Because I'm not going to let Jill take care of him any more."

"She quit, didn't she?" he asked, afraid Kori was going to blame him and his suppertime questioning of her.

"No. . . ."

"I can almost hear the 'but' in that."

She hung the ball, and came back to unbuckle and pick up the baby, who exchanged his whine for a fussy whimper. "There, now," she murmured at him. "Hush a baby."

"But what?" asked Peter.

"But—I don't want her taking care of him."

"Why not?" She did not reply, and he said, "You think she killed Evelyn."

"No I don't. Well . . . maybe. I mean, I know it wasn't you, and it couldn't be Frank, or his Mary, or my Danny, or our Gordon. So that leaves her." Kori sat down, and Jeep cuddled himself against her, finding his thumb and falling asleep almost before he could begin sucking it.

"You think it's her because she's the closest thing we have to a stranger in the house?"

"You make it sound unfair," she said. She put the sleeping baby back in his seat. "But suppose I'm right? Suppose she's the carrier of some kind of grudge against the McKay family? Jeep's a McKay, you know." She touched the sleeping baby on his arm and stood. "I can't take that chance. Give me another ornament." He gave her a small stuffed fabric Santa, and she stood with it awhile, studying the tree. "This could have been one of our better trees," she said. "But I'm all distracted. Maybe I should just pull the plug and go to bed." But, instead, she looked for and found a place on one of the upper branches for the Santa.

"You don't need electricity, if you're really into tradition," he said, slipping a hook through the loop of a purple ornament shaped like a raindrop. "In fact, I'm surprised you've never thought of candles."

"I've never experienced a tree with candles on it, so it's not part of my tradition. And even if it was, I think I'd go with electric lights since I don't want to spend Christmas day in the barn, watching smoke rise from the ruins of my house." She took the purple ornament from him.

"Christmas in a barn would be even more traditional," he pointed out—wickedly, as he was not a Christian. She threw him a look, but he had arranged his eyebrows into a shape of innocence, underlined by his next selecting a lamb-shaped ornament.

The baby woke fussing and began to cry, heartbroken, longing sobs. "Awww," she began, but before she could pick him up again, Peter did.

"Here now," he said, holding him up against his shoulder clumsily, half-smothering him on his sweater. "You settle down, now, okay? And you," he said to his wife, "keep decorating, or we'll be here all night."

"We're almost finished." Kori had come to hover, but Jeep had stopped crying, so she couldn't exactly demand he surrender him. Peter nodded toward the lamb in his lap, and she took it and went back to the tree. The ornament was old and some of the paint had worn off the lumps that were meant to be curls.

"This used to be my favorite when I was a child," she said. "I think I felt sorry for it; it's a clumsy sort of lamb and that spot of red on its mouth looks like lipstick."

He began to whistle softly the melody of a very rude song about a lonely Scotsman and his sheep.

She let him have one chorus, then hung the lamb and said, "I know your childhood memories of the season are unpleasant, but mine aren't; and I hope you'll agree that it's better to pass my soppy sentiment than your anger and pessimism to the rising generation." Which wasn't fair, as the rising generation could not have understood the words if Peter had sung them, and was nodding off to the melody. But it did stop the whistling.

He shifted from a sitting position to a lying-down one and Jeep, one small fist buried in the fabric of Peter's sweater, made a little mew of content and went of sleep. He began very stealthily to remove the remaining hooks from his sweater, hoping she wouldn't notice and say something about how the baby could have put an eye out on one of them.

She was funny about him and the baby. He was sure that while he was at work she doted on Jeep, but as soon as he came home she put the baby so far into the background that he came close at times to forgetting he was there. And when he did have occasion to hold him, she stood close, and took him back as soon as possible. Was she afraid he'd swing his son by his little heels and dash his brains out on a stone?

He looked down at the downy pale head resting on his chest. There was a faint sound, rapid, regular. The kid was snoring. He suppressed his laughter; he didn't want Jeep to wake up and start crying again.

Peter hadn't liked being a child and still didn't much like being around other people's. So he had been glad when she agreed there would be no children in this marriage. But, it had happened, and now he was sort of used to the idea. He glanced over at his wife. She had pulled the box of ornaments closer to the tree and was busy fitting a hook into one shaped like a French horn. What was the point of all the mess and work of Christmas, anyway? It was never like in the movies or on television shows, everything ending in love and happiness. All his childhood memories of Christmas concluded with drunken violence on the afternoon of the twenty-fifth, if they got that far. And his later years had been marked by a cherished neglect of the holiday. But her—even now, so exhausted she could barely stand, she struggled on to decorate a tree, celebrating a Christmas already marred beyond any repair.

He had known when he married her that he had taken a woman who began planning Christmas in September. He had moved from sufferance to mild pleasure in the season, but surely this year even she should be feeling they could skip it. Maybe he would insist the tree come down as soon as everyone left.

He looked down again at his son. It wasn't as if they were doing it for him, trusting little jerk, sleeping on his big, bad, heathen father's stomach. He was far too young to appreciate Christmas. Peter moved his hand, found the pudgy little leg. It felt cool. He looked at Kori. "Uh, hey."

"Hmmmm?" she said dreamily, turning around, but not really looking at him.

He looked significantly at the baby, then at her.

"What?"

"He's asleep."

"He should be, this far past his bedtime."

"Shouldn't you put a blanket on him or something?"

She smiled, that superior smirk women lay on a man who lets on he knows something about babies. He sighed and looked up at the ceiling, and an uncomfortable silence fell. Then something blocked the light and there she was, arms open, fluffy blue baby blanket spread between her hands. "Here," she said, draping it over both of them. "You're right, it's a little cool in here." She bent and kissed him.

He wanted to pull her in for a better kiss, but that might squash the baby. So he just smiled up at her, and she kissed him again.

She returned to her task of decorating the tree, whistling snatches of "Silent Night" between contented silences. He felt himself becoming drowsy and, alarmed, struggled back awake. All he needed to do was fall asleep and roll over, dumping his son onto the floor.

He made motions like he was about to get up, and she came quickly to take the baby from him. "There, baby, there," she murmured, and Jeep tucked his head under her chin and made a brief, noisy business of sucking his thumb. Peter wanted to ask for him back once he got to his feet, but didn't know how and instead stood beside her to admire the tree. Despite her doubts he found it beautiful, softly radiant, like something out of a magazine.

"You're good at things like this," he said. "And it's nice that one of us is, for the kid's sake."

"You're good at what you do, and I've had occasion to be glad of that."

There was a sound many centuries away, as of birds twittering, or perhaps of a quill scratching on vellum, too faint for them to hear.

They lit a pair of kerosene lamps and carried them up the stairs. Michael, who had been sleeping beside the hearth, rose and trailed behind, panting—he'd finished the hero's supper Gordon gave him, even though he'd already received a plate of homemade custard from Kori and a generous slice of chicken from Peter, all in addition to his usual evening snack of kibble, eaten before he'd known about the other treats to come. He dropped with a heavy sigh onto his strip of carpet outside their bedroom door, and Peter stopped to stroke his nappy fur as they passed him on their way in.

The master bedroom had a bay as big as the one in the parlor below it. Kori went to look out and saw that snow was climbing halfway up the windows. She held the baby with one arm and put the palm of her other hand on the chilled glass to feel the wind vibrate it. Recalling those few minutes lost in darkness just yards from this room, she shivered and sent up a brief prayer for those without relief from the cold this holy night. Then she turned back gratefully to the warmth.

The master bedroom was generous in size, papered in softest ivory with a narrow blue pinstripe. The bed was also generous, and elaborate. Her decorator had described it as "classic revival early French provincial, probably."

It was old, a proper antique, but nearly king-size, with a high headboard of blue-stained wood carved into pilasters, flower garlands and two medallions set with Aladdin lamps. Its matching footboard was nearly as high as the headboard. Softening its classical features were lace-edged pillowslips and an ivory down comforter with lace ruffles. It was a heady, sensuous bed, and would have surprised people who thought they knew them, as they were not demonstrative in public.

But, tonight they were sharing the bed with an infant, which put a damper on lovemaking. Kori arranged the baby between them "so he doesn't fall out; he can roll over now, you know."

"No, I didn't know," he grumped.

"I'll move the crib in here tomorrow, so it's just for tonight," she said, misinterpreting his grump. They undressed, blew the lamps out and climbed into bed.

He lifted himself carefully over the baby to kiss her once she was settled. "Just so it doesn't become a permanent arrangement," he said, kissing her again, more warmly.

"Hmmm," she purred and stroked his face and the back of his neck, a promise of pleasures pleasantly forestalled. He rolled away, and she pulled the comforter up over her shoulders. She reached out to check on Jeep, who was making the little snoring sound that meant he was deep asleep. "Who did it, Peter? Was it one of us?"

"I don't know," he replied, grunting as he searched for a comfortable position, "but I'll find out. Did you see how Frank moved to keep me from talking to Mary tonight? Something's wrong there. I don't think Mary was in the bedroom when he went up for her before the lights went out. If he went up the front stairs—and I'm sure he did, they're much closer to the parlor than the back stairs—then why go *past* the oriel bedroom to knock on the bathroom door? No, he checked the bathroom and she wasn't there, so he went to knock on the bathroom door. Then, as you suspected, he went from there down the back stairs. He says she wasn't in the bathroom. If not, where was she? Possibly, down in the library confronting Evelyn. If so, when did she come down? And where did she hide, waiting for you to leave Evelyn alone? And how did she get back up, with Gordon in the kitchen and Jill haunting the front hall? We know she did, because we both heard her calling from upstairs right after the lights went out."

"Have you found out why she was so upset about Evelyn coming?"

"Frank says it wasn't Evelyn Biggins, it was Evelyn McKay. Her quarrel was with the whole McKay clan. She won't tell Frank any more than that, and he's scared to let me talk with her about it."

"Oh, Peter, it sounds as if Frank's afraid Mary did it."

"So am I. But there's also Jill to suspect. She was right on the spot for opportunity."

"But she's so funny and gentle! I can't imagine her hitting a helpless old woman on the head."

"How many times have you seen some puzzled soul tell the TV interviewer that he never thought someone as nice as old so-and-so would go berserk like that and kill fourteen co-workers? But if you really don't like her for it, there's Danny, of course."

"How of course? You said yourself he wasn't faking hypothermia!"

"He may have been trying to get back out to the Bronco, not into the house. His grandfather was Judge Malcolm Bannister, a well-known figure on the bench and in the state legislature. But he was also the McKay family lawyer. Danny says his father expressed an unusual interest in Evelyn's homecoming. Maybe they have a family tale of their own about the McKays."

"I can't imagine Danny killing someone in cold blood."

"Well, then, look at Gordon."

"Oh, for heaven's sake. . . ."

"I know, I know. He has no motive whatsoever. On the other hand, Frank is damn sure Gordon wasn't in the kitchen when he came through there, and Gordon can only insist Frank is mistaken. Frank may be lying to cover for Mary, but if he isn't, where was Gordon?"

"The way you tell it, it could be any one of us."

"I wish I could tell it in a way that would show it was only one of us. Then I would know which one it was."

She reached across to touch his face. "I'm so scared. I like these people, but maybe one of them is a murderer."

He took the hand and kissed it. "Shall I tell you about the time I got to interview a serial murderer? He was a good-looking guy, intelligent, very charming. Even the judge apologized for sentencing him to death."

"Pooh!" she said, lying back on her pillow. Then, "I wish this hadn't happened at Christmas."

"When would you prefer? Spring, when the meadow is brisk with foals? Summer, when everything is sweet and lazy? Fall, when the whole house smells of pumpkin pies?"

She rolled over, turning her back on him. "Oh, never mind! And a merry Christmas to you, Mr. Scrooge!"

"Bah," he sighed, yawning around a grin. "Humbug."

Chapter

7 †

Kori, who slept in only when she was sick, woke as usual a little after six the next morning. She slipped out of bed without waking Peter, gathered her clothes, Jeep's necessaries, and the baby, and trod lightly out of their bedroom, down the hall and down the dark back stairs to the kitchen. Jeep was vastly amused at the strangeness of it all and crowed with delight all the way, chuckling when she went, "Shhhh!" at him.

Kori tried the lights in the dining room and was not surprised when they did not go on. The lines must still be down. She went back to the kitchen and peered out a window. The sky was clear, sprinkled with fading stars, and just starting to lighten in the east; the storm was over.

She put a baby bottle to warm in a pan of water on the stove, spread a padded plastic changing sheet on the floor and cleaned up Jeep, making faces and laughing at him and at his motor noise. She dressed him in new green overalls and an ivory knit sweater with tiny wooden buttons. His carrier seat was brought from the parlor and she buckled him into it. By then he was starting to fuss, so she put a bib on him and gave him a graham cracker to play with to keep him quiet while his bottle finished heating and she got dressed.

She did minimal ablutions in the kitchen sink, got into jeans, red cotton sweater and one sock, and was looking about for the other when Gordon came into the kitchen.

He was wearing a bright blue sweater that set off his fair
hair nicely, and was carrying his razor and a toothbrush.

"What are you doing up?" she asked.

"I couldn't wait to see what was waiting for me under
the tree. Happy Christmas, pet." He kissed her and she
smiled after him as he went off to the downstairs bathroom. She was holding Jeep, feeding him his morning
bottle when Gordon came back and began to fill the kettle
with water.

"It's sad when someone we know dies," he said without looking at her, "but hard lines when it's a relative—
and truly terrible when it happens at Christmas. I'm sorry
about Evelyn Biggins."

"Yes." She pulled the nipple out of Jeep's mouth to
watch him make empty sucking motions, then put it back
in. "Worst of all is knowing it wouldn't have happened if
I hadn't invited her here in the first place."

"You don't know that; perhaps someone had to follow
her up here to do it."

She thought about that a little while. "If so, he hid in
the Bronco and rode out here with her and Peter, because
the blizzard was closing the roads behind them. No, Gordon, it wasn't someone who followed; it was someone
waiting here for her to arrive." The thought made all her
muscles go rigid. Jeep twisted his mouth away from his
bottle and started to cry. "There, baby, there," she murmured, turning at once back into Mother, bending over
him. He started nursing again, comforted, but wary.

She looked up to see an echo of fright on Gordon's
face. "Does Peter suspect anyone?" Gordon asked.

"Right now he suspects everyone."

"Perhaps that means he won't solve it."

"Are you hoping he won't?"

"Are you sure you want to know who's responsible?"

"Oh, yes. And I want to know why, though there

couldn't be a reason good enough. She was a nice lady, and my only living link to this house; my last cousin. It wasn't fair, Gordon; we'd only just found each other, and now she's gone forever. I want to know who killed her. I want to testify at the trial, and see the murderer sentenced to years and years in some truly infamous prison." Jeep began fussing again, and she put his bottle on the table and lifted him up on her shoulder, patting his back.

Gordon turned away to check the kettle. "Does it never occur to you to sell this place?"

"Why should I want to leave here?" She looked around the kitchen, which was large and oddly shaped, colored in friendly creams and oranges.

"My dear pet, when you were six years old, your parents were shot dead in the parlor of this house by your Uncle Nicholas, who, because you were a witness, kept you here under his thumb for fourteen years, while he brokered drug deals as a hobby. When Peter began investigating him, he arranged for you to be taken away and murdered, which attempt culminated in my being shot and his being killed in the front yard by one of his own vicious dogs. I had a hard time sleeping in this place last night, owing in part to the legacy of that blackguard. And if that's true for me, it must be doubly true for you, hm? And was true even before that harmless old woman arrived and had her skull fractured in the library."

Kori turned in her chair so she could look out the window, still patting Jeep. "Any house as old as this has had lots of things happen in it," she said, "not all of them pleasant. But not all of them unpleasant, either. For instance, there was you." She turned back and smiled at him, but he didn't return the smile. "Oh, okay, Uncle made you come, and I know you hated him even more than you feared him. But your coming saved me; you were my father and my mother and my teacher and my friend. You brought me safely through, then introduced me to Peter and helped me understand that his peculiar behavior was only—how did you put it? The result of a cold and rigid personality being suddenly smitten. . . ." She had to stop to keep herself from laughing. "Poor, dear Peter! And there were the horses. They gave me some physical freedom, just as you were my intellectual way out. Yes, some parts were scary, but I survived. Anyway, other people have died in this house, but nobody else moved out because of it. No, Gordon; this house was built for my great-great-grandmother, and my family has occupied it ever since. I like knowing that, and now that I have a son, I want him to grow up here, so he'll feel secure and let his roots grow deep."

"Knowing your ancestors has become important to you, hasn't it?"

"Do you think it should be otherwise?"

"Not at all. I'm concerned because you have some very lofty expectations of your ancestors, especially the more distant ones. Finding the truth about them may be dangerous to those expectations."

She grinned ruefully. "Don't worry; what I've learned in the past twenty-four hours swept away a lot of my illusions. The truth is much more interesting than lofty expectations, anyway. And it makes them more real to discover that some of them were strong characters, who knew what they wanted, tried hard to get it, and devil take the consequences!" Jeep burped loudly and laughed. She tucked him back into her arm. He put a small, fond, supporting hand on his bottle when she gave it to him, but only sucked half-heartedly at it, offering a messy grin when she looked down at him. "I *like* this house!" she cooed to him. "It likes *me*!"

Gordon went to the refrigerator. "It likes you—the house?"

"Yes. Surely you've gone into a house and felt it surround you all warm and friendly, and into others that were cold and distant."

"I attribute that to the people who live in it, not the house itself. Surely you don't believe a house might be a living entity."

"Maybe I do, in a way. I think people leave psychic marks, as well as physical ones on a house."

He stared at her, eyebrows raised. "Gammon!"

"I'm serious. I once saw a television program on abused children. The camera followed this woman who visited her old family home, and the current resident asked if she knew anything about the ghost. It seemed the house was haunted by a little child who wandered about at night crying as if its heart would break. The visitor began to cry herself, saying, 'That's me, that's me.' She had been terribly abused by her father in that house. Ever since I saw that, I've wondered if perhaps ghosts aren't a house repeating a lesson it's learned."

"I had no idea you believed in ghosts at all." Gordon lifted a plate out of the refrigerator. "And if your theory is true, it's a wonder anyone can sleep in any old house, what with all the 'psychic memories' emanating from the walls." On the plate, covered with clear plastic wrap, was a coffee cake set with candied fruit and drizzled all over with white icing. He removed the wrap and put the plate on the table.

"Isn't that supposed to be served at brunch?" she asked.

"I made two, one to serve to people who couldn't wait for the formal brunch. People who go out into the early dawn to feed horses." He turned and opened a drawer. "It's got almond paste in it," he tempted.

"I'll have a large slice, please." Kori spied her sock

under a chair and began reaching for it with her toes.
"Did you hear a ghost wailing last night?" she asked.

He smiled. "No, nor a chain rattling."

"Neither did I. Nor has anyone else who slept in this
house ever complained about being kept awake by
ghosts." She pulled the sock toward herself and said,
"Quick, the kettle!"

Gordon reached and cut the heat back just as the kettle's rumble began to rise into a shriek.

"Good morning," said a new voice, and they turned to
see Danny, tousled but wide awake, stuffing his shirt tail
into his trousers. "Merry Christmas."

"What are you doing out of bed?" said Kori.

"I'm fine; I feel fine, really. I was told last night that if
I felt okay I could go with you this morning to do chores.
And if I don't, then I'm supposed to wake him up so he
can come with you."

"*Peter* said to wake him?" said Kori. Unlike Kori, Peter treasured any opportunity to sleep late.

"Perhaps he thinks there might be a ghost in the barn,"
said Gordon. "Sit down, Danny, and I'll make coffee."

"Thanks. That cake looks terrific."

"Cut yourself a slice. Tea, pet?"

"Thanks." Gordon set the Mr. Coffee machine to work,
then went to a cabinet to get a small teapot, a red carton of
Typhoo tea and a small strainer.

"What's this talk about ghosts?" asked Danny, cutting
a generous slab of cake. "It's Christmas, not Halloween."

"Christmas in England used to be a time for ghost stories," said Gordon. He poured a little of the simmering
water into the pot to heat it and poured it off again.

Kori said, "*A Christmas Carol* is a ghost story."

Danny made a skeptical face, then changed his mind.
"Well, yeah, I guess it is. You don't think this house is
haunted, do you?"

Kori had been inspecting Jeep's bottle to see how close to empty it was. She turned to smile at him. "No, of course not.'

"Are you sure? This is the first time I've slept in the big house, and I had weird dreams all night long."

Gordon added five teaspoons of loose leaves from the tea carton to the warmed pot, then filled it with boiling water. He put a needlepoint tea cozy with a Santa Claus face on it over the pot, and brought it to the table along with three dessert plates, forks and spoons, and sat down to wait for the leaves to steep. "Which of course must not be attributed to the fact that you nearly froze to death yesterday," he said.

Kori paused in the act of thumping another burp out of Jeep. "Sometimes—," she said, and stopped.

"Sometimes what?" asked Danny.

"Sometimes I think the house is . . . waiting for something."

"For what?"

"I don't know. But I'll know when it happens."

Water began to trickle from the coffee maker into its pot, filling the kitchen with its warm fragrance. Danny looked out at the snow-covered lawn, rosy with dawn. "It's so pretty, it seems a shame to go out and spoil it by making tracks in it."

Kori said, "And while waiting for the thaw, we should try hard not to think about the horses starving to death in the barn. Here, hold Jeep a minute." She handed him over, and bent to the task of putting the retrieved sock on. Danny sat Jeep up on his knee and began bouncing him.

Gordon was about to warn of the dangers of bouncing a baby who had just been fed when another voice said sharply, "Danny Bannister, hand me that baby before you drop him!" and they all turned to see Jill in the doorway. She, in jeans and blue sweater woven with snowflakes,

also had the look of someone who has made a sketchy toi-
let, but her face was pink with determination. She came
into the kitchen and held out her hands to the baby.

Danny, not liking the dangerous look in her eye,
handed Jeep over.

"Good mornin', my little dumplin'!" Jill crooned, and
Jeep laughed and reached for her face with both chubby
hands. She looked slantwise at Gordon. "Has he been fed
yet?" she asked in a tone that implied the baby had fallen
into a nest of child abusers.

"He's had a bottle," said Kori, "and most of a graham
cracker."

Jill nodded briefly, disappointed.

Kori continued, "He'll be going back to sleep in a little
while. I want you to let him sleep until I get back."

"Why would I wake him up?" Jill, angry again, was
being her most volatile. "You think I've forgotten how to
be a good nanny? That I don't know what a crab he turns
into when someone wakes him up?" Jeep's mouth turned
down and he made an unhappy noise. "No, Jeep's own
loving nanny wouldn't wake the baby, now would she?"
soothed Jill. "Not for anything, no, no, no, no."

Kori stamped a stockinged foot onto the floor. "Gordon, I want to leave Jeep here in the kitchen with you
while I'm in the barn."

Unhappy Gordon, caught in the middle of a quarrel
whose terms were lost on him, said, "I suppose so. But
I'll be getting very busy here shortly. What do I do if he
wakes up?"

Jill said, "I'll take care of him. *Since*," she continued,
cutting off Kori's interruption, "I'll be here helping you
anyway."

"So long as he stays here with Gordon, you may care
for him," agreed Kori. "Come on, Danny; let's get those
horses fed."

† † †

It was bitter cold out. The early sun provided dazzling light, but no warmth. The snow was drifted waist high in some places and was only an inch or two deep in others, a tribute to the strength of yesterday's wind.

They stopped at the barn door to slap snow off themselves.

Kori said, "We'll send Michael in first," because she knew why Peter was insistent she not go to the barn alone. If it had, in fact, been some stranger who came secretly to murder Evelyn, that person might have been trapped afterward by the blizzard and be hiding in the barn.

With the command "Search!" Michael bounded off to explore every corner of the barn while Kori and Danny shivered outside. As a refresher drill, Michael's trainer had occasionally sent someone in a padded suit out to the ranch to hide in one of the buildings. Michael never knew when this would happen, but he loved to find a stranger and make him yell for mercy. So, whenever Kori sent him on a search mission, he looked hard.

Kori always praised him lavishly whether or not he found anyone, but failure wasn't as exciting, and he came at a disappointed trot this morning to get thumped and stroked.

"Sorry, old boy," said Kori. "Maybe next time."

"If Michael was smarter, he'd be happy there wasn't anyone in there," said Danny. "Anyone who'd bash an old lady on the head wouldn't mind doing it to a dog."

He held the door for her, and followed her over the high threshold. They stood silent a moment inside the dark barn, letting eyes and ears adjust. There was the faint sound of large animals at the far end, but nothing else. There were no footprints on the raked ground, or any other evidence that someone had been there. The part of the barn they had entered was a big exercise arena with a fence marking a walkway around it. Small, high-set windows provided patches of light across a dirt floor.

The barn was T-shaped, a large crossbar on a shorter upright. The box stalls were in the upright. As they approached them, the horses began to call out. Those whose winter coats were kept clipped complained that the barn was exceedingly chilly, and they, with the others, wished to express their annoyance at having had no supper the night before.

"Huh-huh-huh," said the stallion from his stall at the end of the row, thumping his door with his hoof. As boss horse, he was resentful not only for himself, but on behalf of the others as well.

"And a Merry Christmas to you too, Coppy," called Kori.

She pulled a handful of sugar lumps from her jacket pocket—the carrots had gotten lost in the snow yesterday—and went back and forth down the row, giving each horse two lumps and a scratch or a pat, spending a minute or two communing, tugging a forelock, stroking a smooth neck, bringing order and restoring good humor. Domestic animals, Kori felt, were owed as much as they give—more, sometimes, in honor of their distant ancestors who surrendered many freedoms to walk in the safety of humankind's shadow. She stopped at her stallion last, and spent more time with him, poor prisoner of his hormones.

That done, Kori said, "I'll wash, you dry."

That meant Kori went up one side and down the other ahead of Danny, pushing a wheelbarrow which quickly filled with night soil and wet straw. Danny followed with fresh straw and blankets for the two mares not allowed to keep their shaggy winter coats. They worked in separate,

efficient, companionable silences, broken only occasionally by rebukes or soothing words spoken to the horses.

Then they went around again, this time with hay, oats,
and water. Cards in metal holders outside each stall reminded them how many scoops of oats and how many
flakes of hay went to each. Horses' needs and appetites
are as disparate as those of humans.

Nearing the end, Danny spoke to Kori, asking almost
the same question Gordon had. "Does the sarge really
think one of us is a murderer?"

Kori hesitated, and Danny immediately asked, "Which
one?"

"If there's one more than the others, he's not saying."

"But you think maybe it's Jill."

"I haven't said one word to make anyone think that."

"No, but you did something. It isn't fair, taking Jeep
away from her. She's real upset over it. And anyway, it's
ridiculous to think she'd hurt a baby."

Kori came out of Copper Wind's stall, closing the door
behind her. "He's my son, Danny. I have every right to be
ridiculous where his welfare is concerned."

Danny kicked at a box stall door, sending the mare inside snorting backwards. "I wish to hell I never told her
you were looking for a nanny!" He kicked again.

"Stop that, you're scaring Blue. And don't blame yourself. She's the one who came out and applied, and I'm the
one who hired her."

"I think—," he began, but stopped and turned away.

"What do you think?"

He kept going. "Nothing. But talk to her, will you? She
knows something, but she won't tell me what it is."

Peter found Frank in the kitchen, eating a slice of coffee
cake and draining his second cup of coffee. Frank was
wearing tropical-weight khaki trousers, a thin white shirt

and a brown cardigan with a braid pattern knit into the front panels. Peter wore penny loafers, his favorite brown cords and a red flannel shirt made soft by many washings. Sunlight flooded the kitchen, which was also full of cooking smells.

"Are we the first ones up?" asked Peter.

"Hardly," said Gordon, counting eggs set out in rows on a dishtowel. "Danny and Kori must nearly be finished in the barn, Jill's been and gone—she's currently putting Jeep into his crib for a nap."

"Mary's up, too," said Frank. "Had a cup of tea and went with Jill to show her a tricky way to fold a cloth diaper. There's one last slice of this," he added, pointing to the remnant of coffee cake.

"Just coffee, I think," said Peter, not sure whether to be pleased by the news that Jill had somehow reclaimed Jeep. He went to lift a mug from the orange mug tree. "When you finish eating," he said to Frank, "let's search the house."

"Better make it just a preliminary look," said Gordon. "We eat in an hour, and I am not in a mood to put up with another disruption of one of my meals." This was said almost lightly, but with enough edge that Peter nodded agreement.

Frank took the last two bites of his cake in one big bite and stood, brushing crumbs off himself. "Can I bring my coffee along?" he mumbled around the mouthful.

"I plan on bringing mine," said Peter. "Let's begin in the parlor."

The big room was dim with the curtains drawn and no lights on, and fragrant with the heady smell of evergreen. A pile of presents waited under the tree, and a fire was laid in the fireplace, waiting for a match. They walked around the room, lifting drapes as they came to windows and squinting out at the sunlit snow, which lay in deep drifts all around and even up on the porch. "If somebody tossed a weapon out into that," remarked Frank, "we won't find it until spring." He dropped the drape he had been lifting and looked around the room. "You know, this is a very modern looking room for a place built in eighteen-seventy-something."

"That's mostly because it's so big," said Peter. "Most front parlors in houses this old were small; it was the back parlor, or living room, that was generous in size; and this is bigger even than they were." Peter tended at times to lecture rather than converse, and he lapsed now into his lecture mode. "The house was built between 1872 and 1873 by Charles McKay and his wife Eugenia. *Bonne Chance* was its name then, Mr. McKay having made his fortune backing forty-niners back in the gold rush days. It's considered a particularly fine example of the Queen Anne style, especially by people who haven't discovered the peculiarities of its construction."

Frank sighed at this reversion to type by Peter. Then he shoved his hands into his pockets, looked around the room with a critical air, and hoped the lecture would not end with Peter deciding he needed to ask Mary something.

Peter continued, "The cut stone surround of the fireplace is not original, but dates to the turn of the century, and was probably commissioned by Charles's son, William, who died in 1919. You'll notice that the narrow frieze of galloping horses shows the progression of their legs correctly, which would not have been the case in the 1870s."

"Hmph," grunted Frank, going to bend for a closer look. "Nice work."

"The parlor is the second largest room in the house—"

"—you mean the largest," interrupted Frank.

"No I don't," said Peter, surprised. "Wait, that's right,

you've never been given a complete tour of this house."
He opened the door to the hall. "There are two ways to
get into the parlor: from the side porch, and this way,
from the entrance hall."

They went out into the hall. Peter pointed out that the
black and white tiles on the hall floor were in fact stone,
quarried locally, and allowed Frank, who was a whittler,
several minutes to admire the birds on the baluster.

Peter finally remarked, "Come on, you've seen that
thing before. We've got a lot of house to cover, and
Gordie's already tender from the way nobody bothered
much with his supper."

They went down the hall, past the locked library on the
left, through a right hand door to the dining room, with its
cut off corners and built in buffets. A bright green cloth
covered the table, and dishes and silverware waited at one
end to be set out.

The room was as chilly as it had been last evening. Peter said, in his lecturer's voice, "We understand that the
management plans to replace the windows this spring, in
order that the guests will no longer have to weigh the nap-
kins down with the water glasses to keep them from
blowing away in the draft."

"How many fireplaces does this house have, anyhow?"
asked Frank, nodding toward the big wooden one at the
far end of the room.

"Six, one each in the parlor, library, dining room—um,
let's see, butler's pantry, nanny's bedroom and the master
bedroom."

"Christ!" said Frank. "Are they all functional?"

"Yes, and half the basement is taken up with the wood
we burn in them. You can get to the kitchen from the hall
or through this door." It was hinged to swing in either direction.

The kitchen was the oddest-shaped room in the house,

both from having suffered the most renovations and having had a nip taken out of it by the addition of the downstairs bathroom. Coming through from the dining room, Peter and Frank came up against a serving counter, on the other side of which stood Gordon at a cutting board slicing something that looked suspiciously like kidneys. Also on the counter, in a deep pan, was what looked like a bowling ball tied in a soiled napkin. Next to it were a big bowl of rutabagas and a big glass jar of pickled eggs. The radio had been turned on, and a chorus was stating firmly that His name shall be call-ed Wonderful! Counselor! The mighty God! The Everlasting Father, the Prince of Peace! Gordon was humming along in a staccato tenor.

"If this is our brunch," said Frank, indicating the soiled napkin and pickled eggs, "I'll have a glass of milk, please."

Gordon laughed, but did not say anything.

"This is one room my wife won't be able to restore," said Peter. "For one thing, it's no longer possible to figure out what it looked like originally, without the blueprints, which apparently no longer exist. For another, Mrs. Gonzales—our cook—would not appreciate having to work with an authentic Victorian kitchen. Nick Tellios did the most recent modernization."

Peter led Frank out into the back hall, a dim and narrow place, with a narrow door that led to a pantry. "You used to be able to walk from the front door to the back door without going through the kitchen," said Peter. "But whoever installed the downstairs bathroom blocked the hallway doing it."

"So the only way from the back door to the front part of the house is through the kitchen," said Frank.

"Well, you could go up the back stairs to the second floor, and down the front stairs," said Peter. "But I recommend that only when Mrs. Gonzales is in a snit."

At the end of the narrow hallway were the back stairs, steep and narrow, and through a low door the even steeper and narrower ones leading to the basement.

"What about from the basement?" asked Frank. "Is there another set of stairs coming up in the front part of the house?"

"Nope. There's a set leading out to the backyard, but the exit is padlocked. Have you seen Katherine's office?"

"Not since it got turned into an office; I saw it when it was a storage room."

The room had begun life as a butler's pantry, the exclusive province of that chief servant of a wealthy household. Through many changes in function, it had managed to retain its small fireplace of faux marble. Now it also had a beautiful antique desk with a thoroughly modern computer on it, and an atrium door that looked out over a side lawn set with huge sycamores. The stone and stucco cottage Danny lived in was visible at the bottom of a gentle slope, and beyond that the barn and pastures. The desk was set so that a glance past the computer could refresh the user's eyes.

A pair of comfortable arm chairs were in front of the desk, and, on the wall behind it, where the potential buyer could not help seeing them, were the trophies Kori's horses had won and photographs of the horses as they won them. The room spoke of comfort, beauty, competence and money. Frank nodded approvingly; he, too, had known the value of setting in getting what was wanted from his "customers."

"Can you go from this room to the bathroom?" he asked.

"No, even though the bathroom's just the other side of this." Peter tapped the wall behind her desk. "You have to go back out into the hall and through the kitchen to get to it. Katherine says she always asks her customers if they'd like to wash their hands while they're still in the barn, but that people nowadays don't know what that means. I think she's planning on cutting a door."

They went out and climbed the steep back steps to the second floor.

Kori came into the front hall alone. Danny, sensing a confrontation in the making, had announced he would go to the cottage and get some of his own clothes, then haul out the snowblower and clear at least a path from the house to the barn. "Don't hold up brunch for me or anything," he said.

She put her boots into the bench seat and her jacket into the armoire, then went into the kitchen to check on Jeep.

Frank and Peter went into the nursery suite. The door let into a room Peter said was called the night nursery, where the children in early times slept. To their left was a long room lined with sunny windows, the day nursery. Straight ahead was the nanny's bedroom, its door ajar. From it they heard women's voices, relaxed and happy. Frank, recognizing Mary's voice, went ahead to pull the door open.

Mary and Jill were sitting side by side on the brass bed, several diapers stacked between them. Mary was in a navy dress with a broad white collar; Jill's royal blue sweater had strategically placed snowflakes, setting off her voluptuous figure. Jeep was asleep in his crib. Before Frank could say anything, soft, fast footsteps sounded behind him, and he turned barely in time to get out of Kori's way as she stormed into the tiny room. She was in her stockinged feet; a faint smell of horse swirled in her wake.

"I thought I told you Jeep was to stay in the kitchen!" raged Kori.

Peter heard more footsteps and turned to see Gordon coming anxiously into the night nursery, still holding a greasy spatula. "I'm afraid this is my fault," he began to Peter, who waved a shushing hand at him.

Gordon's face tightened. He turned on his heel and walked out.

"I was only trying to do my job," Jill was explaining. "Jeep was fussing and wanted to be in his crib. What's wrong with giving him what he needs? And his crying was getting on Gordon's nerves, I could tell." Her voice was perfectly calm and reasonable.

"I don't understand what the problem is," Mary put in, puzzled.

"I don't want her alone with the baby," said Kori.

Mary's glance flew to Jill, shocked by the implications in that statement. "But nothing happened. I came up with her, I've been here all the time."

"She's showing me how to fold diapers," said Jill, reaching for one, her reasonableness now edged with desperation. "See? You do it this way instead of—"

"—Diapers be damned!" interrupted Kori, making a rare lapse into strong language. "When I say I don't want you taking care of Jeep, I expect to be obeyed, do you understand?"

Poor Jeep, wakened by the noise, began to whimper.

"Maybe we should continue this out of the baby's sleeping room," suggested Mary.

Kori went to lift Jeep gently out of his crib. "Mary, will you take him? Take him to your bedroom; he'll go right back to sleep if you sit with him a minute."

"Of course." Mary took Jeep and wove her way through Jill, Peter—and Frank, who looked anxiously after her, though he did not follow.

When she was gone, Kori turned on Jill. "Danny says you're hiding something."

"He doesn't—," Jill halted, blinking. "I mean, he came up and talked to me after supper last night. And I'm not hiding anything."

"Where is it?"

"I don't know what you're talking about."

"Get out, then! I'll find it."

"But. . . ."

"Out!"

Jill came out to shrug up at Peter in a worried way, as if she were afraid of what Kori might do when she didn't find anything out of the ordinary in the little bedroom. Frank stayed by the door to the hall with an uncertain air, still not sure whether to go after his wife or stay on duty with Peter.

Through the half open door Kori could be seen. She moved swiftly, tossing things out of drawers and sorting through them with ruthless efficiency, unmaking the bed in a brief series of swooping pulls. She found nothing until she lifted back the mattress on Jeep's crib. On the springs lay something blue: the missing photo album.

"There, you liar!" said Kori in angry triumph, coming out and holding the album up with one hand.

Jill shrank back, and Peter took her by the arm. "Why?" he asked.

Jill showed him a face honestly frightened. "Maybe when you look in there you can tell me."

"I was just going to put it away," said Jill, shamefaced. "It was sitting there on the windowsill and I thought it came from upstairs, so I brought it up. And I was curious, so I opened it. There's all kinds of old pictures in it, some of them really old, like over a hundred years, all people I never heard of—but some of them look like me." Jill was sitting beside Kori on one of the two couches in the parlor.

The photo album was an ordinary inexpensive one with a padded blue vinyl cover and thick, soft, black paper pages. The photographs in it had been attached with old-fashioned "corners."

Peter and Frank, on the other couch, leaned forward as Kori opened the album.

On the first page was an enlarged replica in brown and ivory of a portrait of a lovely nineteenth-century woman whose standup collar was edged with ruffles. She wore a dark-colored, tight-fitting jacket, and her light-colored hair was dressed high on the back of her head, falling into complex curls down the back of her neck, and brief curls onto her forehead. Her stiff pose was due both to the severity of her corseting and the photography methods of the time, which required long exposure. Someone had written on the margin of the photo, *Eugenia Margaret McKay, 1872.*

Great-Jean in her youth had beautiful eyes under level eyebrows, a short, upturned nose, and what in her day was called a "cupid's bow" mouth: thin, deeply curved top lip and full under lip. "Uh-oh," said Kori; the resemblance to Jill was remarkable.

Peter got up and came around to the back of the couch for a closer look. His lips formed a soundless whistle, at which Frank got up and joined him, leaning both elbows on the back of the tufted silk. "Well, I'll be damned," Frank murmured, eyes shifting from the photo to Jill and back again.

"And she's not even the one," said Jill. "It's further on."

On the next page was another large photograph of Jean, much the same in middle age. She was wearing a pinstripe suit with a plain long skirt. The sleeves of the jacket were puffed big at the shoulders, her waist was pinched improbably small, her hair was gathered loosely onto the top of her head. She was seated with careful negligence in a carved wooden chair, showing just the toe of a highly polished shoe. An elderly, wide-jawed man whose big silver mustache bristled aggressively was standing beside her, one large hand on her shoulder. The photo was labeled *Great-Jean and Charles, 1910.*

On the opposite page was a photo of the house in the wintertime, looking very much as it did now, except a tree that at present towered over the roof was only middling in size. Among the other photos on that page was a candid waist-up shot of two smiling young women bundled in shapeless wool coats and long striped scarves. They were wearing cloche hats that shaded their eyes. On the shorter of the two, the recurved smile was again apparent. "But this can't be her," said Peter, "that hat looks like something out of the twenties; Jean would have been an old woman by then."

"It's Inez in 1927," said Kori, touching the bottom margin of the photograph. "The tall one is Evelyn."

Peter reached over her shoulder to turn the page. Jill made a noise like clearing her throat. In the upper left corner was a studio portrait labeled "Inez, 1931." Her hair was bleached to gilt and set in even waves, her level brows plucked to thin arcs. The upturned nose was the same as Jeannie's, and the cupid's bow mouth. But here also was the square face. Between Great-Jean and Jill there had been a family resemblance. Inez was the mold from which Jill was cast.

"That's what I saw when I opened the album, and I couldn't think what to do."

"You'd never seen a photograph of Inez before?" asked Peter.

"I never even knew there was a lady named Inez. I

never even heard of that *name* before. I just opened this
thing and there was this person looking back at me like
someone took a picture of me dressed up for a costume
party I forgot I went to. I wanted to show it to Danny, so I
put the album in my room. Then Captain Ryder said it
wasn't an accident, what happened to Mrs. Biggins, and I
got really scared. I mean, I'm not related to these people,
so why do I look like this Inez person?"

"Because you are related," said Kori. "You must be."
She stood and walked off a little way, turned and regarded
Jill. "There's no way you couldn't be. Evelyn told me
Inez ran away from home in 1932. Could you be her
granddaughter?"

Jill shook her head. "No, my grandmother was named
Ellen. I remember her; I was almost eight when she died.
My mother looks like her, a little, but not me."

"What about your other grandmother?" asked Peter.

"Her name was Suzanne, and she died before I was
born. My mother showed me a picture of her once; believe me, she wasn't this lady. Anyway, she was born in
Wyoming. No, it's my mother's people, the Friars, who
are from around here; so it's got to be the Friars who gave
me this face."

Kori said, "Friars? There used to be a Sarah Friar who
worked out here as a cook."

"Sure," said Jill. "She was my great-grandmother."

"Then," said Kori slowly, "your grandfather's name
was—"

"—James. Jimmy, my Grandmom called him."

"Where is he?"

"He's dead. He was a sailor on the USS *Arizona* when
it got bombed at Pearl Harbor." Jill drew up her shoulders. "It makes me feel funny when we study history and
I see that picture in our history book, the *Arizona* tipping

over, black smoke coming out of it. That's my grandfather, burning to death."

"I'm sorry, Jill," said Kori. "Peter, do you want to ask her anything?"

"Not right now. You may go, Jill."

"Thank you, sir." Patently relieved, Jill hurried out.

"Jimmy," breathed Kori when the door closed behind her.

"Jimmy Friar? What about him?" asked Frank.

"He grew up out here with Evelyn and Inez. Evelyn said little Jimmy Friar was Great-Jean's second favorite after her. You remember I told you that, Peter."

"Yes, but what are you getting at?"

"He was a little boy when Evelyn and Inez were little girls, so that puts him in the same generation as them. Maybe he ran away to sea when Inez told him she was going to have his baby."

"No," said Peter, "that won't work. If he ran away, then he never married Inez. And the baby—Jill's mother—would probably have been put up for adoption, and Jill wouldn't know who her genetic grandmother was, much less be talking so casually about grandfather Jimmy Friar and great-grandmother Sarah the cook."

Kori flipped all the pages over and found the promised genealogy chart in a clear plastic sleeve.

"No, Evelyn didn't put Sarah and Jimmy on here at all."

"Why should she?" asked Frank. "They weren't McKays."

Peter's crooked smile tweaked a corner of his wide, thin mouth. "Not officially, maybe. But Katherine's right: you can tell looking at her that Jill's a McKay."

Kori looked at the long line of names under Charles and Jeannie McKay's. "Lloyd, Phyllis, William, Margaret, Andrew—all those children," she murmured. "I

thought I was the only descendent left—but now there's
Jill. I wonder where she belongs on this chart?"

Peter leaned in for a look, giving her a very faint whiff
of his aftershave. He must put it on *before* he shaves, she
thought distractedly. "Maybe Andrew had a fling in the
neighborhood before he went off to France," Peter said.
Andrew, born in 1880, died in 1918, "gassed in France,"
Evelyn had written in small letters beside his name.

Kori paged back and found the big photograph Evelyn
had mentioned, of the whole McKay family in 1917. It
had that slightly blurred quality that comes when a copy
is made from the photograph rather than the negative.
The family had gathered on the lawn in front of the house
on a summer afternoon in an era when a group photograph was a grand occasion, and before people had
learned to put on similar expressions for such photographs.

They were standing in two rows with the house behind
them and a circular bed of snapdragons and forget-me-
nots in front of them. Evelyn had printed their names directly on the picture, making some of them hard to read.
Kori turned the album a little sideways and began spell-
ing them out: "William, Annie, Great-Jean, Marva—"
Evelyn's chart had said she was Andrew's wife
"—Andrew. There he is, poor fellow. He must have been
one of the last to die; the war would be over in November.
Did you know you were going, Andy, and use that as an
excuse for adultery?" Andrew was handsome in a solemn, square-faced way, with a dark moustache. He was
wearing a high-collared, old-fashioned army uniform.
Marva, a smiling, petite figure in a long white dress and
big, strange hat, was shyly holding his hand. Kori gently
touched their faces. "No," she said, "not you."

Peter reached over her shoulder to turn back to the studio portrait of Inez. "Why hasn't anyone ever said,

'Golly, don't that Jill Yeager look a whole bunch like Inez McKay?' "

Frank replied, "Because Jill is two generations away; by the time she got old enough so the resemblance was obvious, people had forgotten what Inez looked like. Inez ran away in 1932, remember?"

Kori said, "And Jill said she and her mother don't look alike. Looks do that, you know. They'll skip a generation. In horses you can get a granddaughter who looks more like her grandfather than her own sire and dam. Not always, of course, but enough times that people will bid up the price of a mare in foal because the sire's father was Bask, even though the mare couldn't finish in the ribbons at a county fair."

Peter stood. "Come on, Frank; let's see if we can finish looking at the house before we eat."

Kori settled back on the couch with the album—then jumped to her feet. Brunch was nearly ready, she couldn't come to the table in her work clothes!

She hurried up to her room, changed into her bathrobe, and trotted down the hall to the bathroom for a fast shower.

But, back in her room she got only as far as putting up her hair when she was again distracted by the album. She sat in the big Morris chair and opened it. How much she had hoped to be sharing the album with Evelyn, listening to her stories about the people in it! Instead, all she had was this collection of black and gray shadows that tricked the eye into seeing people. She had learned their names; here were glimpses of their faces. Who are you? she thought at them. Look at me, tell me who I am. But the faces remained in shadow, speechless and unfathomable.

"I want to know who stole Evelyn from me," whispered Kori. "So I can remember to hate him forever." She turned the page and found a photo of Evelyn at a birthday party. As guest of honor, she stood behind the elaborate cake, which had eleven candles. None of the six other girls present had as elaborate a dress, as big a hair bow or as homely a face as Evelyn. "Poor thing," murmured Kori, and paged back to the big group photo to look for her. There she was, much prettier at age seven, in a short white dress with a dropped waist, holding hands with a smaller girl whose blond hair was dressed into long curls. Inez, squinting into a sun that had set more than seventy years ago.

She turned the album sideways and began to study the names, putting them to the shadowy faces. Sarah Friar was there, in front and a little to the side, stout and pleasant faced, next to a surly faced man in overalls, labeled Edward Friar. Sarah was holding in one strong arm a baby in a white dress. "Jimmy" Evelyn had printed, and Kori recalled that in those times children were dressed alike until they were three or four.

In the back row, near the end, was a homely woman in a light ruffled dress and a hat as peculiar as Marva's. There was no name written over her head. Probably a servant, thought Kori, there too briefly for her name to be remembered.

Kori heard a timid tap on the door and went to find Mary standing there. "I hope you don't mind," Mary said, "but I put the baby back in his crib. Jill's downstairs helping Gordon."

Kori made a guilty grimace. "I hope *you* don't mind," she replied, "but I had forgotten all about him. It must have been a job to get that crib reassembled."

Mary chuckled. "Long ago, my son Frankie wrote me a letter from boot camp describing how his drill sergeant used to leave the barracks when he wasn't satisfied with the way the bunks were made. That room reminded me of his letter. Did you find what you were looking for?"

"I sure did. Look, it's the album Evelyn brought." Kori went to the chair and picked it up to show a page to Mary. "See?"

Mary stared, made a wordless sound of shock or fright, turned and fled.

"No, wait!" said Kori. She glanced at the album, but there was no scary picture on the page, just the big photo. She looked around the room to see what else might have caused that reaction, half expecting to find Peter had somehow come in and gotten himself into a state of undress without her noticing. But she was alone in the room.

She tossed the album onto the bed and went to the oriel bedroom. The door was almost closed. She knocked, but there was no reply. She pushed the door open and saw Mary sitting on the bed, looking bereaved and frightened.

"Mary, what is it, what's wrong?" asked Kori, crossing to her.

"Nothing, just some old memories. You know how they can sneak up on you sometimes?"

"I suppose so. Was it the album?"

"No! I mean, no, of course not."

"Is there anything I can do to help?"

"No, no. I'll be all right if I can just sit here awhile."

"Should I make your excuses at brunch?"

"Oh, no, it's not that serious." Mary offered a travesty of a smile. "I'll be fine a few minutes, really."

"I'll just leave you alone then."

"Thank you, Kori."

Chapter
8 †

Kori went back to her room and put on a pair of gray wool slacks and a red-plaid silk blouse with a very large bow at the neck. What was wrong with Mary? She hadn't looked the least bit frightened until she saw—what? The album? But it had been Jill who had taken and hidden it, not Mary.

Kori went out again and down the hall, then up the front stairs, which were as broad as the steps from the first floor. The banister here had been carved by some master craftsman into the shape of a rope. It even sagged realistically between its supports. Kori let her hand run over the smooth twist of rope-shape as she climbed, absently drawing comfort from the familiar sensation, turned through the landing and climbed again.

As she neared the top, the light changed, becoming brilliant, as if she were about to enter a large, sunlit space.

"By God, it's a ballroom!" She paused to listen. Frank's voice continued, "You son of a bitch, that's why you brought me up those goddamn back stairs, and through those crummy little servants' rooms in the back first. All right, I'll admit it, I'm impressed. All the times I've been in the house, you never brought me up here before. How come?"

"Well, Jesus, Frank, it was bad enough I married a woman who bought me a Porsche for a wedding present; how would it look if I led you up here and showed you I now own a half interest in my own private ballroom, too?" Peter's reply was light, even bantering, the defensive tone nearly undetectable. Peter's father had worked on an assembly line most of his life.

As Kori came the rest of the way up the stairs, her head came over the top of the low wall that marked the boundary between the stairs and the ballroom floor. There were two coffee mugs resting on it.

The wall opposite the stairs was set with five square windows, the adjoining wall had three; they were without curtains and so allowed an undiminished flow of light from the outdoors.

The room was immaculate, painted a pale and chilly peach. A chimney disguised as a pillar near the far end was the only break in the open space; in a square alcove beyond the pillar was a wet bar. The hardwood floor was pale from a recent refinishing and smelled faintly of wax. The ceiling was not high, but that only made its size appear greater. It was by far the largest room in the house.

"Good morning," said Kori, and the two men whirled, startled.

"What are you doing up here?" asked Peter.

"Looking for you," she said to him.

"What's the matter?"

Kori glanced significantly at Frank, but Peter said, "It's okay, tell us both."

"Well, I was in our room, and Mary came to tell me she'd put Jeep back in his crib. I showed her the album and she—well, she acted like it scared her to death. She actually ran back to her own room. I went to see what was wrong, but she said it was nothing, just old memories." Kori didn't know how to describe her feelings about the veracity of Mary's explanation, and so stopped with a shrug and helpless expression.

"I'll go talk to her," said Frank.

"I'll come with you," said Peter.

"No! I mean, no, better let me go alone. She won't talk to you, Pete, believe me on that."

Peter, frowning, gestured assent, and Frank vanished with a hasty thumping down the stairs.

Kori began walking across the floor as they waited for Frank to descend out of earshot.

"What did she see in the album, do you know?" asked Peter finally.

"The big photo, the one of everyone in the front yard. I can't think what about that photo could have frightened her," she added, stopping and patting the fluted pillar as if testing its solidity. "Have you found anything suspicious up here?"

"No, but we're just looking for places to look."

She turned, leaning against the pillar. "Do you really feel guilty about owning a ballroom?"

"I don't think so. It just seems like a case of conspicuous consumption. Who puts on private balls anymore?"

"Nobody we know, but just wait until Jeep gets old enough to invite some of his little friends over on a rainy afternoon. We can send them up here and hardly be aware they're in the house."

"I suppose." He seemed to be about to add something, but Kori had stepped away from the pillar and was leaning on the counter at the wet bar.

"Hey, what's this all over the place?" Her tone was that of outraged housekeeper, not suspicious clue finder.

"I don't know, what?" he asked carelessly, coming to lean over beside her. The serving area was paneled in real boards of knotty pine. The back wall had a small octagonal window over a row of elaborately carved wooden books that had once held beer steins; the wall to the left had a vertical row of three matching hooks. Behind the counter were an old sink, an old-fashioned icebox and a set of shelves that had once held glassware. The floor behind the bar was of the same hardwood as the ballroom floor but it was streaked from one side to the other with a thin layer of dust or dirt.

"That," said Kori, pointing to the floor. "This place was perfectly clean yesterday."

Peter considered that and said, "It looks like a spill that's dried." He lifted the counter hatch and entered.

"Be careful, watch where you're putting your feet; you'll have it all over the place."

Peter lifted a foot and tried to find a clean place to put it down. "I can't help stepping in it," he said; "the whole floor back here is covered with it." He took two big steps out, lowered the counter flap and looked over it. "It didn't feel gritty, like something dried up," he said; "it was soft, like dust. It looks like it blew out from under that wall."

"What? Oh, Peter, I hope not!" Kori was alarmed at the notion of a break in the fabric of her house.

Peter stooped and reached under the flap to move the back of his hand along the wall in question. "I don't feel a draft," he said. "Of course, the wind's died down now. But look, from the way it's concentrated right along here, I'd say there's a crack or some sort of opening along the base of this wall. Have you had dust in here like this before?"

Kori shook her head. She felt sick. Not my house, too, she thought.

Peter leaned forward and rapped on the paneled wall. "Is this original, do you know?"

"Oh yes. And see those old-fashioned stein hooks? Hand-carved and very popular in the late 1800s. But my decorator said the sink and icebox date to no earlier than 1925. Ferris must have installed them." Kori was struck by a thought. "Wait a minute, how can a blizzard blow in dust? Shouldn't it be wet from melted snow, not dusty, if the crack goes through to the outside? And wait again!

This isn't even an outside wall! On the other side of this wall is a chimney!"

"There's no chimney going up this side of the house," said Peter, surprised at her.

"It doesn't come out the roof; I don't think it ever was a functional chimney. Evelyn said Great-Jean McKay kept insisting the builder make changes to his plans even as the house was being built. That's why there are all sorts of odd, unused corners to it. I told you uncle made a linen closet out of that little space by the back stairs. This is another one."

"Are you sure it's a chimney? How big is it?"

"About five feet by six feet, and three stories tall. If you pace off the side porch, you'll see that on the outside the bay extends along the well into where the parlor is inside. Years ago I asked my uncle why the library bay was longer on the outside than the inside. He told me it was a sealed-up space that had once been a chimney. I think now he was guessing, but it was a good guess."

Peter looked at the dust on the floor. "Is that the sort of dust you find inside a chimney?"

"I don't know. Anyway, this never was used as a chimney. Let me in there." Peter stepped back so Kori could lift the hinged counter and go in. She stooped and ran her fingers through the stuff on the floor. "You're right about one thing; this is dust, not dirt." She turned, still squatting, and traced a line between two boards up the wall. "But look, here's a place where the boards are only touching, not fitted together. Maybe this is where the dust came through." She wiped at the crack with the finger and looked at it. "Yes, it's all dusty."

She started to straighten, dusty index finger extended to show him, and rapped her head sharply against the lowest hook. "Ouch!" she said. "You'd think after all these years I'd learn. I don't know how many times I've done that!"

She left the bar, rubbing the top of her head and frowning. Peter went in and peered closely at the panelling. "You're right; this pair is only touching, not fitted together like the others."

"Tongue and grooved is the term the architect used." Kori was walking in a small circle, biting her top lip and rubbing the sore spot on her head.

"I wonder why it's different in just this one spot?"

Kori, still wincing, said, "Maybe Jeannie made another one of her changes after the panelling was ordered, and they ended up just a quarter inch short somehow."

"Maybe." Peter was looking closely at the join.

His wife grumbled, "Her grandson wasn't any better at house planning; the entrance to the bar should be at the other end, where you don't have to duck around those dumb hooks when you come in, but, no, he had the sink put in at that end instead!"

"Hey, what's this?" Peter was tracing the line where the two boards joined to a height a little over his head. "After this point, it's tongue and groove again. And look, there's a join of boards, across here, this way—" his finger moved left "—but not this way." His finger moved right, tracing the join. "But here, the boards aren't tongue and groove, and here they are again. You know, this looks like it's a door."

"What's a door?" asked Kori.

"Here, this shape," said Peter, running his hand over a place on the wall. "See, here, these boards aren't tongue and watchamacallit, and here again they aren't either." His hand was moving downward, and he squatted to follow it to the floor. "And here's another crack in this quarter round." He looked at Kori. "Is it a door?"

"Of course not. Who'd want a door that opens into a chimney?"

"Why are you so sure it's a chimney?"

"What else could it be?"

"An access panel," suggested Peter. "Maybe there's wiring, or heating ducts, behind here."

"It's never been accessed in all the years I've lived here," said Kori. "And why make an access panel invisible? There isn't a knob or anything. Move over, I want in again." She came in and reached up for the highest stein hook.

"What are you doing?"

"I'm going to take those hooks down right now. Uff, that one's too high. Can you reach it?"

She was in one of her do-something-right-now moods, and he knew better than to quarrel. He reached up and tried to unscrew the hook. "It won't turn," he said. "Shall I break it off?"

"No, never mind, that one's out of reach of most people's heads. Try the next one."

"You know, I think someone's already taken some down. Look, there's a hole here and here, between these two hooks. Or maybe there used to be a door handle here."

"I tell you, there never was a door here! Unscrew that second hook; I'll get the third."

Peter found the second hook would turn, if stiffly, and as Kori bent to turn the lowest hook, there was a subtle shift in the panelling.

Kori leapt backwards in astonishment. "There *is* a door!"

"Sure," said Peter. "I told you there was. I bet this was a secret storage place for hooch. You did say that sink and ice chest were installed in the twenties? During Prohibition."

Kori said doubtfully, "Evelyn wrote that there were some big parties out here in the twenties, and she hinted that spirits were very high during them. Open it, let's see what's in there."

Peter turned the second hook a little more, and the door opened with a very traditional creaking noise. An icy breeze trickled out, and Peter moved back. A little spill of dust came out onto the floor.

"What is it, what can you see?" asked Kori, crowding in to look around him.

"It's too dark to see," said Peter. He moved forward again to peer in. "And cold as a well-digger's. . . ." He backed out, swinging with one hand and wiping his face with the other. "Gah, cobwebs all over everything!"

"Hey!" she said, dodging the swinging arm. "But just imagine finding out something new about a house you've lived in all your life!"

Peter went again to the doorway, but hesitated. The light was poor in the wet bar and the space beyond the secret door was all in darkness. "It doesn't feel right. It's as if the space is bigger than it should be, or like there's no floor in there."

Kori said, "Wait," squirmed by him, and was gone.

Peter reached into his pocket and pulled out a coin. He tossed it into the opening, where it ricocheted with a muffled metal-on-metal sound, then struck again well below floor level, and again, still farther down. After a considerable pause, there was a faint, final *tup* as it hit something far below. He turned to say something, but Kori was not in sight. Almost before he could wonder where she had gone, he heard footsteps and she came hurrying back across the ballroom floor. She was carrying one of the rechargeable flashlights.

"May I look first?" she asked, breathless with hurry and excitement.

"Be very careful, it seems to be hollow," he said, but then made a bow and came out of the serving area.

"Brr, it's cold!" she said, stopping at the entrance and shining the light through it. "Why, it's a staircase, a spiral staircase!"

"Don't go—," said Peter, but she was gone. "Damn," he muttered, and there was a little silence.

Kori appeared back around the door, and turned a white face to him. "Oh, Peter, this is terrible! Down there, oh help, it's another one, I think!"

"Another what?"

Bur Kori handed him the flashlight. "Take a look. It's about halfway down."

He went through the secret door. After a few seconds, Kori asked, hoping she had been mistaken, "Do you see her?"

"Yes."

"Who is it?" Her voice quavered. "Is it anyone we know?"

"No, I don't think so," he said. "From up here, I'd guess that body has been there a long, long time. I'm going down; you wait here."

"No, I—I have to see," she said, and he studied her only briefly before making a gesture of surrender. When he started down the narrow, winding stairs, shining the flashlight on the steps, she was behind him.

The stairway felt sturdy. It was metal, thickly laid with dust, its thin railing draped in cobwebs. There was no sign that anyone had been there for a very long time; the long-unbreathed air was cold and musty. Peter sneezed, and she said, "God bless you!" In a quieter voice, she added, "God bless us all."

She stopped a few steps above to watch him step onto a miniature landing, where the body lay crumpled on its side, face turned away. Its hair was a bright blond under the dust, short, set in rows of waves.

Kori asked, "How long ago, can you tell?"

He swept the light over the body, which was that of a small woman, her skin opaque and dried to a dark leather. Her dress was long, a green probably closer to a medium shade than its coating of dust made it appear. It was a backless model with narrow shoulder straps, the skirt in three bias-cut, clinging layers. The fabric had a shine which made him think of silk. "I'm not much on fashion, but this hair and dress look like before the forties. Thirties, maybe?"

"That long ago? But would she still be so—whole?"

"It can happen." He moved the light over the body. The corpse's back showed a rich brown through its coat of dust.

"She's so dark; was she African American?"

"I doubt it. A caucasian will mummify to this color. We had a case in town some while back, found him in an attic." Peter leaned forward to look at the turned away face.

Kori chafed her arms under the thin silk of her blouse and asked, "Can you see who it was?"

"Not in this light."

"Was she young? Pretty?"

"Hard to say, *fy'n galon*." Peter moved the light along the body again, more slowly. The skin had split where one hand was curved sharply inward at the wrist, exposing the delicate arrangement of bones. The skin seemed otherwise intact, although the flesh beneath it had dried away. Peter lifted the skirt and heard a quick intake of breath, then silence as Kori managed to stop herself from objecting. Cobby, low-heeled shoes that might once have been silver had dried and shrunken, but were still too big for the yet-more-shrunken feet. Sheer stockings hung in filmy folds around the spindly, drawn-up limbs, and a garter on the top thigh had rotted into shreds. There was no slip, camisole or panties.

"What's that?"

"What's what?"

"There, behind her knee. Something shiny."

Peter looked over, reached down and picked up an old pair of scissors. "Was she stabbed, I wonder?" he said.

"No, of course not," said Kori. "She fell. These stairs are tricky, so narrow and going around and around like this—Say! Charles and Great-Jean's oldest son fell down some stairs. Could this be—no, she obviously isn't a little boy, and anyway I've seen Lloyd's grave."

"Inez, probably, since she's the one who went mysteriously missing. The clothes appear to be right. Though she's awfully small to be Evelyn's sister."

"No, that's right, too," said Kori. "Evelyn said she was a tiny, blond whirling dervish, never still. Poor thing, she's been still a very long time, waiting for someone to find her."

Peter shone the light over the corpse, absorbing detail. He was looking very much like a policeman.

Kori asked, "Does this change any of your ideas about what happened to Evelyn?"

"It might. What I need most of all right now is to understand what happened to this lady here."

"Can you tell whether or not she fell?"

"Not for sure. I want our medical examiner's expert opinion. Meanwhile, I don't see any bloodstains on the dress." He shone the light on the scissors, which also appeared unstained, but when he tried to work them, they were frozen in their almost-closed position. He put them into a pocket and moved carefully around the tiny landing to squat at the corpse's head. "Hn," he grunted, a sound of discovery, and leaned forward for a closer look at the top of the blond head. He touched a place very gently with his fingertips, wincing as he did so. "There's a break in the skull right here."

"Then I was right, she fell. You don't stab someone in the top of the head."

"Nor do you normally crack the top of your head in a fall down some stairs. In fact, this is virtually the same kind of wound, in the same place, as Evelyn's."

"No!" Kori sat down hard, took a deep breath of dust and coughed it out again. "No, it's impossible. Inez disappeared in 1932. How could the same person kill two women going on sixty years apart?" She tucked her trembling hands in behind her elbows.

Peter sat back on his heels. "Maybe it wasn't the same person. Maybe this was an accident. Maybe it's only a coincidence that two sisters died in the same house in the same manner. *If* this is Inez, of course. And if this is murder. But if it is, I'd prefer one murderer to two, I think." He sighed and stood up, shone his light around. "Who would have known about this secret stairway? Did Evelyn ever hint at something like it?"

"No." Kori's voice still sounded rough. "She did say Inez used to sneak in and out of the house. Maybe this is how. According to Evelyn, remember, when Inez disappeared, everyone thought she had run away from home. Her parents notified the police, advertised rewards for her return, and hired private detectives to look for her. If this secret passage was known, surely they'd have looked in here and found her and saved all that other fuss."

There came a knocking on the wall against Peter's back. Peter returned the knock backhanded. "Hello! Who's there?" he called.

"Hey in there!" came a faint reply. It sounded like Frank.

Peter raised his voice. "Can you hear me?"

"Barely! We're in our bedroom! You seem to be on the other side of the wardrobe! What's going on?"

"We're in an old stairwell! Does the back of that wardrobe open?"

More thumping, the sound of a hand scuffing on wood. "It doesn't seem to! Why, does it open from your side?"

"Never mind, never mind!" Peter did not wish to offer Mary a look at a mummy in an evening gown. "We're going on down to the library level!"

"What?"

"Down! Down to the library!"

"Right!" There was a faint scrambling noise, then silence.

Peter waited a bit, then reached for a wooden handle low on the wall. He shone the light up and around, and Kori saw the handle was fastened to the bottom of a wooden rectangle somewhat wider than a door, set into slides. Peter tapped gently at the wood to test its thickness. "Very clever," he said. "This is the back of the wardrobe."

Kori followed the lantern's beam as it shifted upward. A cobwebbed length of slender rope attached to the panel ran up through some rings and over a pulley at the top, then down again, terminating in a cylinder of rough-cast metal about twelve inches long. "A sashweight," she said, having watched some carpenters replace the parlor windows two summers ago.

"Yes." The beam moved to the other side of the door to show a cobwebbed fragment of rope hanging at the edge of the panel. The matching sashweight was missing. "The weights would make the door easier to lift. But I bet with one missing it would jam. That's one reason no one ever discovered this entrance to the stairwell."

"Another is that very few people try to slide up the backs of their wardrobes," said Kori. "I know I never did." The oriel bedroom had been here all the years of her growing up. She was shivering, in reaction to the discovery of this second body, with cold, and because she was thinking of all those years of hanging her clothes within reach of the corpse of a cousin.

Peter shone the light around the edges of the slide. "I wonder who designed this?"

"The same architect who designed the rest of the house, I would think," said Kori, standing and brushing at the back of her slacks. "At Great-Jean's request, of course. Evelyn said Great-Jean worked with the architect who designed the house. She was a romantic young woman in a romantic age; a secret stairway would be just the sort of thing she'd ask for. When I first interviewed Jill, she asked if this house had a secret passage. But Jill isn't really romantic; she just watches too many old movies."

"And you answered her incorrectly; this house does have one. If the house has always been in your family, how did the secret come to be lost?" He went down two steps and turned to help Kori step over the body on the landing.

"I don't know."

They were nearly at the bottom before they heard a thumping and someone calling from the library side.

"Stay where you are, *fy'n galon*," said Peter. "Let's not trample all over the place before I have a chance to study it. *Hey!*" he shouted abruptly, and she jumped, because she hadn't moved. "We hear you! Just wait a minute, okay?" he was speaking to Frank, on the other side of the wall. The noise stopped.

The cast-iron staircase took up most of the floor space at the bottom. The walls rose up into dimness, unfinished, plaster dried in oozes between the laths. The floor and objects on it were covered with a heavy layer of dust. There was a door marked with a quaint old latch to their left, and close to it an oblong leather suitcase lay on its side. It was held closed with straps and they could see old-fashioned travel stickers on it.

"Look," said Kori. "I bet that belonged to Inez. Evelyn was right, Inez set out to run away; only she never got out of the house."

"That dress she's wearing wasn't made for travel. And why is her suitcase down here and she up there?" asked Peter.

"Well, she'd been out the night she disappeared, so that's why she's still in an evening gown. Let's say she went to a party and met someone utterly fascinating. Evelyn said she'd been threatening to run away; maybe he offered to help her do it. So she came home and packed a suitcase. She brought it down the secret stairway and was about to unlatch the door, but she'd packed in a hurry, and suddenly remembered she forgot something essential, like a toothbrush or perfume. So she hurried back up." Kori made a gesture supposed to represent someone running up a spiral staircase. "But in her hurry she tripped and fell, and after an hour or so of waiting in his car the new boyfriend thought she'd changed her mind, and went home."

Peter shone the light up the stairs. "Was the oriel bedroom hers?"

"Evelyn said it was. She said her own was the nursery complex. So it fits; the bedroom with an entrance to the secret passage belonged to Inez."

"To have fallen hard enough to fracture her skull, she should have fallen down rather than up the stairs. But the body's already on her bedroom level; why was she up higher?"

Kori considered that and shrugged. Peter let the lantern's beam wander. The floor was cluttered with oddments: an old metal vase, a stack of magazines, a croquet mallet, a teddy bear. There was a fresh dimple in the dust at the foot of the stairs; he squatted, picked up the dime he'd tossed in earlier. "What a sweet hideout this would make for a kid," he said.

"In the summertime, anyway," said Kori, shivering. "But you're right; I wish I'd known about it when I was a child."

Near the far corner of the stairwell was the missing sashweight. It had left a bold trail of dust to its present position. A few inches of pale line were still attached to it. Peter shifted the light upward in a dizzying search for the broken rope one floor up.

The thumping started up again. "Peter?" came a muffled query.

"Yo, Frank!" called Peter.

"What are you doing in there?"

"Finding it's a more complicated puzzle than we thought!"

"What? I can't hear you; is there a way in from here? I'm in the library on this side!"

"Go up to the ballroom; I'll meet you there!"

"What?"

"Up! To the ballroom!"

"Hell—right!"

Peter turned to his wife. "Lead the way, *fy'n galon*. Then go get Michael and set him to guard that third-floor door. We don't want anyone wandering in to mess things up."

Chapter

9 †

"This is a hell of a honeymoon, this is," grumbled Frank. "A body in the library, secret passages—you ever get the feeling you're in the wrong movie? I signed up for a Mexican travelogue; here I am in a remake of 'Murder for Christmas.' Mary is gonna file on me all over again!" He was shining his battery lantern over the second corpse, but speaking to Peter, who was standing five steps up, holding the second battery lantern.

"On behalf of the management, I apologize. Frank, what did Mary say was bothering her?"

There was the slightest hesitation before Frank exclaimed, "She's got the megrims, that's all! She's scared, she's upset, she's ready to walk back to town, and I don't blame her! A big part of it is being cut off like we are, no phone, no road out."

"I guess what's been happening is enough to give anyone a bad case of nerves."

"Sure," said Frank. "And maybe some of it is this house. Old houses get to some people; they think they're creepy or something."

Peter's left eyebrow lifted. "Funny she didn't act like she found this house sinister until she found out Evelyn was coming." Peter waited for Frank to entangle himself further, but it had been Frank who taught Peter that trick, so when the silence had gone on long enough, Peter sighed and returned to business. "What do you think of our latest discovery?"

"Interesting." Frank stooped for a closer look. "Left here back in the late twenties, early thirties, judging by the hair and dress."

"And," said Peter, "as with Evelyn, there are some puzzling aspects about this one. Take that knock on the head. It's a lot like Evelyn's, and as hard to explain. Also, our corpse isn't wearing any underwear."

"Ah," said Frank, taking a confirming peak, "and you think maybe she was murdered in the nude and moved here hastily dressed. Well, I happen to know the present generation didn't invent the panty line. If you were an old movie buff, you'd see a lot of slinky dresses with not one elastical dent to mar their flowing lines. When a 'Forty-Second Street' chorine wore something like this gown here, she'd leave her garter belt at home. What else strikes you as odd?"

Peter shone the flashlight up at the empty eyebolt. "See that place of line hanging there? There used to be a sashweight attached to it, to match the one on the other side, to assist in opening this sliding door."

Frank studied the setup. "Okay, so the sashweight broke loose several decades ago. Probably gave the people living in the house quite a start, if they were home at the time."

"So why is there a freshly-broken trail of dust down on the floor, made by said sashweight?"

Frank took the flashlight and went to shine it on the floor. "Hmm," he said, and turned to shine it upwards again, at the fragment of line. It was thickly draped in cobwebs that obviously had not been disturbed in a very long time. "Okay, it appears that the rope broke a long time ago, but the sashweight hit the floor only recently." He reached up to grasp the end of the fragment. "Let me amend that statement. It looks as if the rope was cut a long time ago."

"Cut?" Peter's voice was sharp.

"Under oath I'd say it's only my opinion, but I'm pretty damn sure. Look for yourself."

They shifted places. "Then maybe—" Peter began, and reached into a pocket, coming out with the scissors he had found under the body.

"Oh-ho," said Frank, reaching for them.

"They're corroded shut. They were under the corpse."

Frank shone the light on the blades. "No apparent stains. You're thinking this is the murder weapon?"

"No, I think the sashweight's it. But that's only a theory; I didn't want to disturb the scene down there so I didn't go for a close look."

"And the scissors enter in because someone cut the sashweight down with them."

"Or, she was cutting it down herself and it fell on her head. That would explain why the scissors were under her."

"Maybe she was defending herself, or threatening someone with the scissors. If someone else cut the sashweight down, he would have taken the knife or whatever away with him."

"None of which explains why the sashweight only just arrived on the floor below."

Frank took the scissors from Peter. They wouldn't open using one hand, so he handed the light over and used both hands. Abruptly, the blades parted. He bent over them and Peter brought the light close. Frank picked out a tuft of something. "They weren't corroded shut, just jammed," he said. "Looks like a fragment of a sashweight cord, maybe." Peter took it, wrapped it in his handkerchief and tucked it away. Frank worked the scissors to loosen their action, then handed them over, too. "Anything else?"

"Down there, in a narrow space between the suitcase and the door, are some footprints."

"Fresh ones?"

"I think so. Again, I didn't go for a look. They're the only footprints in here, except for ours. Do we move the body first, or go on down?"

"The body. I always try to get them away from the scene; otherwise, I feel like they're sneaking a peek at me. And in this case, I want to look at it some more in a better light."

But when they finally managed to wrestle the wardrobe slide up enough to crawl through, they found Kori on the other side of it with most emphatic instructions that they were to report to the dining room. "Some of us," said Kori, "are hungry, and Gordon won't let us eat until we are all present. He went to a lot of trouble, and things are starting to overcook; so can't the unfortunate Inez wait just a little while longer?"

Frank and Peter came into the dining room with that slightly damp look of the hastily washed-up. The others were waiting with various expressions of anxiety on their faces.

"Well?" Gordon asked Peter.

"Well, what?"

"What's this about a secret stairwell with something terrible in it?"

"We have found a circular staircase hidden inside an extension of the square bay on the east side of the house. It has an entrance in the library, in the oriel bedroom and in the wet bar on the third floor. There was a body on the second floor of the staircase which has apparently been there a very long time."

"How long?" asked Mary.

"Perhaps since 1932," replied Peter.

"Oh, ish!" Jill turned away.

"I was only just born in 1932," remarked Gordon.

"Do you know who it is?" asked Danny.

"Not yet, not for sure. Anyone here want to venture a guess?" Peter shot a warning glance at his wife who therefore said nothing. No one else said anything, either.

"Fine. What's first on the menu, Gordie?"

"If we will all take our places," invited Gordon, and they all sat down. The table was covered with a green cloth and set with dishes edged in a holly pattern. Fat red candles in a nest of holly formed the centerpiece. Each person found on his or her plate a "Christmas cracker," a tubular, tissue-wrapped article which gave a sharp snap when the tabs in the fringed ends were pulled and which contained a streamer, a paper hat and a tiny gift.

Jill watched Gordon open his and unroll the pink beret it contained, then did the same for the one in front of Jeep, who was in his plastic carrier on the table between her and Kori. It contained a red poof which, put on the baby, was immediately torn off in an ecstasy of amusement.

Mary picked her cracker up and studied it moodily. She said, "I know, I know," in a rude way when Kori offered to show her how to open it. She pulled the tabs, unrolled the tissue and brought out a beret in a bright yellow tissue. She put it on the table beside her plate and dropped her napkin over it.

"We had these at birthday parties when we were little," Frank said, unrolling his to discover a blue beret, which he put on. "I got a prize, too," he added, holding up a small top. "What'd you get, hon?" She held it up and he said with mock enthusiasm, "Hey, everyone look; Mary got a *diamond ring*!" Mary didn't join in the laughter, but put the ten carats of plastic into her lap, out of sight. Frank, abashed, unfolded his napkin and put it in his lap.

Kori shook out her hat, which was an orange garrison

cap in just the wrong shade for her red and green plaid blouse. She put it on sideways, bowed proudly at the laughter from Peter, Danny and Frank, and tossed her streamer over Jeep so he'd have something else to grab and tear.

Jeep, unable to wait like the others, had already had a bowl of gluey baby oatmeal. Now he was given a corner of toast to entertain himself with. The food for the others was, Gordon assured them, typical of an English country breakfast—"prewar"—served buffet style. It featured shirred eggs, Canadian and streaky bacon, grilled sole, even kidneys—which only Gordon took a serving of, the others being too fastidious—plus toast, muffins, honey, and three kinds of jam. Nobody claimed to be hungry, but last night's supper had seen no justice done to it, so they guiltily filled their plates and dug in.

They talked little for the first fifteen minutes, then Peter said, "Ahhh," and got up to refill his coffee cup.

Frank sighed, "No wonder John Bull weighs three hundred pounds. Any more bacon over there, Pete?"

"Two strips," replied Peter, surreptitiously putting the third into his mouth.

A few minutes later Kori said, "Now, if we may adjourn to the parlor, we'll find gifts waiting under the tree."

But Peter said, "Frank and I haven't finished with that stairwell, yet. No, I'm sorry, this is business. You go ahead; we'll join you later. Mary, we'll need your camera again."

The body was photographed in place, then the wardrobe was emptied of clothes and suitcases. A clean white sheet was spread on the carpet and the body, light and brittle, was carefully maneuvered through into the bedroom, and put on the sheet.

"The skull has a dent in it about halfway between the hairline and the crown," said Peter, on his knees beside it.

Frank gently probed the place. "The hair looks clean; evidently it didn't bleed much. You think she died instantly?"

"Hard to tell. It's bleeding inside the skull that does it, slowing things down until you die. It can take minutes or hours. This break isn't as bad as Evelyn's; I'd guess she lasted a little while, anyway."

"Could she have woken up between being hit and dying?"

"Possibly. Why?"

Frank sat back on his heels. "Oh, I was just thinking. Suppose she didn't know about that stairwell, didn't know she was in the house. Could she have figured out how to get out?"

"Maybe. It's not hard to find and operate the doors, if you know where they are. Or have a light."

"Yeah, but if you don't, and you've got a terrible headache from that knock on the head, and you're crying and scared and falling over things in the dark—Christ, I hate a murderer!" Frank shook himself. "But it must've been over a long time ago, judging by the look of her. That hairdo hasn't been fashionable since I was a kid. Marcelled, I think they called it. What do you think?"

"What we need right now is a photograph of Inez. There's a couple of them in that album." Peter straightened. "It's in our room; I'll go get it."

He brought the album to Frank who sat on the bed to open it. He turned the pages until he came to the studio portrait of Inez. "No wonder Jill got scared when she took a look at this. Not a nickel's worth of difference between them. You could almost think somehow Jill posed for this." He looked up at Peter. "What do you think? She was right there in the hall, wasn't she?"

"She took the album, and looked in it. But that happened after Evelyn was dead."

"Unless she went poking around in Evelyn's suitcase earlier. Or maybe she already knew. Maybe that's why she took the job as nanny out here."

"Maybe. But I don't think she came out here with the intention of killing her. It's too likely she'd get caught. If she did it, it's because she went in there to talk to Evelyn, who said or did something that scared her or infuriated her, and she just swung blindly. One big question is, with what? And where did it go?"

"Huh." Frank returned his attention to the corpse. "Well, she wasn't Inez's granddaughter, if this is Inez." He tilted the portrait of Inez, trying to see a likeness.

It had been taken in a studio, probably after time spent in the sun, because even the face powder could not disguise the deep tan of her skin, which made the artificially lightened hair all the more brilliant. It was cropped short, and pressed into even rows of waves across the top of her head and down the sides, a style identical to the corpse's. The level eyebrows had been plucked and repenciled into a thin, arched line and her mouth re-drawn with lipstick.

"What do you think?" asked Peter.

"Could be." Frank put the album on the floor next to the body, and helped Peter turn its drawn and terrible face upward. It more nearly resembled a mummy just out of its wrappings than the girl in the photograph, but besides the similarity in hair, the eyebrows were plucked to the vanishing point. The prominent jaw bones and the horizontal line they made from neck to chin led one to believe the fully fleshed face would have been square, and what could be seen of the ears in the photo matched. Human ears are almost as individual as fingerprints; Frank was satisfied.

"Hello, Inez, you poor, sad kid," he said.

"It's a shame to find the corpse of a young person," agreed Peter. "Even one that died as long ago as this."

Frank sat back and looked out the window without seeing anything. "Sisters," he murmured. "Murdered fifty-eight years apart. *Why?*"

Peter said, "If we knew why, we'd probably know who."

Frank didn't reply, but kept looking out the window. He looked old, and sick at heart.

Inez was photographed again in her new pose, then folded into her sheet, and put out on the porch beside her sister. Peter and Frank, each carrying a battery lantern, went back to the secret stairwell, entering through the wardrobe.

They stood awhile on the miniature second floor landing and surveyed the stairs going down. Footprints indicated that a man and woman had gone nearly to the bottom of the circular staircase, then come back up again. Where their footprints broke the level surface of dust, they exposed the open-diamond pattern of the iron steps. Peter took a photograph before he and Frank started down.

The stairs were supported on a central pillar of scaling cast iron, to which the steps were fixed like daisy petals, sticking out without risers. A metal railing followed the outside curve of the staircase, supported every other step with black iron worked into the shape of a morning-glory vine, blurred and softened now by dust and cobwebs. Frank and Peter went slowly down the stairs, stopping on the bottom and next-to-bottom steps.

The floor below and the objects on it were covered with dust, except the suitcase, which was merely dusty.

"See how the suitcase made a ripple in the dust where

it fell?" said Peter, and there was the flash of Mary's camera, pressed again into police work.

"So it must've fallen recently," nodded Frank. "Maybe the sashweight knocked it over." The start of the trail made by the sashweight was near the corner of the suitcase; Frank ran the beam of his lantern along the trail.

Peter also moved his light away from the suitcase. In the corner nearest it was a long-necked vase on its side, almost touching a small heap of rags. A step away from them, along the far wall, was a low stack of magazines, on top of which was a small bottle or jar. Next to the magazines was a porcelain candle holder sitting on a little box that was probably kitchen matches. In the corner was the sashweight with its brief trailer of rope. A Teddy bear lay near it but along the adjoining wall, on its back, legs upraised. If it had brought its feet down, they would have touched the handle of the croquet mallet, whose head was partly under the stairs. The room was like a shoebox stood on end, three stories tall, but small in its other dimensions. Peter turned in every direction, taking pictures.

"Damn quiet in here," said Frank.

"And cold," said Peter. "You could almost believe we're in a building some distance from the house."

"There's where Inez got the scissors, I bet," said Frank, pointing with his lantern's beam. "See those magazines? I can remember my mother saying how when she was a little girl it was a favorite pastime to cut out pictures from old magazines and paste them into scenes in scrapbooks—or on the wall, until Grandma caught them at it. That's an old-fashioned pot of glue on top of that stack."

"I don't see any pictures on the walls," said Peter, flashing his lantern in that direction.

"We look, and we'll find them under the dust on the

floor," said Frank. "Those laths are rough and that old glue was terrible, didn't hold worth spit."

"Let's look at the footprints, first," said Peter. He violated the blank face of the floor with a single step that brought him to beside the suitcase. Frank went back up the stairs a little way to point his light from a higher angle.

The footprints in front of the door were made by a woman's broad-heeled shoe. There were only a few, seeming to indicate that someone had come in and backed out again without turning around. The toe of the left shoe had come onto the blank space left by the suitcase as it tipped over. "So Evelyn came in after the suitcase tipped over," said Peter, and took two pictures.

"You sure it was Evelyn?"

"Unless Mary wears a size nine."

"No, she was complaining just before the wedding about how hard it is for her to find shoes in her size—just to call my attention to how small her feet are. She's filled out some over the years, but her hands and feet are still little."

Peter nodded. Mary was probably not more than an inch over five feet tall, and even for someone that tiny, her hands and feet were noticeably small. He said, "Jill's feet aren't that little, but neither are they this big. And Katherine wears a six, I think. Anyway, look at the shape; these footprints look like those granny laceups Evelyn was wearing."

"That would mean Evelyn knew about the secret staircase. Funny she didn't tell Kori about it. And why did she open it?"

"Maybe she was just taking a quick peek to see if the door still worked," said Peter. "And to see if it had been discovered. She may have started to come in, then someone coming into the library made her back out quickly. It was the sharp closing of this door that sent the draft upwards, forcing dust out the cracks in the wet bar."

"And the wardrobe," said Frank. "The bottom of it was all dusty when I was in there trying to find out where your voice was coming from. It was clean when I hung up my suitcoat in there yesterday. I think we may safely assume that the person who spooked her into backing out was her killer. If she'd come on in here and shut the door, she'd be alive today. But then she'd have had the unpleasant experience of stumbling over her sister's body as she climbed up the stairs."

Peter squatted to brush away dust from the suitcase. It was longer and not as high as modern suitcases. Its half dozen colorful travel stickers named cities ranging from London to Omaha. The heavy straps around the suitcase were buckled, but not tucked into their keepers. He groped for the handle and raised the suitcase back on its bottom. "It's not empty," he reported.

There was a length of what appeared to be clothesline tied to the handle. Peter took another picture before he pulled a segment of it through his hand to find it stiff and dry, filthy with dust and cobwebs. Its length was over five feet. He looked closely at the end, which appeared to have broken, rather than been cut. "What do you think, Peter? Kids playing?"

Frank said, "I used to get as much fun out of a length of clothesline or a refrigerator carton as a real toy. Only that's sashcord, not clothesline."

"It is?" Peter looked closer. "All right, it's thinner than clothesline and it hasn't got that stuffing in the middle." He turned the beam of his flashlight upwards, moving it until it rested on the cobwebbed sashcord hanging from its metal ring. Then he bent and picked up a tarnished silver-mesh clutch purse that had been under the suitcase. He opened it to find a lace-edged handkerchief, a flat, mottled, blue-gray cigarette case with the initials IM engraved on it, seven outsize dollar bills, a rectangular cigarette lighter with a hammer-style igniter, a rather withered lipstick, a small, thick compact that proved to hold loose powder and a tiny puff, and what looked like a library card, but was in fact a driver's license—in the name of Inez McKay. He handed it to Frank.

"If this is Inez's purse, then this is probably also her suitcase," said Frank, handing it back. Peter put the license back in the purse with the other items, snapped it shut and laid the purse on top of the suitcase. He experimentally pushed a button back on the suitcase and the flipper lifted. "But, let's open this later, out where the light is better," he said, snapping it shut again.

They went next to the corner where the open mouth of the vase pointed to the heap of rags. After Peter photographed it, Frank picked the vase up by the rim of its mouth and blew to clear the dust from it. It was a substantial article, about sixteen inches tall, of lacquered brass lightly etched with ivy. "Well, looky here," said Frank, holding out the vase to Peter. There was an old, thin smear of something dark in and around a shallow dent in the bowl. "I wish we had a kit in the house; I could win a twenty-dollar bill if you'd care to bet this wasn't blood."

Peter came for a closer look. "I don't like sucker bets, never have."

The heap of rags turned out to be a single garment, a large and full-length woman's white cotton nightgown with a faded blue ribbon around the neck. Beyond the dust, it was stained and dirty, and the ruffle around the bottom was hanging loose in front.

"Someone rescued this from a trash bin, I think," said Frank. "To play Princess, or Bride, maybe."

"No connection with the vase, you think?" asked Peter.

"What kind of connection could there be?"

Peter shrugged. "For all we know, this room may be misleading us into a whole series of non sequiturs." Peter wrapped the vase in the nightgown and put both beside the suitcase. Frank, meanwhile, had gone to look at the stack of magazines. The pot on top proved to be Best Mucilage, dried to a cement-like hardness, permanently securing the brush that went through a hole in the cap.

The top magazine, swept carefully with Frank's hand, was revealed as the May 1897 *Harper's*. Inside was evidence of scissors at work. "Looks like you were right about the clipping," said Peter, coming to look.

The box under the candle was marked Lucifer Safety Kitchen Matches, and by its rattle there were still some inside.

The sashweight was about twelve cylindrical inches of gray and brown metal, coarse and pitted, a twin to the one on the second floor. Peter took two photos, one from far enough away to show most of the trail it had left in the dust, the other a close-up. The rope tied through its loop was just a few inches long, stiff and dry, slightly frayed at the loose end. By tugging gently on it, Peter made the weight roll a quarter turn, revealing a thick dark stain, which, while dry, was nevertheless fresher than the one on the vase. There were a few gray hairs stuck to it.

"Yeah," muttered Frank as the strobe flashed. "Yeah, yeah, yeah." They stepped over the trail it had laid in the dust and continued their circuit of the room.

The toy bear had an arm missing. When picked up, it startled Peter by making a sound like a lonesome calf. "Moo?" he asked.

"When it comes from a bear, it's supposed to be a growl," said Frank. "When from a doll, it's 'Ma-ma.' "

"Ah." Peter put it down.

The last item looked at was innocent of any suspicious stains, though the handle had a long crack in it. "My grandfather would not let his daughters play croquet with any man who was not serious about them," noted Frank.

"Croquet?"

"That is a croquet mallet you swing idly in your hand."

"I know, but what could be sinful about croquet?"

"To help a young lady improve her stroke, a young man would stand immediately—and I mean up close—behind her, his arms around her to guide her hands. It was enough to send a girl's father into fits just thinking about it."

Peter laughed for the first time that Christmas. "I must buy my son a croquet set for his sixteenth birthday, and explain the uses of the game to him. He stands right behind the lady, you say."

Frank snorted and said, "I hope your next kid is a girl, so I can come over some day and listen to you explain the uses of the game to *her*. Come on, let's go look in Evelyn's room. Maybe she brought something even more interesting than that album."

Chapter

10 †

Frank and Peter went down the front stairs together. There was the sound of talk and recorded Christmas music from the parlor.

Peter opened the door, just as french horns ceased harking to herald angels. Everyone was gathered around the tree: Kori, with Jeep in her lap, beside Mary on the loveseat, Gordon leaning against the corner of the bay, Jill and Danny crosslegged on the floor. Michael was gnawing contentedly on a big rawhide chew behind the loveseat. There was the bright litter of Christmas wrapping and ribbon all around them. Jeep was laughing and using a rattle shaped like a jester's head as a hammer on his mother's shoulder.

Mary, sitting rather stiffly amid the general merriment, turned a frightened face to Peter and Frank. "What did you find?" she asked.

"The body is Inez McKay's," said Peter. "*Fy'n galon*, here are three gifts we found in Evelyn's suitcase. I'd like us to open these before we go any further."

Her face changed. "All right." She leaned forward to hand Jeep to Danny, who took him a little clumsily, but sat him on his knee and began making squeaky noises and funny faces to entertain him. He was leaning slightly toward Jill, as if to include her in the fun, but was careful not to look directly at her.

Kori opened Jeep's gift first, a rattle of clear plastic with tiny stars instead of beads inside it. She held it out to him, but he was too interested in laughing at Danny to look at it.

Peter tore open his present to find a Parker ink pen and mechanical pencil. Kori said, "She hinted about that in her last letter. She wrote that a man in your profession probably has access to all the ballpoint pens he can use."

"So you had mentioned that I was a police investigator?"

"Not at first." Kori's smile broadened. "When I did, she wrote back that when I told her in my first letter you had a talent for finding people she had assumed you were a credit manager."

Frank tried to turn a snort of laughter into a sneeze, Jill made the strangled sound that was her giggle, Danny pretended his laugh was at something Jeep did, Gordon cleared his throat busily, and even Mary smiled.

"Open yours, *fy'n galon*," said Peter.

Kori squeezed the package between her fingers, estimating its contents, then slipped the ribbon off and pulled loose the tape. Inside, in an antique silver frame, was an old photograph. It was an artful portrait of a young woman in a dark dress whose face was more interesting than handsome, her long hair flowing in loose waves about her shoulders. She was curled into a deep leather chair with an open book in one hand, looking off dreamily into the distance. Shelves of books rose up behind her. "Why, this was taken in the library," said Kori, touching what appeared to be a segment of the tiled fireplace. In the left foreground, very out of focus, was half a round table with something tall standing in the middle of it and so also cut in half. On the photograph Evelyn had written, "The Only Picture of Myself I Ever Liked."

"Oh, Evelyn," murmured Kori, and handed it to Peter.

Peter studied it for a long minute, holding it close and then at arm's length, then handed it to Frank without comment. Frank looked, shrugged, and gave it back to Kori.

"I think," said Peter, collecting their attention, "I'd like us all to adjourn to the library."

"Why?" asked Jill, suspiciously.

"There's a suitcase we found that I want everyone to see, because some of you may be able to tell me something helpful about its contents."

"But your presents from me and Jeep—" began Kori, gesturing at the tree.

"We've got all day for that," said Peter. "Come on, everyone; this won't take long. Oh, *fy'n galon*, bring that picture."

They all trooped down the hall, each taking care to disguise eagerness or fear by feigning an air of simple interest. Michael trailed behind, but was not permitted into the library.

There weren't enough chairs for everyone to have one, so Frank turned one of the big club chairs away from the fireplace, seated Mary and sat on the arm beside her. Danny handed Jeep back to Kori, then went behind the half wall and brought the black enamel chair for Jill, seating himself on the floor beside it. Meanwhile, Gordon seated Kori in the second club chair and took up a position behind it like a sentry. On the floor were a suitcase and a dirty-white bundle of flannel. Peter picked up the bundle, which turned out to be a nightgown, and unwrapped the brass vase from it. When he saw how everyone focused on the vase, he turned and put it on the table, then turned back to find their attention had shifted to the suitcase.

The suitcase had been wiped clean and its travel stickers shone bright, but mice appeared to have chewed on a corner.

"This is what I want you to look at first," he said,

touching the suitcase with a toe. "I opened it and pretty much closed it right back up again. It seems to be mostly clothes and since I don't know much about antique clothing, I wouldn't be able to tell if there's anything significant about the contents. I'm hoping you ladies, especially, can tell me something." He knelt beside the suitcase and unbuckled the straps. The tab fasteners were not much different from modern suitcase closures, except there were three of them.

The suitcase was lined with a gray fabric. The contents were all jumbled together and badly wrinkled, and a musty smell rose like a cloud of steam as the lid fell back. Jill made that sucking sound written *tsk*.

"She must have been in a terrible hurry to have just thrown them in any old which way," said Kori.

Mary stirred herself and said, "I remember my mother helping me pack to go on my honeymoon. We had to fold everything so carefully, because in those days a dress would wrinkle if you looked at it. I don't understand why modern people have gone back to 'natural fabrics,' they're awful."

Peter lifted out the top item, a pair of pajama bottoms in peach. "I got down our copy of *What We Wore*, and according to it, women's pajamas were just coming into fashion in the thirties. It's a good book, but it somehow failed to list what a wealthy young woman would toss into a suitcase in 1932 on the occasion of suddenly leaving home." The book in question, a large volume, lay on the rent table, held open to a later page by the Dornford Yates book, *Blind Corner*. Peter glanced at it, then at his audience. "Which is why I asked you to help. Hey, here's the top to those," he added, pulling it free and handing it to Kori.

The bottoms were passed on to Jill, who on taking them said, "Ooooh, this is soft! Feel it, Danny!"

Danny put out a reluctant hand, touched the fabric, and nodded.

Except that the bottom featured a drawstring at the waist instead of elastic, there was nothing odd about them.

"Silk, don't you think?" Kori asked Mary, handing the tops to her.

"Hmm, yes. Expensive, I'd say." Mary touched fine lace trim on the short sleeves and round collar. Frank peered at the garment but said nothing.

They looked at Peter for questions, but he only shrugged, so the pajamas were handed back. He put them on the open lid of the suitcase and lifted out the next item, a brown linen skirt, well over knee-length by the look of it, ornamented to the left front with big brown buttons. Time had put orangey flecks of something near the hem in front and it was so wrinkled he had to shake it out before they could even see what it was. "What do you think?" he asked, looking around the skirt.

"Size six?" said Kori, and both Jill and Mary nodded. When Peter looked dissatisfied, Kori said, "I'm sorry, but so far, these are just old clothes."

The next item was a coat that matched the skirt, cut to hang straight. It was unlined, with a self-scarf ending in very long fringe. "Interesting," said Kori. "I like the fringe."

Mary only shrugged, and Jill wrinkled her nose to show she didn't think much of it.

"Well, how about these?" asked Peter, lifting out another pair of pajama bottoms. But these were costume pajamas, suitable for wearing to one of those new-fangled cocktail parties. They were an ice-blue color with enormous legs folded into a thousand knife pleats. There was a row of tiny, self-covered buttons from the waist to the hip.

"Ohhh," breathed Jill, but Kori took them when Peter held them out.

The top was a halter with a wide-lapel effect. He turned it around so they could see it was backless.

"Now that's slinky," said Kori, watching as Mary reached for it.

"Very nice," agreed Mary, fingering the fabric. Kori was trying the pleats in the trousers to see how they were arranged, smoothing them over her knee, holding Jeep back with one arm so he wouldn't drool on them.

Peter smiled and lifted out the bolero jacket with draped front and deep armholes that matched it.

"Wow!" declared Jill, reaching for it. Then, looking at what Mary was holding up, she said, "But you couldn't take this jacket off, could you? Not in those olden days. I mean, what would you wear under that top?"

"Just what you'd wear today," said Peter, remembering Frank's comments on the lack of underwear on the corpse. "Nothing."

Jill gave her strangled giggle and nudged Danny with the toe of her shoe. "Whoa, I didn't know they invented going braless so long ago!"

Kori asked, "What shoes did she bring to wear with this?"

Peter dug into the suitcase and came up with a pair of brown cobbies with an ankle strap.

"Uh-uh," said Kori and Mary shook her head in agreement.

Peter dug some more and came up with a pair of heeled boudoir sandals in a pinky beige.

"I don't think so," smiled Kori and again Mary agreed.

"Those are all the shoes in the suitcase," said Peter, rummaging to confirm that fact.

"Those silver shoes she was wearing would have done,

I suppose," said Kori. "Is there a blouse to go with that skirt and coat ensemble?"

Peter lifted up a lovely silk teddy in a creamy beige with rich lace trim in a bone color.

"No," said Kori, and from behind her Gordon cleared his throat to cover an embarrassed laugh.

Peter picked up a crumpled bundle of black fabric and shook it out. It was a sleeveless black dress of thin chiffon with a black silk underdress. A little longer than knee length, it had two deep flounces of chiffon around the hips, higher on one side than the other, and a little chiffon cape with black and yellow-buff flowers appliqued on it. A wad of fabric that had once been a black and buff rose was on one shoulder and a long filmy scarf hung from the rose.

"That was very attractive in its day," said Mary.

"Oh, not just in its day," said Kori. "I bet I could wear that to the club next week and no one would think anything of it. But you'd want black shoes with it, surely. Unless you could find something in exactly that buff color, maybe with black inserts. . . ." She sat back, absently patting Jeep, seeing herself in that outfit, and Peter let the silence grow until she became aware of it and sat up.

"Sorry! What's next?"

There came several pairs of underpants, some with closed legs, some open, all with elastic in the waist. They were of tan silk and richly trimmed with lace. A sheer, one-piece batiste undergarment was displayed. It buttoned at the crotch, which made both Jill and Kori wince. Then came two pairs of rolled-up silk hose, one black and one tan; and a garter belt, a camisole, a full-length slip, and one final item of lingerie.

"Was this called a bra back then, Mary?" asked Peter, holding up the tan article. It had ribbon straps and not much by way of cups.

"I think that's a later term," said Mary. "But don't take my word for it; I was too young in 1932 to need one. That's an early version. When I did get old enough to want one, they had become so, er, uplifting, my mother thought they were awful."

Frank grinned rakishly, and Kori looked down, trying not to giggle.

Peter said, "In that book they show the occasional bit of underwear. There's a young woman in 1917 wearing a kind of all-over corset, to make everything smooth and flat. In the next illustration, late thirties, there's a for-real girdle and a Valkyrie sort of brassiere. I suppose this model represents the interim it took to figure out how to cantilever. . . ." He gestured, and Mary, not sure whether to laugh, take him seriously or blush, looked away. Buxom Jill became interested in the snap fasteners of the jacket, her cheeks crimson.

Kori bit her lip and asked, "Anything else in there?"

"We're almost at the bottom. Ah, here's the blouse you asked for." He lifted out a pink percale blouse with cap sleeves and mother-of-pearl buttons. It had a pattern of small red rosebuds all over it, and a white collar around a very wide neckline.

"Not with that brown outfit," said Kori. ''Is there another one?"

Peter lifted out a short-sleeved cotton blouse with narrow yellow and pink stripes on a white background. Kori frowned doubtfully, and Peter lifted up a matching wrap-around skirt that fastened with a snap at the waist then with three yellow string ties down the left side.

"That's sort of cute," said Jill.

"A summer vacation sort of thing," agreed Mary.

"A honeymoon outfit," guessed Kori. "I suppose the brown would do for a hasty wedding before a Justice of the Peace. But it needs a blouse of some sort. Something silky in brown or peach."

But they were down to the bottom, and all that was left in the way of clothing were a pair of light gray cotton gloves, and two squashed hats. One was a pale yellow straw, so crushed nothing could be told of it except that it had been small, the other a flatened maroon felt.

"Well," said Mary.

"That's it for clothes," said Peter. "Comments, ladies?"

Jill said, reaching, "Can I see that hat? No, the red one. Thanks."

Mary said, "She must have just thrown everything in—those poor hats!"

"Yes, she was in a terrible hurry," said Kori. "How else could she have forgotten a blouse to go with that skirt and coat. And why bring gray gloves—and that pink blouse?"

"Maybe they had different ideas about what went with what," said Peter, poking at the blouse.

Jill was fooling with the maroon hat, turning it around, trying to decide if she liked it. It had a curious resemblance to a cartoon airplane, the brim wide on either side, narrow in front and back, and she was determined to try it on. One wing was folded under and after one failing attempt to straighten it, she wriggled her fist inside the crown to open it. A small wad of paper fell out, rolled across her lap, and fell on the floor. Danny picked it up.

Kori said to Mary, "Would you have worn that blouse with the brown outfit?"

Mary frowned. "I was only eight in 1932," she reminded her. "But no, it doesn't seem to me that blouse would go with that outfit at all."

"See?" said Kori to Peter. "What else is in there?"

Peter handed round in turn a toothbrush with a wooden handle, toothpaste, a jar of cold cream, bottle of Narcissus perfume, a mirror, a comb and brush in real tortoise-shell, an "eyelash art stick" with a little brush, and a box of talcum powder complete with big puff. Jill, wearing the hat, which with its broken "wing" looked ridiculous on her, unscrewed the perfume, sniffed delicately, and made a face. She held it under Danny's nose and he, getting a whiff, screwed up his face and sneezed, setting off her strangled giggle.

"No lipstick?" asked Mary.

"That was in her purse, along with cigarettes, lighter, driver's license and seven dollars cash."

"Only seven dollars to run away from home on?" exclaimed Kori. "How about jewelry? Maybe there was something she could sell."

"I hadn't thought of that," said Peter. "But there isn't any in here; she must have forgotten it. There's just one more item." He lifted out a black leather appointment calendar with *1932* printed in Art Deco–style gold letters in the lower center.

"That's an odd thing to bring along," said Mary.

"Especially when you're running away from all that," said Kori. "May I see it?" She handed Jeep to Gordon, took the book and opened it to find each page devoted to a week's worth of engagements, with an inspirational verse at the top. She leafed through quickly. "Busy lady," she said. "Parties, movies, a picnic, dates with Joe, Frankie, Lew, Marvin and Amos. Fickle, it appears." She stopped, put her hands on the open book. "I'm sorry, I'm being mean. And disrespectful. After all, poor thing."

"When's the last entry?" asked Peter.

Kori flipped back, then forward a few pages. "July nine. 'Car to be serviced. Hal 8 P.M.' No, look, the next page is ripped out." She looked closer, then held up the book so Peter could see the torn edge.

"Maybe she was the sort who used calendar pages for shopping lists," said Peter. "Any other pages missing?"

Kori turned back, searching. "I don't see any," she said.

"Is this the missing page?" asked Danny diffidently, holding out the wad of paper he had been idly picking open.

Peter, one eyebrow lifted, took it, and the appointment calendar. Frank rose and came to help him smooth it and fit its one jagged edge against the torn remnant in the book. "Sure is," said Frank. "Where was this?"

"Inside the hat," said Jill in a scared-solemn voice, pulling it off and handing it over.

"Hn," grunted Peter, looking into the hat as if for more clues, then tossing it down into the suitcase. "What day did Inez disappear, anyone know?"

Kori said, "I do—I think. I found a newspaper story about it. It was a Saturday." She touched her chin, trying to recall the date.

"It was in the summer of 1932," said Frank. "It had been a hot one, I remember. July, August. . . ." He frowned, thinking.

"It was in July," said Kori. "Somewhere in the middle, the fourteenth, sixteenth, eighteenth. . . ."

Peter consulted the torn calendar page. "July 16 was a Saturday."

"Then it was the sixteenth."

Peter looked again at the calendar page. "She had a date with Henry B. on that Saturday."

"Who was Henry B?" asked Jill.

"Not Biggins," said Kori. "Henry Biggins was Evelyn's fiance."

Peter looked at Frank, who shrugged, then began putting the clothing back in the suitcase. "So, what do you think of the contents of this suitcase?"

"Remember I said she'd forgotten something and rushed back up for it?" said Kori. "The suitcase proves it. She went back for her jewelry case, or a blouse, or her black shoes, or maybe all three. And fell. She must have fallen."

"Maybe she rushed back to tear out the calendar page," said Peter.

Kori, feeling rebuked, looked into her lap. Jill and Danny looked at one another, puzzled by Peter's tone. "Maybe Henry B. was the name of the boy she was running away with," said Mary.

"And she didn't want her parents coming after her till it was too late," agreed Jill.

Frank said, "Come on, Peter. You've got something in mind, don't you?"

Peter nodded. "I know some of it now. That is, I know how Inez came to be in that stairwell."

Kori raised her head and said, "Evelyn killed her, didn't she?"

There was a mild chorus of objections, soon ended as everyone looked at Peter.

"Yes," he said.

"How do you figure?" Jill asked Kori.

"Because Evelyn was the only person who knew about the secret stairwell. Those *were* her footprints in there, right inside the library entry, weren't they?" Peter nodded, and Kori continued, "She came here knowing about it; that means she's always known about it. When Inez went missing all those years ago, why didn't they look in there? Because no one knew about it—except Evelyn. And she didn't tell anyone to look in there because she didn't want Inez found. Whether Inez was killed in the secret stairwell, or Evelyn put her in there after, it had to be Evelyn who did it."

"But how? Why?" asked Mary in a distressed voice.

Kori shrugged and looked at Peter.

"Let me try a scenario out on you," said Peter. He closed the suitcase and walked back to the rent table, resting one hand on it as if he were an old-time lecturer addressing an audience.

"A little before our son was born," he began, "Katherine decided she wanted the house to reflect the generations of people who had lived in it. While doing her research, she discovered that the house was built by her great-great-grandparents, Charles and Jeannie McKay. But she couldn't find the original plans, and so didn't know what additions or alterations had been made in the more than one hundred years since. At her request, I began a search for someone who might tell her more about the house in its earlier days, and found Evelyn Biggins, who had been Evelyn McKay, born in 1910 and raised in this house. Evelyn had actually known Eugenia. She called her Great-Jean, because she was her great-grandmother."

Kori turned and reached up for Jeep, who came with a glad squeal and outstretched hands.

Peter continued, "From Evelyn, Katherine learned that Great-Jean had been deeply involved in the planning of the house, that she made demands for changes in it right up to the time she and her husband moved in. One feature Evelyn knew about, but didn't mention, was a secret stairwell. I suspect it was a last-minute addition, because there's no basement under it, and instead of going between walls like the traditional secret passage, it climbs outside of the house, disguised as an extension of the square bay."

"*That's* why it's so quiet in there; it's an addition!" said Frank, looking over his shoulder at the bay. "Sure! I bet you anything that if you check it out, you'll find its beams and studs are not a continuation from the rest of the house."

Peter straightened and walked around behind the table, continuing. "Great-Jean's child Lloyd died at the age of seven. Evelyn said it happened after he fell down some stairs. That hidden staircase is of cast iron, narrow and very steep; a fall there is both more likely and more dangerous. I conclude the passage was sealed up because Lloyd McKay fell down those iron stairs and died. It would be a natural act on the part of a parent to seal the stairwell against a second accident; and given the guilt she felt for having it built in the first place, Jeannie McKay might well never again speak of the place where her son died, even after the other children were grown and it was safe to unseal it.

"Her surviving son, William, inherited the property on the death of his father in 1906. He was only two years old when his older brother died and would have no memory of the incident—or the stairwell. William spent his time and money on racehorses, and for that and other reasons his mother disapproved of him. So she never told him the secret.

"In the passage of time and as a result of the great flu epidemic, in 1919 the house came to William's son Ferris.

"Ferris was an important man in his community, a banker by trade. He married Annie Stuart, and they had two children, daughters, Evelyn and Inez. Evelyn was the older by two years, a good girl, but big and homely. Her sister was her opposite, small, outgoing, blond and very pretty, a whirling flash of high spirits and misbehavior." He glanced speculatively at Jill, who frowned and reached for Danny's hand. "Someday around 1925, some workmen came to install a sink in the ballroom serving alcove. Evelyn and Inez were about nine and eleven. As children will, they went up to play and explore after the men left for the day. The men would have left their tools behind, and it is likely the children would have played with them. There are some holes in the panelling up there where some extra-large screws used to be. It's not too big a reach to see them as both tempting and easy for inexperienced hands to manage with a screwdriver. Perhaps it took quite a while for them to realize that they had opened the entrance to a secret stairwell. They may have already known the old wooden stein hooks could be twisted, but it was only after the screws were removed that they discovered that twisting the hooks opened a hidden door. The secret staircase was far too exciting and wonderful a secret to share with the grownups in the house."

"How do you know that?" interrupted Danny.

"Because if the grownups were told, or found out about it, they would have resealed it on the grounds that it was dangerous. But it wasn't resealed. Or, the girls would have boasted about it, showed it to their friends, and the secret would not have been lost again. In either case, they would have looked in there for Inez after she disappeared. No, the girls must have managed to keep it to themselves, then and through the years that followed. They stopped playing in it as they matured, but Inez found it helpful when she came in drunk and needed to slip upstairs without being caught.

"Then came a summer night in 1932." Peter turned and took the vase in one hand. "July 16, a Saturday. Evelyn was supposed to be at a party with her fiance, Henry Biggins, but was too sick to go. It had begun as a summer cold, but had gotten worse and she was shaky with fever. She changed into her nightgown and, as was frequently the case when she was not feeling well, she decided to take refuge down here, in the library." Peter gestured toward the alcove with the vase. "She brought pillows and a sheet or light blanket and made herself a nest of them on the bench seat in the bay. In the summertime, in an era before air conditioning, it was cooler downstairs.

"*Fy'n galon*, may I have the photo Evelyn sent you?" She began fishing around Jeep's feet in her lap for it.

"We had a drought that summer," said Frank suddenly; "no rain for weeks and weeks. I remember because I had to water our garden every day before I could go play with the rest of the gang. No hose and sprinkler for us back then, but a backyard pump, a bucket, and a dipper. I'd go out before breakfast, but it was already hot. We thought it would never rain again. Our street wasn't paved, and every time a car would go by the dust would rise up and hang in the air for half an hour. People sat out on their porches half the night, waiting for it to cool down enough to go to bed." He stopped, suffering again that hot, dry summer, oblivious to the drifts of snow outside the windows and the surprised looks on the faces of the people around him, then suddenly blinked and came back. "I'm sorry. Go on."

Peter took the photo, consulted it, then put the vase down very carefully in the exact center of the table. "Evelyn remarked to Katherine that the library was just as she remembered it. But it wasn't, until now. This vase is just barely identifiable in the photograph Evelyn gave Kori, standing as I have placed it, in the center of this table." There was an uncomfortable stir as Peter adjusted the vase by turning it until its stained dent faced his audience. Jeep whimpered softly.

"Evelyn would have been nearly prostrate, suffering from severe congestion and a high fever. No one was at home; both her parents and her sister were out."

Jill cleared her throat and said, "It was mean of her

folks to go out and leave her there alone if she was that sick."

"Maybe they didn't know how sick she was," suggested Kori, her voice gentle.

Frank added, "And maybe it was an important party. They were a high-class family, and social obligations were a moral duty. In 1932 Franklin Roosevelt was making his run for president on the Democratic ticket, and good Republicans like I'm sure they were, they were probably helping raise funds for Herbert Hoover."

"Still, to think of her all alone in the house, coughing and coughing, burning with fever . . ." Kori trailed off, frowning. Mary made an unhappy gesture, and Peter continued.

"Pneumonia can come on fairly quickly. It's possible she didn't appear dangerously ill before they left. It's possible she didn't realize how sick she was until everyone had been gone some while. But she must have been glad to hear the front door open at last." Peter moved from the table to the door. "When she went to the library door, she saw it wasn't her parents come home, but Inez." Peter opened the door, but didn't go through it. Michael, in the hall, sat up attentively, waiting for orders. Peter said, "Inez was, as usual, a little drunk, and instead of offering sympathy or rushing to call a doctor, she came rustling over in her green silk gown to tell Evelyn about her evening, and who she'd been out with."

"Henry B!" said Jill.

"Yes. Inez told her sister she'd been out with Henry Biggins."

Jeep made the start of a fussing sound, but Kori shifted his position and soothed him with a murmur. "Now, Evelyn had grown from a big and clumsy child to a big and homely woman; even with the McKay name and fortune, she hadn't exactly been the belle of local balls.

Henry Biggins, local attorney, was a very eligible bachelor, and she, Evelyn, had caught him. Maybe Inez hadn't really set out to steal Henry away; she just wanted to play the vamp. But her sister wasn't a part of the liberated set; Evelyn felt she had been betrayed. She may have shouted that Inez had made it impossible to continue the engagement. Her one chance at happiness was gone.

"I'm conjecturing, but it's not hard to see how an exchange of words could escalate into a shoving match, especially if one sister were drunk and the other burning with both rage and fever." Peter, pretending to push and be pushed, moved forward abruptly and stepped on Michael's toes. The dog gave a loud yipe and bounded up. Peter stumbled back into the room, bumping into the table. Jill jumped from the black chair to the table and grabbed the vase up out of the way with one hand reaching to fend him off with the other.

"See?" he said.

"Only you have to turn it around," said Peter, reaching for the vase. "It was the taller one who hit the shorter one, which is why the wound is right on top of Inez's head."

"You're saying it wasn't premeditated," said Frank.

"There wasn't time to come up with a real plot," replied Peter. "She probably just grabbed the first thing suitable for her purpose, which was the vase."

"Or maybe it happened like what we just saw," said Kori. "One of them bumped into the table, or was pushed into it, and Evelyn grabbed the vase to keep it from falling and—well, it was in her hand and she was furious."

"Whichever," said Peter, "it took only one blow to drop Inez into darkness forever."

A silence fell, weighty with the image of a small blond vamp, her whirling flash forever stilled. Jill sat down.

Peter put the vase back in the middle of the table. "What to do? How to explain? Maybe she could load the body into Inez's car and take it away, run it into a ditch so it would look like an accident—But it was getting late; suppose she came back to find her parents waiting to ask her where she'd been? No, better to hide the body somewhere in the house, for now. And where better than the secret passage?" Peter walked toward the bay, and everyone stood and turned to watch. "She dragged the body into the bay, opened the door, and pulled it inside—then got another idea. Inez had threatened to run away from home. So all right, she would do it. Quickly, quickly,

183

stumbling over her nightgown, Evelyn hurried up the circular staircase."

Such was everyone's fascinated attention that their heads rose, following the sick and terrified Evelyn up the iron staircase to the oriel bedroom.

Peter continued, "She grabbed a suitcase, opened drawers, and just grabbed, not paying close attention—after all, it didn't really matter; Inez wasn't ever going to put on any of these things. But in the course of packing she came across the appointment book. Did it tell? Yes, there was the name, written for anyone to see. She ripped the page out, then, worried a missing page might bring as many questions as the name Henry B., tossed both the wadded up page and the book into the suitcase.

"Evelyn brought the suitcase down the spiral stairs, then took off her nightgown and—"

"—why?" asked Jill.

Peter came back and picked up the nightgown, shaking it out to display it. "Because when she dragged the body by the arms into the stairwell, its head brushed against her nightgown, staining it."

Jill made a face and flapped a hand to show she wished she didn't ask questions that brought grisly replies.

Peter lifted the ruffled hem of the nightgown to show its tear and continued, "In addition to the stain, the ruffle has been ripped free, probably caught by a clumsy foot when Evelyn climbed the stairs to get the suitcase. There was no need to think up an explanation for the damage; it was an elderly garment, overdue for replacement. She tossed it into a corner, along with the vase with its smear of blood. The next day being Sunday, her plan was to plead sickness, wait until her parents went off to church, then take everything away and hide it somewhere."

"The quarry," said Frank. There was a rock quarry not far from the ranch, abandoned since early in the century, deep and nearly full of murky water. Long used as a dumping place for the stripped remains of stolen automobiles, it was also notorious as a place for courting couples to park, and had once been the choice of an unhappy couple for a double suicide by drowning.

"But Evelyn didn't drive," objected Kori. "She said so in one of her letters."

"Which is not to say she couldn't," replied Peter. "Her sister had an automobile, her great-grandmother drove an old-fashioned electric. I think it probable that she at least knew how. But as it happened, the trip was never made. Evelyn was far too ill the next day to speak of the events of the night before, and as soon as she was well enough, she was shipped off to Arizona. The body not having been found, she just decided that it never would be and it was safer to leave things alone."

"But wait," said Danny. He cast a glance at Jill, and tried to put his question delicately. "I mean, what about the . . . smell?"

Peter said, "According to Frank, that summer was a scorcher, remember? After weeks of hot, dry weather, the stairwell must have been like a kiln. Inez was small and thin. In a matter of twenty-four hours all the moisture would have been baked out of her; that's why we found her so intact. She mummified before decay could set in. The entrances to the stairwell are in here, in Inez's bedroom, and up in the ballroom, places that probably went unused during at least the next few days. Any faint smell that did drift out would have been attributed to the sickness in the house."

"What sickness?" asked Jill.

"Evelyn's pneumonia," said Kori.

"You mean they didn't take her to the hospital?" Jill was appalled by this further evidence of parental indifference.

"In 1932, people were treated at home," said Mary. "My brother died at home when he was nine. The doctor came every day toward the end, but couldn't save him."

"I didn't know you had a brother," said Frank, surprised. "What did he die of?"

"Tuberculosis."

Kori said, "But I thought they could cure that! Put them in a sanitarium and give them vitamins or something."

Mary walked away from Frank to near the rent table. She put a hand on it with the same tentative gesture Evelyn had used. "Sanitariums took months to cure TB and they cost money. My father had lost his job and was doing day labor, when he could find it, at rock-bottom wages. My mother took in sewing to help put bread on the table. We tried caring for Patrick at home, but he needed special food we couldn't afford, and everything clean and fresh, which was impossible. He got sicker and sicker. You talk about Evelyn and her coughing. Dear God, you don't know. . . ." She stopped, touched her mouth with the ends of her fingers. "Finally, the doctor told us the only thing that would save Patrick was a trip to Switzerland. There was a sanitarium up in the Alps, he said, where the patients slept in rooms with no windows, and spent their days outdoors in beds surrounded by snow. Something in the clean cold air cured them. Mother came out here to ask Ferris for help. He refused, told her she had made her bed and must lie in it. Three months later Patrick was dead."

There was a sick silence, then Kori asked in a puzzled voice, "Why out here?"

Frank said urgently, "That's enough, Mary!"

"It doesn't matter; you see, they have the picture. . . ."

"What picture?" asked Kori.

"In the album. The same picture my mother used to

have, of everyone in the front yard. I saw the names written above the faces, and I was so frightened I couldn't think what to do."

"Your mother is in that picture?"

"Yes, she's the one in the back, on the end."

"The one with no name written over her," said Kori; and, handing Jeep to Danny, she came to take Mary's elbow and asked, pleased and excited, "Was her name Alice?"

"No name? Then you didn't know. Oh, my. Yes, she was Alice McKay. She was plain, you see, and the tail end of the family, so it was thought she'd remain at home and take care of her parents in their old age. But she met Terrence O'Brien, and ran off to marry him. Oh, they were so angry with her." Mary said it softly, shaking her head, remembering a tale often told.

"Then Evelyn was wrong, there *was* another child!" said Kori.

Mary frowned. "Evelyn said there wasn't? But she *knew* my mother; Evelyn was in third grade when my mother eloped!"

Kori's face went blank. "But that means. . . ." She turned to Peter. "Evelyn told me a Mrs. O'Brien came to see her father, claiming to be an aunt, but that Ferris only gave her a few dollars and told her not to come back. She may not have seen it happen; she described it as something her father told her. But if she knew who Alice ran off to marry, then she probably knew this Mrs. O'Brien was Alice. And that her father refused to save his own cousin from dying."

Frank asked sharply, "*Evelyn* told you about it?"

Kori nodded distractedly. "She said Mrs. O'Brien couldn't have been a relative, because an O'Brien would have been a Catholic, and the McKays didn't marry Catholics back in those days. Maybe they didn't tell the children—Evelyn and Inez—what Alice had done. But Ferris wasn't a child; he *must* have known her when she came to the door!"

"Of course he knew!" Mary blurted angrily. "And she knew, they all knew! But the McKays washed their hands of my mother because she dared marry Terrence O'Brien against her father's wishes! And they let my brother die because she wouldn't leave him and come home like a penitent sinner!"

Jeep began to cry, real sobs. Peter took him, but Jill came quickly to take him from Peter, and went back to her place, rubbing his arm and making soothing sounds.

Kori's eyes were like open sores. "How wicked, wicked! Just because Terrence O'Brien was a Catholic . . ." She put both her hands on her cheeks and rocked as if in pain. "Oh Mary, oh Mary, I can't believe we let your brother die! I am so sorry!" She burst into tears.

It was Peter who took her in his arms and let her sob on his shoulder. Mary stood beside her stiff and unaffected, deaf and blind with fear and misery.

"Why?" Kori squeezed the word out.

"I warned you," said Gordon, speaking for the first time. He thrust his way forward to say to Kori, "I told you not to go looking into your past. But you insisted, and now you've stirred up this ugly mess and we—" He stopped short, taking a sharp breath through his nose.

"That's enough, Gordie," said Peter. He stroked his wife's head. "Are you all right, *fy'n galon?*"

She nodded, unable to speak, and he fished for his handkerchief. She took it, mopped and blew, and turned away to hide her red face and swollen eyes.

Jill said, "The more I learn about these people, the more I hope they're not really relatives of mine."

Frank took Mary's hand and patted it, looking at the others with an angry glare.

"I'm sorry for you, Mary," said Gordon. "For all of us."

Kori mourned, "I wish I'd known. I would never have insisted you come if I'd known."

Jeep's crying subsided to a hungry fuss. Frank, with a series of nudges and nods, led Mary back to the club chair, made her sit, and sat down himself on the arm, putting a protective hand on her shoulder. Peter asked, "Mary, is it possible Evelyn recognized your name when Katherine told her who the other guests were?"

Mary shook her head, a tiny, trifling gesture. Her chin was up, her mouth turned down. "I doubt she had any idea I existed, much less who I married."

"But you knew who she was."

"Everyone knew the McKay girls, if only by reputation."

"And you knew Inez had disappeared?"

"Everyone knew. There were posters about it everywhere."

"You also knew that Evelyn nearly died of pneumonia?"

Again the trifling gesture. "I think I must have back then, but the memory's gone now. I did know she was sent out west for her health." The bitterness in that last sentence was pungent.

"I knew someone who caught pneumonia," said Jill suddenly. She cuddled Jeep defensively as they swung around to look at her. "I mean, she never came close to dying. They just gave her shots and made her blow into a bottle of water for a couple of days, and she was fine."

"Antibiotics hadn't been discovered in 1932," said Peter. "Pneumonia is an infection of the lungs that can kill, and Evelyn nearly died of it. When she was well enough to travel, she was shipped off to Arizona, where the climate was considered good for weakened lungs." He was gathering their attention to his lecture again, and moved to distance himself from them. "After a while, Henry Biggins wrote to her there. God knows what her reply was, or what she thought of him. But in the end she married him, and no one ever came to talk to her about her sister."

Peter looked at his wife. "Fifty-eight years later Evelyn gets a letter from a distant relative living in her old home, asking about the house in the old days. The first thought in Evelyn's mind is, 'She can't possibly know.' She replies in a way calculated to discourage further inquiries. But Kori Price Brichter persists, and she's courteous, interested, without suspicion. Evelyn thaws a little." Peter walked back to the table. "But then Mrs. Brichter says she's thinking about a restoration project, and fear strikes Evelyn to the heart. What if that old wardrobe in the oriel bedroom is removed, or the panelling in the wet bar is taken down, or the library bookshelves are emptied and refinished? Is the body still there? What about the vase, and the nightgown? There's no statute of limitations on murder. Evelyn allows Mr. Brichter to persuade her to come for Christmas, not because she wants to help, but because she must know what there is to be found. And to stop Kori from finding it, if necessary. Paranoia accompanies her; Peter Brichter is a police detective; suppose they already know and this is a trap to bring her back so she can be arrested?"

"Crazy," murmured Danny.

Jill said sadly, "After all those years of thinking she was safe." Jeep's fussing again turned into a wail.

"She must never have felt completely safe," said Gordon. "Sometimes, in the night, memories must have strolled out to speak to her."

"She didn't mean to kill her," said Jill. "She swung because she was sick and mad and scared."

"Possibly," said Peter. "But having done it, she was anxious not to be caught for it. That's why she came, and that's why she was angry to find there were other guests in the house, and that's why she took advantage of an opportunity to be alone in the library. She hinted about the album so Katherine would go get it, and give her a chance to find out if anyone had discovered the secret stairwell, and, if not, what was left to find in there. Katherine was probably barely out the door when Evelyn was reaching for the latch to the secret passage. She opened the door. . . ." He stopped.

"And then what?" demanded Frank, his grip on his wife's shoulder now hard enough to make her reach up to loosen it.

"I don't know. Probably she heard someone come into the room, and closed the door so hastily it sent a gust of wind up the staircase, forcing dust out into the wardrobe and under the door on the third floor. Then, before she had time to turn around and see who it was, something heavy landed on her head, killing her in the same way that she had killed her sister all those years ago."

Frank jumped up and moved to confront Peter across the rent table. "Well, hell, you're no good!" he barked. "We're barely any further along than we were! You bring us in here and you set off on that long song and dance, and I thought, by God he's solved it. But he hasn't. You haven't."

"We've solved half of it," said Kori, reaching to take Jeep from Jill, jogging him against her. "We know who killed Inez. And we know it wasn't the same person who killed both of them. That's progress, isn't it? It's better than what you've been doing, going around hinting wicked things about Gordon, trying to cover up for your wife. How unnecessary, and cruel! And unprofessional!"

"Now pet—" started Gordon.

"Don't you now-pet me!" Jeep turned his face away from the shouting. His wail took on a heartbroken quality. "After what he said to you, I should think you'd join me in baying at his heels." She shifted the baby as if to smother his crying against herself and said, "I'm sorry, I'm sorry," and fled from the library. Jill followed her out, throwing Peter a look that made him frown after her.

Mary said, "I want to say it here and now, in front of you all: I didn't kill Evelyn Biggins."

"They know that," protested Frank, but Danny looked at Gordon then at his hands, and Peter said nothing.

Mary stood and walked out of the room. Frank followed, pausing before going out of the door to say, "God damn each and every one of you."

Peter went looking for Jill. He found her with Kori and Jeep in the day nursery. Jeep, drawing deeply and contentedly from a bottle, was restored to his good-natured self. Kori was holding him, seated in a big comfortable rocking chair. Jill was seated cross-legged on the floor, folding a pile of receiving blankets. The day nursery was all the way at the back of the second floor, and lined with windows that let in the winter sun. The room was painted in rust and cream, hung with framed posters from the Chicago zoo. The row of windows was underlined with shelves already filled with a bright assortment of toys. There was a smell of baby lotion; between that and Jeep's state of semi-undress, Peter concluded a diaper change had also occurred. None of the three seemed aware of his arrival.

"Jill, may I speak with you a minute?"

Jill looked around, startled. "Oh, hi. Um, sure, I guess so. Where?"

Kori said, "Why not stay here? I need to go see how Gordon's doing. . . ."

But Peter interrupted with a gesture. "No, stay. I may need your recollection of some things."

Kori looked down at Jeep, and Peter added, with his crooked smile, "He can stay too."

Peter looked around for somewhere to sit, but the chair was the only suitable adult-size seat, so he leaned against the door jamb, tucking the toe of one loafer into the instep of the other. "Jill, I want you to think back to yesterday evening, and tell me everything that happened from about ten minutes before the lights went out until we found Evelyn."

Jill took a deep breath, gathering her wits. "Okay, I was in the parlor with the hors d'oeuvres tray with you and Captain Ryder. The captain said he was going to see if Mary—Mrs. Ryder—wanted to come down, and he left. So then I was going to the kitchen with the empty tray but I only got as far as the front hall when Kori came out of the library. She said she and Evelyn were in the library and didn't want to be disturbed. I took the tray into the kitchen—"

"—was Gordon there?"

"Yes, he was slicing up a roasted chicken."

"Did you tell him about Evelyn being alone in the library?"

Jill screwed up one side of her face. "I may have. I know I said something about wondering what they were talking about in there, Kori and Mrs. Biggins. I left the tray in the kitchen and came back to the front hall and fooled around with the holly garland, getting it just right. I was just going to plug it in when Kori came down, so I asked her to wait to see if it looked okay. And that's when the lights when out." She turned to Kori. "You told me to go upstairs, right? So I did, and I found Mary outside the oriel bedroom, and I was leading her down the back hall—she can't see when it's dark—when I heard Jeep crying. I went in and got him, then we went for the light and, since we were there, we came down the back stairs and picked up Dr. Ramsey in the kitchen." Recalling the details of this journey made Jill relax and become fluent. "We got to the library door and there was some kind of fuss because Evelyn got hurt—we didn't know she was dead yet. So Mary and I went on to the parlor and I was thinking I should have brought Jeep's blanket along, so I gave Jeep to Mary and took the flashlight and went up for it, and on my way I saw the album, so I took it along. I sort of remembered Kori had it with her coming down before the lights blew, so I was thinking it belonged upstairs. But I didn't know where, so I brought it with me into the nursery and left it there. I didn't look in it until later, after Danny got found and we knew he was going to be all right. I was putting the blankets away and I remembered the album. I went and got it, only I got sort of curious, y'know? And I looked inside and Jeeze! I couldn't think what to do, because by then everyone was pretty sure someone hit Evelyn—Mrs. Biggins—on purpose, and I was pretty scared someone would think I had a what-do-you-call-it, motive, if they saw that picture."

"What kind of motive?" asked Peter.

Jill said warily, "I don't know. I mean, what kind could I have? I never knew any of these people."

"Except Sarah Friar."

"No, she died back in the thirties. I don't know anything about her, hardly; I've never even seen a picture of her."

Kori said, "I can show you one. She's in the album, Jill, in a big picture with her husband and Jimmy as a baby."

"Really?" Jill sounded pleased.

Kori said, "And I can tell you one thing about her. Evelyn said her great-grandmother made puns with her name, because she was a cook."

"What kind of puns?" asked Jill.

"Friar," said Kori. "You know, fries things."

Jill gave her strangled giggle. "Fryer! That's funny!"

Peter said, "But it doesn't explain where you got your face. You not only look like Inez, there's a family resemblance to Jeannie. Are you sure there's no McKay blood in your background?"

"Are you kidding?" Jill scoffed, relaxed and still amused by the pun made of her great-grandmother's name.

"How about Klee?" persisted Kori. "That was Jeannie's maiden name."

"Uh-uh. I did a thing in high school, looking up the family tree, for a project and ran my mother's family back to England around 1850. There was a Clark, but no Klees or McKays."

"What about your father's line?" asked Gordon.

"I didn't trace him. But I know they're all from Wyoming; my dad was here just long enough to marry Mom, start me, and cut out."

Peter said, "May I ask a question without you getting mad and walking out of the room again?"

Jill sobered. "Okay."

"What made you decide to be a nanny out here?"

"To be near Danny."

"Danny says you didn't decide you needed to work near him until you found out Mrs. Biggins was coming."

Jill didn't reply, but Peter said nothing more, and raised an eyebrow at his wife to keep her silent as well. The room filled with the silence, like a balloon growing bigger and bigger.

"I only wanted to talk to her," Jill said.

"And instead?" prompted Peter gently.

"Nothing. I didn't even get to see her. She arrived while I was putting on my costume and went down to the library with Kori, and from there she goes to being put out on the porch to freeze, poor thing."

"Why did you want to see her?" asked Kori.

"I don't know exactly what it was about. I only know there was something from way back."

Kori made an impatient noise, but Peter said, "Just tell us what you know about it."

"It's kind of a family joke," Jill said. "About how the McKays owe something to us. To my grandfather, actually."

"Sarah's boy, Jimmy, right?" asked Peter.

"Yeah. Anyway, it was him who told his wife, my Gran'ma Ellen, that there was something owed us from the McKays."

"Did he say what it was?"

"No. That's why I wanted to talk to Mrs. Biggins. From what Mom and Gran'ma told me, it was a secret bargain. When Sarah had her second heart attack, she told her son—that's Jimmy—that he had something important coming from the McKays when he turned twenty-one. Jimmy mentioned it in a letter to his wife, my gran'ma Ellen, but told her not go asking for it, because, it was supposed to be a surprise. Y'see he was on his ship on his birthday so nothing happened. And he never did get home to pick it up—Did you know he met my gran'ma through a pen pal program? They wrote for over a year, and he asked her to marry him by letter, even though they'd never seen each other in person. She met his ship in San Francisco, and they got married there, and started my mom on their honeymoon. Only that was all they got of each other, except more letters, because of Pearl Harbor.

He never came home, not even his body, so the surprise never got handed over."

"Any idea what it was?" asked Kori.

"Gran'ma thought it might be stocks and bonds, but she was too proud to go ask about it. But I'm not. Danny told me this real old lady who used to be a McKay was coming to visit, and I thought maybe I could ask her if she knew anything about it. I was hoping she did, and knew who had it, and if we could still get it even though Gran'pa was dead, so we could sell it and I could go to cosmetology school."

Kori said, "It was money, Jill."

"Really? Are you sure?" Jill's hands clasped in a greedy gesture. "Is it a lot? Do we still get it?"

Peter said, "Whoa, there. How do you know it was money?"

"I don't know for sure; in fact, I may be wrong. I'm only assuming."

"Why assuming?"

"Because Great-Jean said Jimmy Friar was trustworthy."

Jill said, "Yeah, so?"

Peter gave a little sigh and pulled out his notebook. There was a crooked smile on his face, as if he, too, knew the answer, but was willing to let his wife reveal it.

"Evelyn said three interesting things about her family. Our family, really. See, there was Jeannie Klee, who married Charles Mckay. They had five children. The second son, William, inherited this ranch property when Charles died in 1906. Jeannie lived a long time after that, and she strongly disapproved of 'Wild William'—that's the first thing, her disapproval. The second thing is, the cook had a little boy named Jimmy that Jeannie treated like a member of the family. The third thing is, she said Jimmy was trustworthy."

Jill looked at her, frowning. "So?"

"So, she said Sarah had an electric personality and left her an electric-powered car in her will. She said Jimmy was trustworthy and—" Kori stopped.

"It was a trust, Jill," said Peter. "There's a trust fund that's been sitting around somewhere for what, sixty, seventy years. The interest on it by now would probably make it a very significant amount."

"But why?" asked Jill. "Did Jimmy do something special?"

"Not Jimmy. William. I think Jimmy was Sarah and William's son. I think that's why Jeannie treated Jimmy like a member of the family, and I think that's why you look so much like your cousin Inez. You and Inez share an ancestor, Mr. Wild William McKay."

"You mean they—messed around? It's kind of weird to think of people back in those days doing stuff like that."

"Well, the words for it have been around a very long time."

"But then how come nobody knew about it till now?"

"Because a double adultery was not something you cared to advertise in those days. William was an important man in the neighborhood, and there would be a big scandal if people found out. Mrs. Friar may have threatened to sue, which, besides the scandal, could get her a substantial settlement. So William probably decided the cheapest way to keep her quiet was to offer money to the baby. He set up a trust fund and directed that it should go to James Friar on the occasion of his twenty-first birthday. Great-Jean knew about it, probably because Sarah went to her first when William refused to help. No wonder Great-Jean disliked William, fathering children on the servants right under his wife's nose!"

"So what happened to the money? Why didn't my grandfather get it?"

Kori shrugged, and looked down at her son, who was fast asleep. "I don't know. Maybe you could look up old court records and find out. Or maybe not—there was that fire in the courthouse in the forties. . . ."

"I know. It made looking up records real hard when I was doing our family tree."

"Me, too. Suppose Annie—Mrs. Wild William— found out about it and made him take the money back. No, that can't be right. Great-Jean wouldn't have stood for that. It must have happened after Jeannie died, so that means Ferris took it."

"Can you do that?"

"I don't think so. I think he must have stolen it some-how."

Jill sat up straight. "You mean I don't get the money? But that isn't fair! After all, if William was the father; he owed something to his kid! Ferris was a cheat, a stinking cheat, to take away money from his own nephew!"

"Jimmy wasn't a nephew, he was Ferris's half-brother."

"Even worse! I hate him!"

"Don't say that, Jill. Don't ever say that!" said Kori.

"Why not? It's true!"

Peter said, "You knew Evelyn was in the library alone. Did you go in to ask her about this?"

"I already told you I didn't!"

Kori said, *"Can you prove it?"*

There was a long pause. Jill's light brown eyes grew gradually larger, as the seriousness of her position sank in. "I can't prove something like that, it's impossible!" Seeking high dudgeon, she found only indignation. When Kori did not reply, even her indignation collapsed. Jill folded her arms tightly and asked the carpet, "Am I under arrest?"

Peter said, "In light of conditions outside, I hardly think I need to lock you in your room to keep you from running away. On the other hand, I think you should be warned that you are a suspect in a murder investigation, and should be careful of what you say and do until the investigation is complete. Do you understand?"

Jill stared at him as if he had grown horns and an arrowhead tail. "Can I go talk to Danny, please?" she asked.

"Of course, if you like."

After she left, Kori looked at Peter and said, "What are we going to do? Is it safe to just let her walk around?"

"She's only a suspect, *fy'n galon.* Unfortunately, not the only one. I think the only way I'm going to solve this is to figure out just how it happened."

Peter went back into the secret passage. He took the suitcase with him, and tipped it onto its side, fitting it carefully back into the outline of its previous position. He put the bundle that was Evelyn's nightgown back into its corner, and the vase so it pointed to it with its open mouth. Then he went up to the second and third floors, opening the entrances to bring a feeble light to the stairwell. Coming down again, he stopped four steps from the bottom and stood awhile, studying the scene, the beam of his flashlight making shadows leap and fall as his attention moved from place to place.

He was surprised no one had asked some questions that seemed obvious to him. For example, why was the body of Inez on the second floor? If Evelyn killed Inez in the library, why would she drag the body up that infandous staircase to the second floor?

Maybe the murder took place in Inez's bedroom. But if so, what was Evelyn doing in Inez's bedroom?

Maybe she was in there snooping, and Inez interrupted her.

No, people seriously ill with pneumonia don't have the energy to go rooting in their sisters' bedrooms. And if

somehow she was murdered up there, why were the suitcase, nightgown and vase on the ground floor?

And since the photograph showed the vase belonged in
the library, how did it end up in Inez's bedroom, ready to
be used as a murder weapon? (When Ferris noticed later
that it was missing, did he conclude his daughter had
taken it as a souvenier?)

No answers came to mind. Or even any more questions. Being blocked in that direction, he thought maybe
he should take a look at some of the other items in the
stairwell.

He came back down and went to the stack of magazines. He opened several and found evidence of scissor-
ing in each of them. He began very gently brushing at the
dust on the floor. In less than a minute he had uncovered
pictures of several children in bulky clothes, two dogs, a
rocking horse, a fireplace, a big chair and a woman in a
straight-up-and-down dress and wide-brimmed hat, with
a fur stole that came to her ankles, all carefully cut out. So
Frank had been right, some children had amused themselves by creating little scenes from pictures cut out of the
magazines. Did that mean anything? Probably not.

He picked up the candle holder and blew on it to remove the dust. It was white porcelain with tiny pink rosebuds painted on it and a gold line around the wax catcher.
A shriveled bit of wick lay in a discoloration that might
have been the last of some candle wax. Someone had let it
burn itself out. He put the thing down and picked up the
box on which it had been standing. Dusted off, it proved
to be a box of Lucifer Strike Anywhere matches. Some of
the matches in it were used.

The bear still mooed when tipped forward. The mallet,
its ends soft and lightly splintered, nevertheless appeared
innocent of murder.

He went to the sashweight. Whoever killed Evelyn

knew about the secret passage, because this, the murder weapon, came from in here. He picked it up by the rope, careful not to disturb the ugly stain near the far end.

That rope.

Peter carried the sashweight over to the suitcase. He picked up the longer length of rope still tied to the suitcase handle. It looked solid enough, though it felt stiff and crisp. Had the years in this place made it brittle? He put the sashweight down on the suitcase, pulled the line tied to the handle tight between his hands, slowly increasing the tension with no result. He let it go slack, then snapped it tight—and it broke. He compared the freshly broken end to the end hanging from the sashweight. They were exactly the same.

So the sashweight had been tied to the suitcase and someone had come in here and broken it free. But how had he come in here to do that without leaving footprints?

There were footprints, actually. He went to look at the footprints right inside the door to see if someone else had come and gone before Evelyn. No one had; there was not the slightest sign anyone but Evelyn had stepped in the dust just inside that doorway.

But if so, then Evelyn had opened the door, found the sashweight and broken the line to get hold of it. Why?

To commit suicide with, dummy. After hitting herself on the head with it, she opened the door, tossed it back in, then fell down dead. No. Think!

She came in here looking for a weapon, because she was afraid, and selected the sashweight. And someone took it away from her, killed her, then opened the door and tossed it in.

That almost made sense. Maybe Evelyn hadn't closed the door all the way, and the murderer saw it as a place to get rid of the weapon, closing the door firmly afterward.

Except it didn't explain why Evelyn went looking for a

weapon in a place that was a perfect refuge. All she had to do was step in here and close the door and she was safe. What would make an eighty-year-old woman choose to stand and fight rather than run away?

He had no answer to that.

And where had that sashweight been all this time? When it was picked up to be used as a murder weapon, it should have left a hole in the dust.

He lifted the suitcase into its original upright place in its clear rectangle amid the dust. Tied to the suitcase, the sashweight must have been within six feet of right here. But he couldn't see where. Had it been put on top of the suitcase? He looked for some indication, but found nothing. Which meant nothing; the mesh purse hadn't left a mark, either.

To hell with it. Back to the original questions. How did Inez's body get up on the second floor landing? Evelyn had no reason to drag her up there; her plan would have been to take the body out of the house, right? Well, suppose she wasn't going to take it out. Maybe she planned to take it up to a third floor lumber room and hide it in a trunk, where some day a curious person could open it and make a horrible discovery.

No.

So someone else moved it. But no one else knew about the secret passage. Right?

He went to put the sashweight back at the end of its trail in the dust. He turned and scooped up the bear, saying, "Tell me, Theodore, what's your theory?"

"Moooo," said Teddy.

"Sounds as good as any of mine," said Peter, and he took the bear with him back to the staircase. He went up four steps and, ignoring the dust, sat down. He played the flashlight around the room, making shadows dance. No answer to his many questions appeared in the dancing beam.

He stood, turned to put the bear on the step nearest his hand, and saw something. A blank space at the back of one of the steps, a dustless place about the size and shape of a foot-long hot dog bun.

He went to get the sashweight and reached up to fit it into the space. A perfect match. "This is where you'd been all that time," he murmured, and went to stand in Evelyn's footprints and looked up at the sashweight, its rope dangling down toward his upturned face.

"I'll be damned," he murmured.

Chapter

12 †

Since Gordon insisted he could not abandon his Christmas feast, now approaching its climax of preparation, Peter came to talk to him in the kitchen. The air was luxuriously expressive of Bird, Bread, Potato, Cabbage, Sage, Turnip, and sharp, sweet spices.

"I suppose this is because of Frank's ridiculous insistence that I wasn't here when he came through yesterday evening," said Gordon. He was at the stove, wrapped again in his big apron, now stained and spattered. He tapped a big spoon on the edge of a pot and put it on a spoon holder.

Peter nodded. "This isn't proving easy for him, Gordie."

"*Him?* What about me? What about Mary? And Kori? She's the one taking the loss of Evelyn personally. It's not easy for any of us!"

Peter nodded. "I know. But it appears there was someone else who took a personal interest in Evelyn. Can you sit down a couple of minutes? I want you to tell me again about what you were doing just before the lights went off. Did you see or hear anything?"

Gordon sighed and came to the table. They both sat down while Gordon thought back. "I don't think so. That is, there were footsteps, voices, doors opening and closing, things like that. But those are to be expected in a house with people in it. No one came in or through, except Jill to get the hors d'oeuvres. And later to return the tray."

"When was this?" asked Peter.

Gordon said sarcastically, "I didn't think to check my watch." But Peter waited, so Gordon made an exasperated sound, thought, and said, "I was nearly finished with the carrots. I was scrubbing the last one when she came in."

"What did she say?"

"Not much, she wasn't here even a minute. Something about not wanting any more hors d'oeuvres because there was no one in the parlor to serve them to. And that Kori and Evelyn were in the library and not to be disturbed. She put the tray on the counter and left."

"Go on from there. What did you do next?"

"I sliced my carrot, as I had the others, put them all in a pan with water and a slice of fresh ginger, and set them to boil. Then I went into the pantry for the jar of honey. I had just come out when it went dark."

"So you weren't in the kitchen when Frank came through."

"Of course I was! I just told you—" Gordon stopped. "How absolutely stupid of me! The pantry opens into the passageway, not the kitchen! It's just outside, a step brings you back in, but even so . . . yes, if Frank came through when I was in the pantry and was at the other end of the kitchen when I came out, he wouldn't have seen me. Then the lights went; and by the time I groped my way back into the center of the room, he would have been gone. That explains things, doesn't it? Neither of us was mistaken!" Gordon threw up his hands in relief. "Would you like a cup of coffee?"

Peter rarely refused a cup of Gordon's special blend, mixed for him at Java, Ltd., a shop in town. "Thanks."

Gordon rose, filled two heavy mugs and brought them

to the table. Peter tasted his. "Gordie, did you know Mrs. Biggins before she arrived this afternoon?"

"No."

"Did you know she was coming here?"

"Certainly. Kori called me—" he stopped to roll his eyes upward, counting back, "—about five weeks ago. She said she'd found a cousin, a McKay who actually once lived in this house. She'd invited her to come for Christmas, and wanted to give a reception in her honor. She asked if I'd be able to come some evening the week after Christmas. I said I'd be honored. Then, maybe a week or ten days later, she decided to have an old-fashioned Christmas weekend, and I was fortunately able to change my plans. I volunteered to do most of the cooking, as Mrs. Gonzales would be on vacation, and Kori is . . . hm? Unreliable in a kitchen."

A smile tweaked Peter's mouth. That wasn't as true as it used to be, but she was still nowhere near the cook Gordon was. He asked, "Did you tell anyone else that a member of the old McKay family was coming home for a visit?"

"No—no, as it happens I didn't. I did turn down another Christmas invitation by saying I was coming out here, but I didn't mention Mrs. Biggins."

"What did you know about Mrs. Biggins before Kori told you she was coming?"

Gordon shrugged. "Nothing. I had no idea she even existed."

"But you did know the McKay family has always owned this ranch."

Gordon twisted a hand to show that wasn't exactly the case, and amended it by saying, "I knew a man named Ferris McKay sold the ranch to Jamie McLeod, Kori's grandfather, sometime around 1936," he said. "I didn't know the McLeods were related to the McKays. And it was an incidental discovery, hm? Something I read when I was trying to find out more about her family."

"Why were you trying to find out more about her family?"

"Because," said Gordon, with great simplicity, "she asked." Peter looked expectant, so he continued, "Back when she was about thirteen and I was living out here as her tutor, she asked if I knew why her last name was different from her uncle's, and how she came to live on the ranch with him. I didn't, but I did some research and discovered that he was the one who had come to live with her, that the ranch was not his, but hers; it had been purchased by her grandfather and left to her mother, and on her parents' death to her. Nick Tellios was only her guardian and would have to turn the ranch over to her on her twenty-first birthday. What neither of us knew was that her parents had discovered he was a criminal and threatened to turn him in, whereupon he murdered them and took advantage of his guardianship of Kori to retire from the Chicago crime outfit he'd been involved in and move down here. I also discovered that he was her uncle by marriage, which, given the fact that I believe criminal traits can be inherited, was and remains a source of relief to me. I had no interest in the McKays as a family, so I never looked beyond the fact that it was one of them who sold the ranch to her grandfather."

Peter asked, "What did Katherine tell you about Evelyn?"

"She said Evelyn was a great-granddaughter of Eugenia and Charles McKay, who built the house in the 1870s or 1880s, I forget which. That Eugenia had still been alive when Evelyn lived here, and that Evelyn was going to tell Kori what the house had been like in those old times."

"Anything else?"

Gordon thought. "That Evelyn was a widow?" He said

this not as a question but as if asking if this is what Peter wanted to know. He lifted both hands. "We didn't talk a lot about it. She—Kori—seemed very pleased to have found Evelyn, and was excited about having her come for a visit, but she knows I'm not interested in history after the reign of Elizabeth the First, and that's what the relationship between the two of them was based on."

"You spent a certain amount of time in this house while Nick Tellios was here, didn't you?"

Gordon's expression tightened. "As little as possible. I stayed mostly in the cottage."

"Still. You were familiar even then with the layout of this house?"

Gordon shrugged. "I suppose so, yes."

"You were permitted to roam freely around it?"

A frown pulled Gordon's light-colored eyebrows together. "What does that mean?"

"I mean, Nick wouldn't assign an escort to follow you around the house."

"No, not normally."

"What did you think of Nick Tellios?"

"Peter. . . ."

"Humor, me, Gordie."

Gordon bowed his head, and his grip on his mug of coffee tightened. "I thought he was the most depraved creature who ever lived. You could tell there was something dreadfully wrong as soon as you came into his presence—remember the first time you met him, those dead eyes? He thought he could buy you as he had bought or blackmailed other officials. He fed on that ability to control others, it was his delight to make a person who thought of himself as honest do illegal things, to become as vicious as he was. I hated him, my God, I hated him!"

"Did you ever think about killing him?"

"Oh, yes, often. But I don't have the kind of nerve it would take to kill someone."

"Say you had discovered a quick, sure way, one where you wouldn't have to be present. Do you know what a deadfall is?"

Gordon blinked at this plunge into detail. He nodded doubtfully. "It's a kind of mechanical ambush, with something rigged to fall heavily on its victim, hm?"

"Yes. You'd have been doing it not just for yourself, but for someone you loved, someone even more desperately trapped than you. And you could do it in perfect safety."

"I see, for Kori. And in perfect safety?" Peter nodded. "Well, yes, I think I might have thought very hard about that."

"Gordon, did you know about the secret stairwell?"

"What, before it was discovered today? No."

"Are you sure?"

"Of course I'm sure! If I'd discovered it, I would have told Kori about it, wouldn't I? Or you, perhaps, because of the body. I don't think I'd have wanted Kori to see something so dreadful as that must have been."

"But you wouldn't have told Nick."

"Ah, you mean if I'd discovered it back then? Probably not. It would have given him an idea for some new wicked scheme, I'm sure. And he might have killed me so as to keep the secret for himself."

"Suppose he already knew? Suppose you discovered he was using it to hide the evidence he was using to blackmail people? Might you have removed the evidence and rigged a deadfall so the next time he went in there he'd be killed?"

Gordon wriggled uncomfortably. "You're asking me to speculate beyond my imaginative capabilities, Peter. I'm a historian, not a writer of fiction." But again Peter waited, and at last Gordon sighed. "Very well. I have found the secret hiding place in which Nick Tellios keeps his blackmail material, hm? Would I have removed the material and substituted a deadfall, if I could have done so in perfect safety?" Gordon clasped his mug with both hands, closed his eyes and breathed heavily though his nose for almost a minute. He opened his eyes. "Yes," he said. "Particularly toward the end. I was in a wretched position, and terrified for both myself and Kori. So yes, I might have done that."

"Did you?"

The timer on the stove began to ching insistently. Gordon started, looked around, then laughed heartily and stood. "Time's up. I shall quickly mark my last answer as No and hand in the quiz. And I'd better get a passing grade, because once what really happened had happened, and Nick was dead at the hands—er, teeth—of his filthy killer dogs, then I would have told Kori, or you, about the stairwell, and we would have dismantled the deadfall. And then there wouldn't have been this shocking Christmas discovery. Because that's what you're really on about, isn't it? Evelyn Biggins was killed in the secret stairwell by a deadfall. Or are we now to pretend that didn't happen, either?"

Peter found Frank and took him into the off-limits library where they wouldn't be disturbed. "All right," he said to his erstwhile boss, "what do you think?"

But Frank said, "You think you know, don't you?"

Peter nodded. "I've come as close as I can get to an answer. This one's hard, Frank; one little shift anywhere and it goes another way."

"So why ask me?"

"Because I'm wondering if you've come to the same conclusion I have. You taught me a lot about being a detective, especially with regard to human behavior. I'd like your input."

Frank sighed. "Okay. First, I'm not sure this one is solvable. The evidence doesn't point so strongly at any one of us that we can eliminate the others. For example, it's not like Gordon to lie. It would take something very important to make him lie. But he's lying when he says he was in the kitchen just before the lights went out."

"I think I've cleared that one up," said Peter, and explained.

"Well," said Frank, "then again, they often tell us the obvious one is the right one. Jill was on the spot—she was last seen standing practically outside the library door, and you told me Danny said she decided to work out here only after she found out Evelyn Biggins was coming for a visit."

"I talked with Jill," said Peter. "She says her own family has a story to the effect that the McKays owed her grandfather, Jimmy Friar, something of value. Kori makes a good case that it was a trust set up for Jill's grandfather." Peter explained, concluding, "But, since no money was ever paid from the trust, a case might be made that it was stolen."

Frank nodded. "Now there's a motive with teeth."

"Yes, but I recall Jill asking Katherine last night as we were decorating the tree what Evelyn's voice was like. It was clear Jill had never spoken with her."

"So she walked in and hit her without saying a word."

"No, because remember, Jill didn't know about the trust, she only knew something was owed her by the McKays. She came out here to ask Evelyn what it was and if it was available to Jimmy's descendents. She admitted as much. Now, I can see her confronting Evelyn in the library, getting a snotty answer, and losing her temper. But to cover up by pretending to guess what Evelyn's distinctive voice sounded like from Kori's description, is a little much, even for the actress Jill thinks she is."

Frank turned away and walked into the bay. He lifted a curtain to peer out at the fading bay. After awhile he sighed and said, "She wasn't in the bedroom."

"I know," said Peter. "No one goes past the room he thinks someone is in to knock at a second-choice door first."

"She says she was in the bathroom. I knocked, but she didn't answer." He dropped the curtains and turned around. "She remembers me knocking and calling her name—she really does, Pete." But the distress in his eyes was dreadful. "She was just too damn upset over this Mc-Kay business to want to talk to anyone. And I'm too upset over her to help her like I wish I could."

"I tell you what," said Peter. "You give me a half an hour, then come into the secret stairwell. Use the library entrance. I'll show you what I think happened."

Frank came out of the library a much older man than when he had gone in. He went to the foot of the stairs and looked up, summoning the courage to go speak to his wife.

The front door opened, and Danny came in, covered with snow.

"Where have you been?"

"Cutting more paths with the snowblower," replied Danny, using a thick mitten to beat snow off himself.

"You should have done that out on the porch," scolded Frank, dodging the stuff flying in all directions.

"I started to, but my hands got cold right away, so I came in."

Frank, abruptly struck by an idea, said, "When you get your outdoor gear off, come into the parlor. I want to talk to you."

A few minutes later, Frank seated Danny on one of the champagne couches, taking the other for himself. He began with a flat statement: "All right, Danny, let's stop fooling around. You had as good a reason as anyone to wish Mrs. Biggins dead."

Danny blinked at Frank. "What reason was that?"

"Protecting your family name. Oh, you like to pretend you don't give a damn what your last name is, but ever since you stopped trying every way you could think of to get yourself sent to prison, you and your old man have come halfway toward being friends. You'd like him to quit riding you about being a horse trainer, and what better way than to save the famous Bannister name from being dragged in the mud?"

"How would I do that?" Danny's expression was both puzzled and wary.

"Suppose Evelyn McKay Biggins knew the rotten details about how your grandfather and her father stole a trust fund set up for Jimmy Friar. Your father might be in a real sweat if he suspected that. After all, there's a street and a school named after the judge; Bannister is a name that means something in this county. He probably told you about it, and asked you to watch Evelyn for any sign she was going to spill the beans. But you saw a perfect opportunity to take care of the problem altogether while setting yourself up with a perfect alibi."

Danny blinked twice, then began to chuckle.

"What's so funny?"

"Wow, I hardly know where to begin!" laughed Danny. "Hell, Captain, you know me, you know my dad; how can you come up with garbage like that?"

"Because I do know you. And your father. He's a damn sharp criminal lawyer who enjoys putting one over on the justice system now and then. And you started life with every advantage, but threw it in your family's teeth. You were a thief, a doper, a good-for-nothing bum from the sixth grade on up."

Danny leaned back, crossed his legs. "You're absolutely right. Then I met Kori's Uncle Nick, who taught me I didn't know the first thing about being bad. He introduced me to heroin, not because he liked me, or hated me, but because Dad sat on some powerful commissions in town and Nick wanted a piece of that action. He couldn't get to Dad directly, so he tried to do it through me. You know, I wish I'd gone to Nick's funeral. It would've been great to join that line of people wanting to toss dirt on his coffin. But, it was knowing him that scared me straight."

"You believe a bad boy can really reform?"

"You mean is it like being an alcoholic? Sure. I always have to watch myself, because the impulse to do it the easy way is there forever. It's just a little bit harder for me than for decent folks to say no when someone offers a joint or a line or a special deal on a watch with someone else's initials on it. Once a bum, always a bum. Except I don't have to act like one."

Danny uncrossed his legs and stood in a single rapid motion. "Kori took me in when I was till shaking from my first lesson in how to straighten out. She trusted me when even I didn't trust me. And you know something? She was right. I can behave like decent people." He began walking up and down, gesturing sharply. "I even found a talent, handling horses. I'm good at it. But all the rest of my life I'm gonna have to hang out with decent people, because I borrow how people around me behave and if I hang out with bums, I start acting like that again." He stopped and bent toward Frank, hands on knees. "And you know something else? I think I *inherited* that problem! Not from my dad, the sharp lawyer, but from my grandfather, the wonderful, famous Judge Bannister! You ought to see my old man wince whenever someone talks about Granddad. He could tell you stories about the judge that would curl your hair! You think Dad gives a tinker's dam about the Judge's reputation? So long as it doesn't come from me, Dad would almost welcome the public learning a little bit about the bad side of old Judge Bannister." He straightened, gestured. "Anyway, I got enough to do trying to make this town forget what a bum I used to be." He set off walking again. "Like you. You haven't forgotten. And you'd *like* to think I sneaked in from the cold and killed that sappy old woman then tried to make it out to the truck again. But I didn't, and you know it. You're just picking on me because I'm a bum. But you, Captain Francis Xavier Ryder, are a jerk, and when Sergeant Brichter tells us who really did it, I wanna be there to see the look on your fat, stupid face!"

Danny strode from the room without waiting for a dismissal.

Kori was sitting in the big rocker in the day nursery, looking at the album Evelyn had brought. Jeep was on her lap, squirming and fussing. He'd just finished a half-bottle of apple juice, he was freshly changed, and not suffering from diaper rash. He wasn't tired nor was nap time approaching. He was being hummed to and gently rocked. All this was virtually guaranteed to make him pleased with life. But he wasn't. He abruptly threw himself backwards against her with a little scream and started to cry. "Here, now, what is it, Jeepers?" she asked, putting the album down and getting to her feet. She put him up onto her shoulder and walked around the big, sunlit room while he quieted, then came back to the seat again to look at the next page of the album. As soon as she sat down, he started wriggling and fussing. She hummed and rocked and turned a page.

Among others, there was a candid snapshot of William,

looking plump and prosperous, on the front porch one
distant summer. Women suffered the corset for the sake
of beautifully tiny waists, thought Kori; maybe men used
that standup collar to keep their chins up. Wild, profligate
William, who died before he was fifty, leaving all those
horses to his rapacious banker son, Ferris. She frowned.
If his son was married with two children when William
died, someone married awfully young. She checked
Evelyn's chart and found that William was barely nine-
teen when Ferris was born. She wondered if perhaps there
hadn't been a sudden wedding and everyone counting on
their fingers when the baby came to see if they could get
to nine months. No wonder Great-Jean disapproved of
Wild William.

Jeep began crying again, so she began singing "The
Twelve Days of Christmas," in an absent-minded way,
jogging her knee in time to the carol. Jeep liked being
sung to and fell into a restless silence.

She turned some pages and found the wedding photo of
Evelyn and Henry. He was broad in the shoulders, bright
and smiling in the eyes, but he wasn't quite as handsome
as Evelyn had made him sound in one of her letters. ("Oh,
my dear, such shoulders! Such a chin! Every girl in town
had set her hoop at him!") Maybe it was the narrow line
of moustache. Kori felt that if you were going to have a
moustache, it was better to have one of those amusing, as-
sertive handlebars like old Charles and his son Wild William did; there was something feral about Henry's thin
black line.

Jeep grew tired of the carol somewhere between the
swans a swimming and the maids a milking and announced the fact in a loud voice. Kori got up and took two
circuits of the room to get him quiet and sat down again,
holding him up on one shoulder. She began singing that

she saw three ships come sailing in on Christmas Day in the morning. He didn't think much of that, either.

Toward the back of the album was a photo of Henry and Evelyn's home in Tucson, taken in 1963—a surprisingly modest house, considering Henry's occupation and the fact that Evelyn was the sole heir of the McKay fortune. Kori turned Jeep around, stood him on her lap and leaned him forward on her forearm so he could see the picture, too, and the novelty of the position made him stop fussing. She began to describe the pictures in animated terms.

"See, there's cousin-by-marriage, Henry Biggins," she said. "And aren't we glad he's a by-marriage relative?" Henry stood in the driveway beside Evelyn and his new 1964 Dodge. He had the sharp lapels and careful hairdo of a shyster. Evelyn looked elegant and upper-class, so out of place beside him that one might think he was a stranger who had stepped into the frame to talk to her about some desert property just as someone snapped the shutter. It seemed an odd photograph to include as a sample of their marriage until Kori realized how flattering the picture was of Evelyn. "Poor lady," said Kori. "She was probably so pleased at finding a nice picture of herself she just didn't notice how repulsive Henry looks."

Apropos of nothing, Jeep started to cry. "There, there, it's not our fault Henry took a bad picture." She stood and began the circuit again. "Hush a baby, hush. Shall we go waltzing?" She began another song, this one about Uncle Walter, who used to sneak out of the house to waltz with bears, setting her feet in time to the tune. But Jeep wasn't interested in dancing, either. She stopped to check his clothes for pins or twists or rough spots. She felt his forehead and found no sign of a temperature. She took his shoes off and rubbed his feet. She jounced him, and steadied him, held him high and low, willing to try anything to stop the crying. Finally she found that a moderately brisk, silent walk seemed most nearly what he wanted. After four brisk circuits of the room, the oxygenation of her brain stirred her to speculation.

Inez had doubtless vamped Henry, which was wicked of her—but why hadn't Henry said no? Because he was young and she was experienced? It was possible Inez was his one wild oat, but Kori didn't think so. He was handsome and eligible; and by the look of him, an experienced oat-sower.

And he certainly was able to take care of himself. After all, when it was all over, he married the remaining McKay girl.

Why had he worked his way back to her? Because he knew quality when he saw it? Not the Henry revealed in the photos. Because she was the only McKay available? While McKay was a name to conjure with in Charter, it meant nothing in Tucson. If he married her for her connections, it must have been the monetary ones. So where were they?

Risking another outcry from Jeep, Kori sat down again and turned back the pages of the album. She looked for and found the photo of Evelyn's parents in early retirement in Chicago. They were looking at the camera over the top of a wrought-iron gate to an imposing brick mansion—the effect of which was spoiled by a closer look. The paint was peeling from the pillars of the portico, the grass was unmowed and an Apartment for Rent sign was nailed to a big tree in the yard.

Once she knew what to look for, she found more clues: Lydia in winters six years apart wearing the same fur coat; Ferris in 1948 with a possessive hand on his big, pre-war car.

Jeep gave her ten minutes of research before he began crying again, harder than ever. Kori got tiredly to her feet.

She sometimes wished that things had worked out the way Peter had wanted them to. It would be nice, at times, to be childless.

She walked and thought. Evelyn had said that her mother redecorated "often" until 1930, when her husband put his foot down. Because they could not longer afford it? The big parties in the ballroom were described in her letters as having taken place in the twenties, during prohibition. A lot of banks failed after 1929; Kori had never heard of the Commercial and Property Owner's Bank before Evelyn mentioned it as the one Ferris was vice president of. Did it fail in the depression? Ferris had taken a job with less pressure in the thirties—maybe by starting all over at some other bank? Bankers must have come cheap after so many banks failed. Did they have enough of the McKay fortune left not to care?

The family fortune had already been diminished by the time it came to Ferris. Wild William, reported Evelyn, had wasted a lot of money in his racehorse operation. Maybe most of his inheritance? Suppose Ferris had attempted to rebuild the fortune by investing in the stock market? And lost it all in 1929? Had there been a certain amount of "keeping up appearances" in the McKay family after the stock market collapse of 1929?

And had that been the motive for the plundering of the trust fund set up for Jimmy Friar? Ferris had the banking skills—and Judge Bannister had the legal skills. Had they split it, or had Ferris taken it all? No wonder Danny's father had been interested in a McKay's return home!

But it hadn't been enough, or Ferris and his wife would not have sold this place and retired to that seedy mansion in Chicago.

Kori had a sudden flash of insight into Evelyn and Henry's marriage. He had married her for her money, and she hadn't any; she had married him because he was an attorney, but he proved to be less than competent. It had been a case of mutual disappointment.

The door to the day nursery opened and Peter came in. "Whoa!" he said. "What are you doing to the kid?"

"Nothing, nothing. He's just feeling cranky. I'm sorry, is it really bothering you? I was hoping you couldn't hear him out there."

"Give him to me."

"I can handle him."

"I'm sure you can, but you look ready for a break. Let me take him, while you go find me a can of baby powder."

Peter put Jeep up on his shoulder and began thumping him with authority. "What's put that thistle in your britches, old fellow?" he asked, beginning to pace.

She came back with the powder and said, "Peter, honestly, you don't have to help; I can handle him. And you're hitting him pretty hard."

He swung the baby down, but didn't hand him back. "Let's talk."

"About Evelyn? Have you found something out?"

"All sorts of things. But I want to talk to you right now about the baby."

"I told you I was sorry. Babies get like this sometimes, crying for no reason. I try to keep him out of your way as much as I can, but with all that's going on right now, it's just impossible. If it's really bothering you, I can take him up to the third floor, back in one of the servants' rooms."

He didn't reply at once, but went to sit on the floor next to the toy shelves. Jeep's loud crying had diminished to a mixture of whining and fussing. Peter assumed a position halfway between a slouch and lying down. He sat Jeep up so the baby straddled his stomach, holding him upright by letting him grasp his thumbs. Jeep, abruptly silent, began looking at the rows of toys, then up and through the windows, at the sunlight glistening on the snow-covered tree tops in the back yard. His cheeks glistened as well, with the tears he had shed. He hiccuped, but remained silent.

"Why do you think you need to protect me from my son?" he asked. He looked at her, and she wondered with a little chill if he was angry.

"That's a terrible thing to say!"

"Jill thinks I'm a terrible father."

"Where did she get such a notion?"

"Maybe because the minute I walk in the door you send her out of sight with the baby. You rarely let me hold him—"

"*Let* you hold him? You never ask to!"

"Why should I have to ask? He's my kid! I'd think you'd be parading him in front of me all the time, trying to get me interested!" Jeep whimpered, and Peter made a prolonged kissing noise at him, then smiled. Jeep smiled back.

"You made it pretty clear a long time ago you didn't want a baby in the house. You said it was a stupid idea."

"You're right, I did. And you never give me a chance to find out if I'm wrong."

"I thought. . . ." She stopped, wondering how to put it. "When we got married, we agreed not to have children," she said. "And then I got pregnant. Accidentally, but pregnant. And so now we have a baby. I know you still aren't too thrilled with the idea, so I agree I try not to shove him up under your nose a whole lot." Peter raised alternate eyebrows at his son, who laughed, completely restored to good humor. Peter shifted his hands so one was supporting the baby's back, then cupped Jeep's chin with the other and brushed tears away with a thumb, a gesture Kori recognized, since he had used it on her. Jeep like the sensation; his mouth fell open in an excited grin. "He's got a tooth," said Peter, surprised.

"Yes, and another one coming on top," said Kori eagerly, but then she cut herself off, stopping in mid-stride her approach as well.

He looked at her. "I'm not an ogre," he said.

"No, of course not."

"I was afraid to father a child because my mother left me with a drunken father who beat on me all the time. Abused children often become abusive parents."

"Yes, I know."

"I don't know how to be the kind of father I'd want my son to have."

"Frank's a good father. Maybe you should imitate him."

"Frank's kids left home to get married years ago. Things are different since his kids were this little, and it was such a long time ago he probably doesn't remember what it was like."

"I mean he was like a father to you. That wasn't very long ago."

Peter stared at her, then at Jeep, then out the window. "He was a good boss," he said.

"And remains a good friend, and a good counselor. It's not that hard, truly. I keep thinking I'm doing everything wrong, but when I talk to other mothers, it turns out we all think that, that all mothers have always thought that, but somehow if you love them and they know it, the kids grow up okay. It's probably the same with fathers."

"So you think maybe you could give me a chance at it?"

"I didn't mean to keep you from it. I apologize." Her voice became high and vibrato. "And I can't tell you how happy I am that we're going to be a real family." She pressed a hand over her mouth and nose for a moment. "Sorry, sorry. Everything makes me cry right now. Even the good stuff." She was so moved that when she traded the powder for the baby she forgot to ask him why he wanted it.

Chapter
13 †

Frank felt behind the books for the edges of the small square, found it and pulled forward. He heard the click as a latch released, and immediately pulled the bookshelf forward. The door was cleverly balanced so as to close it-self; he had to simultaneously release the latch and pull forward to get it open. The mechanism was uncompli-cated, but nearly impossible to discover by accident.

The room beyond was dark, and smelled, oddly, of fresh baby.

"Peter?" he called. "What'd you bring Jeep in here for?" There was no answer. "Dammit, you said to meet you in here, so here I am!" Frank peered up into the dark-ness. "Yo, Pete!"

A faint light glimmered briefly on the far wall, shining from above. A voice muttered, "Damn rechargeables . . . Come on in."

Still peering upward, Frank took a step into the room. His left foot came forward in a second step, aborted when a solid object connected with his foot and shin, and which fell away. Something both soft and hard hit him on the ear and shoulder. He leaped back into the library as the some-thing thumped onto the floor in the stairwell, making a sound like a lost calf. "What the hell!" he exclaimed.

"Well done," said Peter, who could be heard coming down the stairs. The bookshelf door had started to close; Frank had to grab fast to stop it. "No, just stay where you are a minute; I want to see what we've got here."

"What who's got where?" demanded Frank.

"It was an experiment," said Peter appearing at the other side of the fallen-over suitcase. He squatted to shine a light just inside the door. "If I'd warned you, it would have spoiled it."

"Spoiled what, goddammit!" Frank stepped up to the doorway and looked around. Jeep was not to be seen; there was only Peter in the space. "What kind of experiment is it that you throw that damn bear at me?"

"I didn't throw the bear at you; you pulled it down on yourself. No, don't come in yet."

Peter rose. He held both battery lanterns, their light not so dim after all, so their beams would show Frank the way. "Watch you don't step in the footprints."

He held one lantern out to Frank, who took a giant step into the stairwell and asked, "What's the suitcase doing back in here?"

"I was resetting a trap. I sprinkled baby powder to represent dust, and see? Your footprints follow the same pattern Evelyn's did. Step in, overlap the mark of the upright suitcase, back out." Peter's light swung upward. "Our murderer tied one end of the rope to the handle of the suitcase, and put the sashweight up there, see? On the back of that step, the one that's right over the door. You can see the outline of it in the dust. When Evelyn opened the door, she did just what you did, kicked over the suitcase. And doing that pulled the sashweight off the step onto her head."

Frank studied the marks indicated, heavy white eyebrows knit together. Slowly, they unraveled. "Well, I'll be go to hell."

Peter said, "I used the toy because I didn't think you'd want a sashweight landing on your cranium just to help me prove my theory. The bear didn't hit you square on top of the head because I used the twelfth step instead of the thirteenth, so I wouldn't spoil the mark the sashweight left."

Frank went to study the mark on the step. He turned round and shone his light on the sashweight in the corner. "And it was the yank from the suitcase that broke the rope?"

"After a hundred and twenty years, that rope's like wet newsprint. It holds when you pull it, but if you yank, it breaks." He showed Frank the break he'd made in the original rope—he'd used a length of string for the bear trick. "I'm sorry I used you as a butt of the experiment, partner, but I didn't want to try it on one of the civilians."

Frank smiled the littlest bit, lifted the suitcase to test its heft and fitted it back into its rectangle in the dust. He reached up to put the bear back on the twelfth step, then booted the suitcase over. The bear was snapped off the step into his waiting hands. "Clever," he said.

Peter nodded. "Evelyn pulled the lethal chuck of metal onto her own head, and staggered back into the library. The door closed, she fell, and we, not knowing about the secret stairwell, thought someone came in from the hall and took the weapon with him when he left."

Frank put the bear down on the suitcase. "This suitcase trick must have been set up a long time ago; otherwise, we'd have his footprints, too. How far in advance did Kori know Evelyn was coming?"

"Since late November. But I was asking around the neighborhood for the name of a surviving McKay as far back as June or July."

"Would that be long enough? I mean, how long would it take for footprints to fill in with dust?"

"Dunno. Longer than that, I'd think. Years."

Frank leaned against the wall and shone his light idly around the little room. "So, since no one knew she was coming back until just a few weeks ago, this couldn't have been set for Evelyn. For who, then?"

Peter tugged an earlobe. "I've been thinking about that."

"Hell," groused Frank, "first we have a murder and can't figure out how it's done, and now we know how, but don't know who the victim was supposed to be."

Peter said, "It could have been for anyone who opened that door. But I don't think so; I think Evelyn was the intended victim."

Frank asked, "Could it have been set by Evelyn herself?"

"If I rigged a deadfall, I'd be damn careful approaching it, no matter how many years later."

"Maybe Inez set it before she was killed. No, then Evelyn would have triggered it when she put the body in here. Unless she killed Inez upstairs?"

"Possibly."

"Sure. The question is, why? But at least this clears Mary, right? She was in this house for the first time in her life only yesterday."

"When did you meet her, Frank?"

"What the hell does that have to do with it?" Frank's temper rose from under its ashes like banked coals blown upon.

"Lighten up, will you? I was just asking. Did you know her when she was a kid? You didn't know her brother; what about her mother? She came out here at least one time, we know that."

"Her mother was a nice lady. Felt sorry for the mosquitoes she swatted."

"Is she—?"

"Oh, hell yes, died in 1952. Her husband died in a car accident in 1949 or 1950, a DWI, though they didn't call it that back then. He was kind of a sad little man, very partial to Irish whiskey. I met Mary in the summer of 1943. I was a shoe salesman at Clark's and sold her two pairs of shoes before I got up enough nerve to ask her what her name was. . . ." He caught the surprised look on Peter's face before the latter could suppress it. "What's wrong with being a shoe clerk? It's an honorable profession."

"How come you weren't in the army?"

"I was 4-F. I had a little bit of a trick knee that finally got so bad I had an operation to fix it in 1968, I'm allergic to eggs, feathers, and sulfa drugs, and I'm colorblind."

"But they took you on the cops."

"During the war years they were taking anything that could walk on its hind legs. Mary threw a fit, but I'd warned her before we got married I wanted to be a cop. And by the first time I came home all beat up from arresting a drunk and disorderly, she was four months pregnant with Terry, so what could she do? Come on, there's other people in this house besides Mary!"

"I know it. And I know it wasn't Mary, Frank."

Frank came nowhere near putting the question as casually as he wanted to. "What persuades you of that?"

"For one thing, while it is just possible Mary could have slipped down the front stairs after we left her in the bedroom, it is not possible that she could have gotten back up unseen. Gordon is very sure no one but Jill came into his kitchen from the time Evelyn arrived until the lights went out, and Jill virtually occupied that front hall from the time Katherine left the library until the lights went out. For another thing, Mary's too short."

"Too short for what?"

"Well, picture her, Frank. She's even shorter than Jill. And Evelyn is what, five seven? Five eight? So here comes Mary into the library, the light of vengeance gleaming in her eyes, and Evelyn, alarmed, opens the secret door and grabs the sashweight to fend her off with.

Mary wrests it from her and—what? Levitates to a height sufficient to allow the blow to fall square on top of Evelyn's head? Convinces Evelyn to hold still a minute while she climbs up on a chair? Asks her please to bend over? For crying out loud, Frank!"

Frank was silent. "Don't tell anyone," he murmured after a while, "but I was a little bit scared maybe it was her."

Peter very courteously and with some effort refrained even from smiling.

Frank became brisk again. "So who, then? You think Jill maybe set that trap a long time ago?"

"She's too young. I'd guess it takes a minimum of six years for enough dust to drift down and smooth away footprints. That would make her what? Twelve? Thirteen? No. Anyway, Kori swears Jill was never in this house until she came out to apply for the job of nanny."

"What about Danny? He's old enough, he's been coming out here since before you met Kori. And once a punk, always a punk. Even he agreed with me about that."

"Sure he did. He probably volunteered the opinion. He's so scared he might go bad again, he refuses job offers from other horse operations, even at double what Katherine pays him, and won't even consider his father's offer to pay all expenses if he'll quit and go back to school. He doesn't smoke or drink or cheat or lie or steal. His one character flaw is sexual jet propulsion. I don't know where he finds them in this age of the sacred chaste, but the sheets in that cottage take a lot of wear."

"I thought he and Jill had found true love."

"Jill thinks so. Katherine would like it if she's tamed him, but I doubt it; in that one area he's incorrigible. On the other hand, in all other respects he's straight arrow."

"All right, then, who else is there?"

"Well, Katherine grew up in this house. . . ."

"Katherine?" Frank interrupted. *"Kori?"*

"No, of course not! Jesus, Frank! But she's known for years there was an empty space the other side of one wall of the square bay. It was her uncle who told her it was an unused chimney. I wondered for a while if he knew better."

"Would Nick Tellios have known anything about the McKays?"

"I doubt it; his connection with Katherine is through her father; he married her father's sister. But it wouldn't be the McKays he was after. I'm remembering the bad old days, when Nick was in charge out here. He might have discovered this hidey hole and kept the secret to himself. He wouldn't have been bothered by the body on the stairs."

"So how does the deadfall come into it?"

"He was a blackmailer, but none of the photographs or letters or whatever he had on the people he was blackmailing ever turned up. What happened to them?"

"I thought we decided he was smart and burned them after he proved to his victims he had them. That way, if they happened to go looking they wouldn't find them, but just decide he had one hell of a good hiding place."

"Yes, but he'd need to convince his victims at first that he did have the goods on them. Suppose Nick used this place to keep his evidence in until he was satisfied his victims were solidly caught. And he set this deadfall up in case anyone happened across it in the meantime."

Frank nodded. "Yeah. Yeah, I like it."

"Of course," said Peter, tugging an ear, "since he left a private collection of gold coins and gems that was the foundation of the current family fortune, you'd have thought he'd have hidden it in here instead of that storm drain halfway across the property. And, since he also left Katherine a letter in which he told her where his private stash was hidden, it's funny he didn't mention this death trap waiting to be found. She was probably the one person in the world he loved, so you'd think he'd have warned her, even obliquely, about opening that door."

Frank threw up his hands. "Well, hell's bells! Who *do* you think did it?"

"Well, I'll tell you," said Peter, and did.

"You know the first part," said Peter, some while later. "Evelyn struck her sister, Inez, on the head with a brass vase one hot Saturday night in July, 1932, and hid her body in the secret stairwell. I came to that conclusion by a fairly roundabout way, but my wife went straight to the heart of it by pointing out that only two people knew about the secret passageway: Evelyn and Inez. If one was in there, the other put her there."

They were all gathered in the parlor, seated on the two couches. Michael had assumed his attentive pose on his strip of carpet, and Peter faced him from the other end of the couches. He was determined not to fall into his lecture mode again.

"The fact remains true for the second murder as well. Evelyn was killed when a sashweight rigged to do so fell on her head—in the secret stairwell. I have found no evidence anyone else knew about that secret stairwell. So it must be that the deadfall was set up by Inez, in revenge for Evelyn's attack on her."

Kori's head came up, forehead corrugated in a puzzled frown. "I don't see how," she said in a mild tone, afraid she was missing something obvious.

Frank reached happily for Mary's hand, but Mary drew her plump shoulders up a trifle and looked at the dead fireplace as if she had never seen one before, determined to have no part in this until she knew what Peter meant. Jill and Danny looked at one another, not sure if this was a joke they should laugh at. Gordon cleared his throat at Peter, a request for clarification.

Frank, now seeing the general lack of understanding, said, "Maybe you want to run that past us again, this time with a little meat on it?"

"I mean the living, breathing, dying Inez did it. Evelyn hit Inez on the head with that brass vase, fracturing her skull and starting a leakage of blood that would put her in a coma and then kill her. But the blow was not instantaneously fatal. Inez woke up in the secret stairwell." Peter began to pace, resolution forgotten. "You spoke about it, didn't you Frank? About Inez blundering around in there, confused and dying, looking for a way out."

"But she wouldn't have been confused!" objected Kori. "She used the stairway all the time!"

"Correct," said Peter. "Inez awoke with a splitting headache in a dark hot place that smelled of old wood and dust, but it was a familiar smell. She put out a hand and touched the wall or the teddy bear or the bottom step of the metal staircase. Oh, yes, she knew right away where she was. She groped her way to the candlestick, found the matches, and lit the candle in it. Then she saw there was a new item in there with her; her suitcase. She opened it, saw the jumble of her clothes. What was going on? The last thing she remembered was having a fight with Evelyn. How bad a fight was it? The top of her head was so painful she could not touch it. And the big brass vase from the library table was on the floor, its bowl dented and stained. And Evelyn's bloody nightgown, that was in there, too. It was Evelyn, Evelyn who had hit her, dragged her in here. She almost laughed; Evelyn thinks she's killed her; Evelyn thinks she's *dead*."

"You mean she didn't die?" interrupted Jill. "What happened to her?"

"Bear with me," directed Peter. "She looks around and

thinks, I'll fool Evelyn; I'll go take some aspirin for my headache, go straight to bed, and be at the Sunday breakfast table in time to give Evelyn the shock of her life."

"But—" began Kori.

Peter gestured, less to silence his wife than to indicate how he was struck by an idea Inez had had. "No, wait. Evelyn certainly won't leave a dead body in the house; she must be planning to come back and move it somewhere. Inez has another idea; she'll hide and leap out at her." He reversed the gesture. "No again; this calls for something stronger than a fright. Evelyn hit her on the head, tried to *kill* her. How about if she drops something on Evelyn's head? Yes, that would even things nicely. So she takes the scissors from on top of the stack of magazines, goes up to the second floor, and cuts down one of the sashweights. She comes back down to the thirteenth step, choosing it because it is the one directly over the door from the library, balances the sashweight on the back of the step, and drops the cord down. She goes down herself and ties the other end of the cord to the handle of the suitcase and stands it right in front of the door. It's a very simple, effective deadfall. Inez is sure that when Evelyn comes in, she will kick the thing over and yank the sashweight onto herself. This, she thinks, is gonna be swell. She goes up to wait. And wait. In time the candle burns down, flickers and goes out. But Inez doesn't notice, because she has long since grown tired of waiting, tired of staying awake, tired even of breathing."

"*That*'s why she was on the second floor!" said Kori. "I wondered about that. And then—" She stopped, and gestured at Peter to go on. This was his story, not hers.

"Fifty-seven years later, Evelyn opens the door and kicks over the suitcase, which yanks the sashweight down on her head. She staggers back into the library, the door closes, she collapses and is found dead just yards from the sister she murdered all those years ago."

"There!" said Kori. "There! Oh, *Peter!*" She was beaming in shared triumph and wiping her eyes with the backs of her hands. "Poor Evelyn! Poor Inez!"

"But," said Jill, trying not to look at Mary, "that means it wasn't—any of *us!*"

"No," said Peter, "it was one of us. It was Evelyn. And it also was her sister, a suspect I didn't know we had."

Gordon said, "They make an ugly little circle, the two of them. 'You killed me, so I'll kill you!' My God!" He shivered.

"But it's a tidy little circle, all the same," said Frank. "And not one of us present is standing in it."

"You never really thought *I* might be, did you?" said Mary carelessly, not looking at him, fists clenched.

Frank kissed her on the cheek. "Not for even three-six-teenths of a second, *ma croidhe*," he declared.

"What's 'machree' mean?" asked Jill.

"It's Irish for 'my heart'," said Frank, and, never one to throw away a splendid opportunity to regain domestic bliss, continued, "Because if she ever leaves me again, she'll take my heart with her and I'll die." Mary's fists unclenched and she groped for his hand.

"Kori says *fy'n galon* means 'my heart' in Welsh," said Jill.

Frank nodded and said, "The best endearments are the same in any language."

"No, it's because Mary's my—what, cousin? No, aunt," said Kori, still smiling through her tears. "All of us McKays get called 'my heart.' "

"I'm a McKay too," said Jill, hinting, reaching for Danny's hand.

But he chose that moment to stand and stretch. "If I go and wash up," he said, "will someone feed me?"

Gordon rose with alacrity. "I have been waiting two whole days for someone to say that," he said.

A short while later, Gordon summoned them all to the dining room, which glowed with candlelight and soft colors. The table stood firm under its burden of silver, crystal and fine china, and the air was fragrant with the holiday smells of rich food. Gordon had brought everything in and made a sumptuous display of it on the sideboards. He stood ready to serve.

Everyone took his or her place, and they saw a place left over. Kori had earlier insisted a place be set for Evelyn, and couldn't bring herself now to remove it.

Frank glanced at the empty place and said quietly, "I always did like poetic justice." He looked at the head of the table and said to Peter, "Good thing I retired, I guess."

"You would have figured it out sooner or later," said Peter. "I couldn't have done it without your help."

"No, I was good in my day, but this was something special. You've outdone any detective work I ever did," said Frank.

"I'm glad I married him," said Kori. "Especially now, having discovered what a murderous pack of thieves my ancestors were. I hope Jeep takes after him."

"No, no," said Jill. "I mean, okay, a couple of them weren't so wonderful. But it was a long time ago, and I think you're a terrific person."

"My mix of McKay blood is richer than yours," said Mary, "and except for a couple of parking tickets, I've never come under the eyes of the law."

"You're very kind, thank you," said Kori. "But if an opportunity comes along to investigate the Prices or the McLeods, I think I'll pass. Meanwhile, I need to apologize to Jill for suspecting her of murder."

Jill hunched a little bit and flushed. "It's okay," she murmured.

"No, it isn't. If you'll stay until I find another nanny, I'll pay to send you to cosmetology school. You're owed at least that from old William McKay. And anyway, Cousin Jill, you're family. We should look out for one another."

Jill's head came up, her light brown eyes glowing. "That's right! So sure, I'll stay, till next fall at least. And really, thanks! Wait'll I tell my mom!" Danny smiled at her, and she smiled back in such a way that anyone could read her mind. I've got until next fall, she was thinking. That's plenty of time.

Peter, at the head of the table, felt very patriarchal. He sat basking in the feeling—but finally Gordon said, "I don't suppose you'd care to serve the wassail, Peter? It's in the big crystal bowl in front of you. I, too, have been laboring, and I think both of us are due our reward."

Wassail is an ancient beverage. This version of it was a highly spiced mixture of ale and rum, served cold and garnished with clove-studded orange slices. Peter filled the small crystal cups with the drink and handed them around. "Does anyone wish to make a toast?" he asked.

"To never another Christmas like this," said Kori.

"Hear, hear," murmured several voices and everyone drank.

The soup was Creme Princesse, made of chicken and asparagus puree, enriched with cream, and flavored with chervil.

The salad came next, a lettuce and chicory toss, with a vinegar and oil dressing; then pickled eggs, deviled eggs, and fresh and deep-fried oysters.

The goose was brought from the sideboard and expertly carved by Gordon. It was overflowing with sage stuffing and garlanded with sausages. With it came "baggies"—mashed rutabagas—boiled potatoes, brussels sprouts, applesauce and, oddly, oat cakes spread with blackberry jam. Gordon was serving a traditional English feast.

They ate their fill and more, and were sighing over the remains when Gordon went into the kitchen and from there ordered all but two of the candles blown out. He came back in holding aloft a tray on which a round object burned with a blue light.

"Plum pudding!" cried Kori.

The candles were re-lit, and the bowling ball–like object was sliced, releasing a powerful spicy odor to tickle even the most jaded palates. It was served with Cumberland rum-butter sauce.

"I don't suppose anyone wants any nuts or cheese?" asked Gordon after a while.

"No, oh no," pleaded Danny. The others just shook their heads.

"In a minute or two I think I'll be able to crawl into the parlor on my hands and knees," said Peter, "where I will open the Christmas gifts my family has waiting for me, and give my wife the present I bought for her."

Kori went with Peter and Gordon to the parlor, put the Mannheim Steamroller Christmas album into the CD, then stooped to reach under the tree for unopened gifts. The first was Jeep's to his father, a plexiglass cube with a photograph of himself or himself and his mother on every side. "For your desk at work," said Kori, and Peter who had pointedly ignored similar items on other peoples' desks, said thanks in a disinterested way, then found himself turning the cube around and smiling at the photos.

Kori's gift to Peter was a new tunic to wear to the Twelfth Night medieval-style event the local Society for Creative Anachronism group would be putting on in two weeks. It was knee-length, made of very soft, buff-colored wool, embroidered in complex twelfth-century Germanic patterns with gold, brown and green silk. She was skilled with her needle, and he smiled over the workmanship for an embarrassingly long time before thanking her.

Gordon, entering into the spirit of the occasion, displayed the gift Kori had given him, a framed page from a thirteenth-century manuscript, half the Lord's Prayer in plainsong. Then Kori showed Peter Gordon's gift to her: the next page! They had ordered from the same catalog.

Peter joined in their laughter, then pulled from under the tree the last unopened gift, the one from him to Kori, with an air that said this was something special. The box was two feet high and maybe half that wide and deep. It was heavy. Kori opened it from the top and lifted the styrofoam cover she found under the lid. A small hand, palm up, fingers deeply recurved, was all she saw. "Oh, my," she whispered and looked at him. He nodded, grinning. Rather than try to lift it out, she dismantled the box, revealing a bronze figurine with an oriental face and a subtly colored costume that might be described as the Far East meets Art Deco. "It's Erte's 'Chinese Legend,' " she explained to Gordon. "You've seen his Miss Liberty that I got two years ago. It's not painted; he does tricks with patina to get those colors. I've wanted Chinese Legend for some while, but couldn't find her." She smiled at Peter. "This must have taken some doing," she said.

He shrugged. "A little. But, as you told someone not long ago, I've got a certain talent."

"Thank you."

"Merry Christmas."

Peter then withdrew with Gordon to the fireplace to continue a discussion that over the past year had grown to include in one massive tangle the American public school system, South Africa, Japan, the Persian Gulf, and the manned versus robotic exploration of space.

Glad her two favorite men didn't require her constant attendance, Kori took Michael into the library with her and collapsed into a chair with a book of Kipling's poems. Mary and Frank had gone up to their room; Danny and Jill to the nursery. Jeep had had his supper and was asleep. There was a pleasant air of justified rest.

Did you have a merry Christmas? asked the house.

Well . . . thought everyone. There were new raw spots that would have to heal before the question could be properly addressed.

On the other hand, I've had worse, thought Peter, remembering a few.

There was my first year here, thought Gordon.

I'll have to call around and see what's needed to get them properly buried, thought Kori. A joint memorial service perhaps. Evelyn will go next to Henry in Tucson, of course. Maybe there's space next to Ferris and Lydia for Inez. How sad that Inez's bright, dervish energy was smashed dark and still before its time. I wonder what sort of old woman she would have made?

"Me own love, me dear heart," crooned Frank.

"Ah, you're the one, you are," murmured Mary.

"In the morning we'll go down to my place and I'll show you the videotape of me at the Nationals," said Danny from the window seat in the day nursery. "Among other things."

"In the morning you and I are going to report for kitchen duty and give Gordon a break."

"Yeth, m'love," he lisped, quoting their favorite Warner Brothers cartoon. "Did you have a merry Christmas?"

"No, of course not. Did you?"

"No, but I've had worse." He looked around, out the window and back across the room toward the door. "Funny, isn't it, how just knowing that stairwell is there makes the whole house seem a different shape."

Kori put her book down, for once unable to escape into the solid meters and bold rhymes of Kipling. *Perhaps tomorrow, or maybe when they come back from Mexico, I will sit down with Mary and explain how it was poverty and pride, not hatred, that kept Ferris from helping save her brother. Maybe that will help the healing. I need the reconciliation, because also out of this mess came the news that Jeep and I aren't the last McKays. Uncle Frank and Aunt Mary*—she smiled and repeated it—*Uncle Frank and Aunt Mary have four children and four grandchildren, all cousins Jeep can claim. And, with Peter deciding he likes Jeep, maybe we'll have another child. And Jill's bound to have children—I just hope she gets married first!*

She leaned forward to pinch a bit of evergreen off one of the branches in the coal scuttle, broke two of the needles and inhaled the sharp scent as she looked around the room. *I don't care what Peter says,* she thought; *next time we paint, this room turns ivory, or pink, or bright orange. Anything but green!*

CHARLES McKAY (1828–1908)
m. EUGENIA (JEANNIE) KLEE (1849–1926)

LLOYD 1867–74	PHYLLIS 1869–1915 m. George St. Clair 1852–1915	WILLIAM 1871–1919 m. Annie Stuart 1871–1919

	Peter Freddie Martha died 1915 in the Lusitania	Ferris 1890–1961 m. Lydia Campbell 1894–1943

		Evelyn 1911–1990 m. Henry Biggins 1912–1973	Inez 1913–1932

0 children

Sarah Clark
1877–1934
m.
James Friar
1871–1927

James, Jr.
1916–1941
m.
Ellen Smith
1916–1978

Judy
1940–
m.
Stan Yeager
1945– (divorced 1972)

Jill
1971

MARGARET	ANDREW	ALICE	
1875–1875	1880–1918	1887–1960	
	m.	m.	
	Marva English	Terrence O'Brien	
	1887–1939	1893–1952	

Margaret	0 children	Mary	Patrick
1891–1930		1921–	1923–1931
m.		m.	
Jamie McLeod		Frank Ryder	
1888–1958		1920–	

Katherine	Terrence	Beth	Helen	Frank, Jr.
1930–1973	1944–	1946–	1948–	1952–
m.				
David Price				
1928–1973				

Katherine (Kori)
1967–
m.
O. Peter Brichter
1955–

Gordon Peter (Jeep)
1990–

TERRIFIC NEW MYSTERIES FROM BERKLEY

___ A LITTLE GENTLE SLEUTHING by Betty Rowlands
   1-515-10878-2/$3.99
Mystery writer Melissa Craig kisses London good-bye and heads for the quiet Cotswolds. But the discovery of a corpse soon shifts her focus from fiction to the dark side of country life, where lust, greed, and a killer dwell.

Look for the next Melissa Craig mystery,
__Finishing Touch 0-515-11059-0/$4.50   (3/93)

___ ASHES TO ASHES by Mary Monica Pulver
   1-55773-768-1/$4.50
Sergeant Peter Brichter's investigating a case of arson that could be a smokescreen for mob drugrunning. But Brichter's new partner seems more concerned with making friends in high places than in solving the crime...and soon Brichter's own reputation is on the line.

Look for the next Peter Brichter mystery,
___ Original Sin 1-55773-846-7/$4.50